A DARKER WILDERNESS

A DARKER WILDERNESS

ANCIENT TERRORS
IN THE CANADIAN ROCKIES

R.D.D. SMITH

Modelbenders Press

This book is a work of fiction. Names, characters, businesses, places, events, locales, and incidents are the products of the author's imagination or used fictitiously. Any resemblance to actual persons, living or dead, or actual events, is purely coincidental.

A Darker Wilderness: Ancient Terrors in the Canadian Rockies

AI Disclaimer: All the text, characters, and plot were created by a human author. Therefore, it is all covered by copyright. AI contributions are described in the "AI Disclosure" section at the end.

Modelbenders Press books may be purchased for business and promotional use. For more information, please contact the publisher. Inquire with the author at **http://www.rddsmith.com/**

PRINTED IN THE UNITED STATES OF AMERICA

Interior and Cover Designed by Adina Cucicov at Flamingo Designs

The Library of Congress has cataloged the paperback edition:

Smith, R.D.D.
A Darker Wilderness: Ancient Terrors in the Canadian Rockies
/ R.D.D. Smith–1st ed.
1. Action Adventure, 2. Travelogue, 3. Thriller
I. R.D.D. Smith   II. Title.

Paperback ISBN 978-1-938590-55-9
Hardback ISBN 978-1-938590-56-6
eBook ISBN 978-1-938590-54-2

FICTION BY R.D.D. SMITH

Dr. Monica Gray, Medical Thriller Series
The Surgeon in the Mirror
Against a Viral Threat
Savior of the War Torn
Beyond the Mind's Horizon
Echo

Global Runners Travelogue Series
Blood on the Equator (Ecuador)
Sebastian's Gold (Portugal & The Azores Islands)
Safari of Shadows (South Africa)
A Darker Wilderness (Canadian Rockies)

Short Stories
The Surgeon's Genie
Freyja $AI
Jack Hunter: One More Mission
Lauren Banister: Sacred Shadows
Guardians of Blackwood

Join our community of readers to receive fascinating news, speculative fiction, and discussions related to the novels.
www.rddsmith.com/free

GLOBAL RUNNERS TRAVELOGUE SERIES

https://www.amazon.com/dp/B0D9WTBFF8

Detective Jenn Moreno pursues the murderer of a global oil executive across her native country of Ecuador. She suspects that the murderer is hiding among the members of an international group of eco-tourists on a running vacation that spans the Ecuadorian Andes mountains, Amazon rainforest, and Galápagos Islands.

In the mist-shrouded Azores Islands lies a secret that men have killed for—the lost treasure of Portugal's King Sebastian. For archaeologist Lauren Banister, this isn't just another expedition. After being betrayed and robbed of credit for a previous discovery, she's here for redemption as much as riches. Going undercover with a running tour group, she thinks she's finally one step ahead of her rivals.

In the breathtaking wilderness of South Africa, a running expedition becomes a deadly chase. What starts out as the adventure of a lifetime—traveling through South Africa's stunning coastlines and exploring the pristine wilderness of Kariega Game Reserve—turns into a fight for survival when the leader of Global Runners accidentally witnesses the brutal actions of Victor Malanga, one of South Africa's most dangerous crime bosses.

TABLE OF CONTENTS

PREFACE:
THE LAND BEFORE BANFF

The Banff area encompasses the traditional territories of multiple Indigenous tribes, which include the Stoney Nakoda—composed of the Bearspaw, Chiniki, Goodstoney, and Tsuut'ina First Nation—and the Blackfoot Confederacy, which includes the Siksika, Piikani, and Kainai nations.

For over 10,000 years, these Indigenous peoples have called the region now known as Banff National Park their home. Long before the establishment of Canada's first national park in 1885, these lands sustained generations through hunting, fishing, trapping, and gathering, while also serving as vital sites for trade, ceremony, and spiritual practice. But the human story represents only the most recent chapter in a much older narrative—one that begins with beings who walked these mountains long before the first people arrived.

The Bow River—known as "Minhrpa" (translated in Stoney Nakoda as "the waterfalls")—formed the lifeblood of this region, providing both a crucial travel corridor and abundant resources. Its banks, lined with Douglas fir trees, supplied the strong, flexible wood from which Indigenous peoples crafted their renowned hunting bows. The river's waters teemed with fish, while the surrounding forests and grasslands supported populations of bison, elk, deer, and other game.

Contrary to common misconceptions of isolation, the Indigenous peoples of this region maintained extensive trade networks spanning hundreds of kilometers. The site of present-day Banff served as an important gathering point where diverse nations came together to exchange goods, share knowledge, and conduct ceremonies. These networks connected mountain peoples with prairie nations and coastal groups, facilitating the movement of resources, tools, and cultural practices across vast distances.

This intimate knowledge of the mountainous terrain—its passes and valleys, its seasonal changes and hidden resources, and the proper protocols for moving through spaces that belonged to powers older than humanity—made Indigenous peoples invaluable to the

European traders, explorers, surveyors, and missionaries who began arriving after initial contact in the 17th century. By the 18th century, regular trade had been established, with Indigenous hunters and trappers supplying furs, hides, and fresh meat to European settlers while serving as essential guides through country that would have been impassable without their expertise.

Tragically, the establishment of Banff National Park in 1885 brought policies designed to exclude Indigenous peoples from lands they had stewarded for millennia. Traditional activities including hunting, gathering, and ceremony were prohibited, and communities were forcibly separated from places that held deep cultural and spiritual significance. These exclusionary policies persisted for decades, causing profound harm to Indigenous communities and severing connections between peoples and places that had been maintained since time immemorial. Over the past fifty years, Parks Canada has worked to reverse discriminatory policies, rebuild relationships with Indigenous peoples, and recognize their essential role in the stewardship of these lands.

Among the Stoney Nakoda, a small faction emerged in the mid-1800s—a group that would come to call themselves the Wapiti. Unlike the majority, who adapted to changing circumstances and eventual life on reserves, this splinter band chose isolation, retreating deep into the wilderness to maintain practices that others were abandoning. Their spiritual leaders believed that certain knowledge—particularly the ceremonies that maintained a connection with the "Ancient Ones"—could not be allowed to fade. These practices required specific conditions: remote locations where the boundary between worlds remained thin, participants willing to undergo profound transformation, and, most crucially, the continued respect for the legendary creatures.

Today, Banff continues its ancient role as a gathering place—a site where ceremony, trade, sharing, vision, and celebration bring together diverse communities. Indigenous leaders, artists, and creators across all disciplines gather here, realizing creative potential and sharing the diversity of Indigenous perspectives and practices that have always been central to this landscape.

The story that follows is fiction, but it unfolds against this backdrop of history both documented and hidden—a landscape where human presence stretches back ten thousand years, where mountains and forests hold memories of countless generations, and where the relationship between people, place, and powers older than both continues to evolve in ways that modernity struggles to comprehend.

Some truths persist regardless of whether they are believed. Some beings endure regardless of whether they are seen. And some ceremonies continue in the margins, carried out by those who remember that the wilderness is not just a backdrop to life, but the external substance of existence—ancient, aware, and watching.

DAY 1

ALBERTA, CANADA

CHAPTER 1

THE CEREMONY

The moon hung full above the pines, its light barely penetrating to the forest floor where fifty figures circled a fire that cracked and hissed against the night. Maskwa stood at the edge of the gathering, his massive frame still as stone, watching everything. He had stood guard at ceremonies like this for twenty years—since he was eighteen and his father had passed the duty to him. He knew every sound the forest should make, every shadow that belonged.

Tonight, something felt different.

The circle swayed and chanted in an ancient rhythm, voices rising and falling together. Most wore animal-skin capes over their regular clothes — jeans, flannel shirts, hiking boots. The old ways and the modern world mixed here, as they always had in the Wapiti camp. But when they chanted, the modern world fell away. The language was older than the trees, older than the mountains themselves.

At the center, Thomas Whitehorse knelt beside the fire, his head bowed, hands pressed together. He wore only deerskin, traditional from neck to feet. His weathered face — high cheekbones speaking to his mother's Nakoda blood, paler skin revealing his father's European ancestry — was painted with red ochre in patterns Ayâs had drawn that morning. Around his neck hung a small leather pouch, the only thing he'd kept from his old life. His mother's medicine bag.

Maskwa had known Thomas for all twenty-eight years the man had been with them. Had hunted with him, built lodges with him, sat at fires through countless winters. Thomas was brother to him. And tonight, Thomas would either become something greater, or he would die.

The chanting grew louder. The circle closed tighter around the kneeling man.

Ayâs moved through the gathering like smoke, her stooped form somehow commanding despite her small size. She was ancient — how ancient, no one truly knew.

Her dirty blonde hair, worked into wild braids decorated with bones and feathers, caught the firelight as she took her position before Thomas. On her forehead, the tattoo that marked her authority: a crude, powerful face, the sacred representation of the Napiyaw.

She raised one gnarled hand, and the chanting softened to a whisper.

Maskwa's eyes swept the darkness beyond the fire. The forest pressed close tonight. Too close. He caught movement at the edge of his vision—a shadow that seemed to shift against the natural flow of darkness. He focused on it, but it was gone. Or had never been there.

The smell hit him then. Musky, like elk, but underneath it something else. Wet stone. Ancient earth. The smell of something that wasn't really there.

They were here. Watching.

His hand moved unconsciously to the knife at his belt, though he knew a blade would be useless if the Napiyaw chose to come closer. They responded to ceremony, to faith, to sacrifice. Not to weapons.

Ayâs placed both hands on Thomas's head. Her voice, when she spoke, carried across the clearing despite its age-cracked quality. "Brother, are you ready to be transformed?"

Thomas raised his face. His eyes shone with tears—not of fear, but of joy. He had waited twenty-eight years for this moment. Had devoted his life to earning it. His voice was strong, certain.

"Yes, sister. My old life here is complete. I am ready for the next stage."

The fire surged higher, though no one had fed it wood. In the forest beyond the light, something moved. Something large.

Maskwa's jaw clenched. The ceremony was working.

Ayâs lifted a gourd from beside the fire, cradling it in both hands like a newborn. The liquid inside caught the firelight—pale, almost luminescent. Nature's milk. Made from roots that grew only in the deepest parts of the forest, mixed with other things Maskwa had never been told. Ayâs guarded the ancient recipe as if her life depended on it. Perhaps it did.

"Look up at me and the heavens beyond," she commanded.

Thomas raised his head, opened his mouth, and stared fully into those ancient eyes. Maskwa saw the trust there, absolute and unshakable. Thomas had watched others attempt this transformation. Had helped carry their bodies to burial when it failed. And still, he believed. Still, he offered himself.

Ayâs tipped the gourd slowly, pouring the pale liquid between Thomas's parted lips. He swallowed once, twice, three times. His throat worked rhythmically. When the gourd was empty, Ayâs set it aside and stepped back.

For a long moment, nothing happened.

Then Thomas's pupils dilated, swallowing the brown of his irises until his eyes were nearly black. His breathing deepened. The circle of chanters picked up their rhythm, voices rising in waves of sound that seemed to vibrate in Maskwa's chest.

"Bring forth, through me, the ancient spirit and protector of the forest," Thomas intoned, his voice already changing—deeper, resonant with something that wasn't quite his own. "Let me be the instrument of rebirth."

The words were ancient. The first time Maskwa had heard them, he'd been a boy, and his father had explained: These are the words that call them. The words that open the door between their world and ours.

Ayâs raised both arms toward the sky. "May you be the next bridge to the Napiyaw, brother."

The chanting swelled. Fifty voices crying out in unison, their sound filling the clearing and spilling into the forest beyond. Thomas rose to his feet, his movements fluid and strange. He lifted his arms, mimicking Ayâs's gesture, reaching toward the moon.

That's when the forest responded.

A howl split the night—long, deep, starting like a wolf but ending in something almost human. The sound came from the west. Before its echo faded, another answered from the east. Then a third from the south, so close that Maskwa felt it in his bones.

Several of the younger Wapiti faltered in their chanting. Maskwa saw fear flash across their faces—saw hands tremble, saw one young woman's eyes fill with tears even as her mouth formed the sacred words. He understood. They were calling something that could destroy them as easily as protect them. Something their ancestors had bound with promises and blood.

And if the ceremony went wrong—if the wrong person were chosen as the vessel—

The Napiyaw might walk away from the Wapiti forever—no one really knew.

The fire twisted, flames bending toward the forest as if drawn by invisible hands. The shadows around the circle grew darker, denser, moving in ways that had nothing to do with the flickering light. Maskwa's eyes tracked the movement and found unbelievable shapes—figures too tall, too angular, standing just beyond the reach of firelight.

The smell grew stronger. That musk, that wet stone scent, now mixed with something else. Old fur. Breath that had never known human food. The smell of something ancient and rare.

Thomas began to chant in the old tongue, his voice rising above the others. The words tumbled from him faster and faster, as if something was speaking through him rather than from him. Sweat poured down his painted face, his body beginning to shake.

"I can see it," Thomas shouted, his eyes wide and wild. "I can see the new world. It will be as it was in the past. Nature will rule, and we will be one with it again!"

The circle responded, their fear transforming into desperate hope. "Napiyaw! Napiyaw! Napiyaw!"

The word reverberated through the trees. And from the darkness, an answer—a sound so deep it was felt more than heard. A rumble that shook the ground beneath their feet.

Maskwa's hand tightened on his knife again. He could see them now, clearer than he ever had before. Three of them, maybe four, moving between the trees. Too large to be human, too purposeful to be an animal. Their eyes caught the firelight—amber and ancient, watching with an intelligence that made his blood run cold.

The trees themselves seemed to bend, branches reaching down as if to touch what was happening below. The air grew thick, heavy with their presence. Maskwa had been at a dozen ceremonies before this one. He had seen shadows and heard howls and smelled their passage. But he had never felt them this close, this real.

Thomas's voice cracked with ecstasy. "Our protector will rise! The destroyers of the forest will be destroyed themselves!"

His arms stretched wider, his head thrown back. His entire body vibrated with energy that seemed to come up from the earth itself, rising through his legs and exploding from his fingertips.

"Napiyaw! Napiyaw! Napiyaw!" The chant became a roar.

The fire surged twenty feet high, a pillar of flame that illuminated the entire clearing. In that moment of brightness, Maskwa saw them fully—

Tall figures, easily eight feet, covered in dark fur that seemed to absorb light. Faces that were almost human but not quite, with eyes that held terrible awareness. Long arms ending in hands with enormous fingers. They stood at the edge of the clearing, three of them visible now, watching Thomas's transformation with what looked like... anticipation? Hunger?

Then Thomas's eyes snapped open, wider than human eyes should go. His mouth opened impossibly wide.

"I am he!" he screamed.

For one heartbeat, Maskwa thought it had worked. Thought Thomas Whitehorse had finally become the bridge between worlds.

Then Thomas coughed, and foam erupted from his mouth.

The foam was white, tinged with pink. It poured from Thomas's mouth and nose, bubbling and frothing as his body convulsed. His arms, stretched wide in triumph just seconds before, snapped inward, fingers clawing at his chest. His legs buckled.

The chanting died. Silence fell over the clearing like a shroud.

Thomas hit the ground hard, his body jerking and twisting. The painted patterns on his face smeared with sweat and foam. His eyes rolled back, showing only whites. His throat made terrible sounds—wet, choking gasps that seemed to pull all the air from the clearing.

Maskwa started forward, but Ayâs raised one hand without looking at him. Wait.

In the forest, the Napiyaw remained. Maskwa could feel their presence, still strong, still watching. But the anticipation was gone, replaced by something else. Disappointment? Anger? He couldn't read them, had never been able to. They were as alien to him as he surely was to them.

The firelight caught their eyes one last time—amber glints between the trees—and then they were gone. Not walking away, not retreating. Simply… vanishing. As if they'd never been there at all.

The musky smell faded. The trees straightened. The air lightened.

They were gone.

Ayâs knelt beside Thomas's convulsing form. Her ancient hands moved over his chest, his throat, his forehead—checking, assessing. Her face showed no surprise, only a deep weariness that made her look, for the first time in Maskwa's memory, truly old.

"Brother," she whispered, so quietly that Maskwa barely heard. "It was not you."

Thomas's eyes found her face. The convulsions were slowing now, his body exhausting itself. His lips moved, trying to form words, but only foam came out. In his eyes, Maskwa saw confusion. Pain. And worse—the dawning realization of failure.

Twenty-eight years. Thomas had given twenty-eight years to the Wapiti, to this life, to this moment. And it wasn't enough.

Ayâs stroked his forehead, her touch gentle despite her gnarled fingers. She chanted softly—not the calling words, but something else. Words of release. Words of passage.

Around the circle, the Wapiti remained frozen. Some had tears on their faces. Others stared at the ground, unable to watch. A few looked toward the forest where the Napiyaw had been, as if hoping they might return, might give some sign that this could still work.

But the forest was just forest now. Dark and quiet and ordinary.

Thomas's convulsions stopped. His breathing grew shallow, labored. Blood mixed with the foam now—internal bleeding, Maskwa knew. The nature's milk was powerful. When the transformation failed, the body couldn't sustain what it had begun.

Ayâs pulled something from within her animal-skin robe. The knife. Maskwa had seen it many times, had watched her use it for this exact purpose at ceremony after ceremony. It was ancient, crafted from bone with a long, slender blade of chipped stone. The blade that ended suffering. The blade that granted release.

She held it up for Thomas to see, giving him the dignity of knowing what came next.

His eyes focused on the blade, then moved to her face. His lips formed words, barely audible: "Not… me?"

"Not you," Ayâs confirmed, her voice cracking. "But you served faithfully, brother. Twenty-eight winters you walked with us. Your mother's people would be proud of who you became."

A sound escaped Thomas's throat—not quite a laugh, not quite a sob. His hand fumbled for the medicine bag at his neck, clutched it once, then fell slack.

Ayâs leaned close, pressing her forehead to his. "Brother, go and find our protector in the next world. You are released."

She raised the knife.

The blade caught firelight as it descended, a brief flash of reflected flame. Then it was over. The stone blade pierced Thomas's chest cleanly, finding the heart with the practiced accuracy of someone who had done this too many times before.

Thomas Whitehorse's body went still.

The circle of Wapiti began a new chant—soft, mournful, a song for the dead. It was not the powerful rhythm of the calling ceremony but something quieter, older. A song mothers sang to dying children. A song as old as the first humans in these mountains.

Ayâs withdrew the blade, wiped it clean on the deerskin covering Thomas's legs, and stood. She seemed to have aged another decade in the last few minutes. Her shoulders bowed even more deeply. Her hands trembled as she returned the knife to its place within her robes.

Maskwa stepped forward, and Takoda appeared at his side. Without words, they both understood their duty. They had performed it before.

Together, they lifted Thomas's body. He was lighter than he should have been, as if the failed transformation had burned something out of him. His face, in death, looked peaceful. The confusion and pain were gone, replaced by a stillness that was almost serene.

Takoda placed his hands on Thomas's forehead, a gesture of respect. "We will carry you into eternity, brother."

The circle parted to let them through. As Maskwa and Takoda walked into the darkness beyond the firelight, carrying Thomas between them, the mournful chanting followed. It would continue until dawn, until Thomas was properly laid to rest in the earth he had loved.

Behind them, Ayâs remained by the fire. Alone now, except for the weight of another failure pressing down on her ancient shoulders.

A dozen attempts. A dozen failures.

How many more would there be before time ran out?

CHAPTER 2

THE PRIESTESS

The chanting faded as the Wapiti dispersed to their lodges and shelters, disappearing into the darkness like spirits themselves. Ayâs remained by the fire, her stooped form casting a long shadow across the trampled earth where Thomas had fallen.

So many attempts.

She kept count of each one, etched them into her memory like scars. Each face, each name, each moment when hope had transformed into failure. Twelve men and women who had drunk nature's milk, spoken the old words, offered themselves as vessels for the Napiyaw.

Twelve times, the ancient ones had come close, drawn by the ceremony, watching with those amber eyes that held the weight of millennia. And twelve times, they had withdrawn, disappointed. Unsatisfied.

The fire crackled, sending sparks spiraling into the night sky. Ayâs stared into the flames and let herself remember.

She had been young once. The thought felt strange, impossible, like a story about someone else. But she had been young—a girl called Giiwedin, apprenticed to the priestess who came before her. That had been in the time before the railroad, before the settlers flooded these mountains, before the buffalo vanished and the old ways began their slow death.

1847. One hundred seventy-eight years ago.

She had witnessed a successful transformation then. Had stood in a circle much like tonight's, had watched as her teacher—old even then, ancient beyond measure— had called the Napiyaw forth. And they had come. Not as shadows at the edge of firelight, not as distant howls in the forest, but here. Present. Fully manifested in the physical world.

The vessel had been a young warrior, strong and pure-hearted. When he drank the nature's milk and spoke the words, the Napiyaw had not withdrawn. They had embraced him. Entered him. And when he rose from his knees, he was something new—something between human and spirit, a bridge that walked in both worlds.

Magnificent and terrible, her teacher had called it. The way things were meant to be.

Ayâs had been fifteen years old. She had watched with wonder as the transformed warrior—no longer quite a warrior, no longer quite human—had walked into the forest with the Napiyaw. The ancient ones had accepted him as one of their own. And for years afterward, he had led the Wapiti, protected them. The buffalo had remained plentiful. The settlers had kept their distance. The balance had held.

When her teacher had finally passed, crumbling to dust one winter morning as if she had only been held together by will, Ayâs had waited for her turn. She had been twenty-three, full of certainty that she would continue the work after her teacher, after the young warrior. That she would find the next vessel, maintain the bridge between worlds, keep the Napiyaw present and powerful.

But the world had changed too quickly.

The railroad came. The buffalo died. The settlers multiplied like rabbits, spreading across the land in waves that never stopped. Her people were herded onto reservations, their ceremonies banned, their children stolen and sent to schools that beat the old ways out of them.

The Wapiti had splintered off from the larger Stoney Nakota nation, refusing to give up the ceremonies, refusing to let the connection die. They had hidden in these mountains, coming each summer to this sacred place to perform the rituals that kept the memory alive.

But memory was not enough. The Napiyaw grew more distant with each passing year, retreating further into the spirit world, their presence in the physical realm fading to shadows and echoes.

Ayâs had tried everything. She had refined the nature's milk recipe, adding ingredients her teacher had never used. She had studied the old songs until she could sing them in her sleep. She had searched for candidates — people with the right bloodlines, the right spiritual sensitivity, the right hunger for transformation.

Some had been born to the Wapiti. Some had come seeking, like Thomas Whitehorse, drawn by heritage and the ache for belonging. A few had been taken — captured and converted because Ayâs had sensed potential in them that they didn't see in themselves.

Twelve attempts. And every one had ended with foam and convulsions and the bone knife.

The fire dimmed, and Ayâs felt the weight of her years pressing down. Her body was ancient, held together by ceremony and sheer stubborn will. The rituals kept her alive because the Napiyaw needed a priestess. But will had its limits. She could feel herself thinning, like cloth worn so often it had become translucent. One day—soon, perhaps—she would crumble to dust as her teacher had.

And if she died before finding the true vessel…

The Napiyaw would fade completely. Become full shadow, full spirit, unable to protect these lands. Unable to reclaim what had been stolen. And her people—the Wapiti, the keepers of the old ways—would fade with them. Another generation or two, and the ceremonies would be performed by rote, empty words spoken by people who had never seen what she had seen, who didn't truly believe.

The old agreements would break. The balance would shatter. And the modern world would consume everything, as it had consumed so much already.

"But not yet," Ayâs whispered to the darkness. Her voice was cracked, tired, but underneath it ran a thread of iron. "I feel you coming. The one who can bridge the two worlds."

She closed her eyes and let her awareness expand, reaching out the way her teacher had taught her. Past the fire, past the sleeping lodges, past the boundaries of the camp and into the forest itself. The Napiyaw were still there, she could feel them. Patient. Waiting.

They had waited for millennia before humans came to these mountains. They could wait longer.

But could she?

A vision flickered at the edge of her consciousness—not clear, never clear, but present. A woman. Not Wapiti by birth, but something in her blood sang with the old world. Something in her spirit was already broken, hungry, seeking. A woman trapped in the wrong life, suffocating under the weight of a world that had never fit her.

She was close. Ayâs could feel it. Days, perhaps. Weeks at most.

"Soon," Ayâs murmured. "She comes soon."

From the forest, a sound—not quite a howl, not quite words. The Napiyaw had heard. They were listening. They believed too, in their own ancient way. They would wait for this one more chance, one more vessel.

And if this woman failed as the others had…

Ayâs pushed the thought away. She couldn't afford doubt. Not now. Not when she was this close.

She opened her eyes and looked at the fire. The flames had burned low, reduced to red embers that pulsed like a heartbeat. Beyond the firelight, the forest pressed close, full of shadows and old promises.

Somewhere out there, the woman was coming. The right one. The vessel that would succeed where others had failed.

She had to be.
Ayâs had nothing left but that hope.

22

THE BURIAL

The burial site was a quarter mile from camp, in a clearing where the trees formed a natural cathedral. Moonlight filtered through the canopy, dappling the forest floor with silver. Maskwa and Takoda had walked this path many times before, carrying bodies wrapped in ceremonial cloth. But tonight felt heavier somehow. More final.

They laid Thomas Whitehorse gently on the earth beside the grave Maskwa had prepared earlier that day. The hole was deep, lined with cedar boughs and sweet grass. Thomas would rest among his brothers and sisters—others who had tried and failed, who had given everything for a transformation that never came.

Takoda knelt beside the body, adjusting Thomas's medicine bag so it lay properly on his chest. His hands were steady, but Maskwa noticed the tightness around his eyes, the way his jaw clenched.

"He was happy here," Takoda said quietly. It wasn't a question.

Maskwa grunted agreement. "Happier than he ever was in Seattle."

They had talked about this before, he and Thomas. Late nights around fires, when the others were asleep and the two men could speak honestly. Thomas had told him about his other life—the cubicle, the fluorescent lights, the meetings, endless emails. The marriage that fell apart because neither of them knew who the other really wanted. The feeling of living in a skin that didn't fit.

"The police stopped looking for him after two years," Takoda said, still staring at Thomas's peaceful face.

"His ex-wife remarried." Maskwa crouched beside the grave, began arranging the cedar boughs more carefully. "She told people he 'found himself in the mountains.' She wasn't wrong."

Takoda made a sound that might have been a laugh or a sob. "He lived with us for twenty-eight years. And then Ayâs told him he was ready. He believed her."

"He was ready." Maskwa lifted Thomas's body, cradling it as if it weighed nothing, and lowered it gently into the grave. The cedar branches cushioned the descent. Thomas looked like he was sleeping, his weathered face finally at rest. "Ayâs sensed the potential in him. Not when he first arrived—he was too broken then, too raw. But after years of healing, of learning the old ways… she saw it."

"And now he's dead." Takoda's voice cracked. "Another one dead, and we're no closer—"

"Ayâs says the right one is close." Maskwa began covering the body with earth, his movements methodical and reverent. "She feels it. A woman this time."

Takoda stood, wrapping his arms around himself despite the warm summer night. "She's said that before. How many times has she sensed 'the one'? How many have we tested?"

"Twelve." Maskwa's voice held no doubt, no hesitation. "But this time is different. The Napiyaw are restless. They came closer tonight than they have in years. You felt it. You saw them."

Takoda had seen them. Three of them, maybe four, standing at the edge of the firelight. Tall and impossible, covered in fur that seemed to drink the darkness. Eyes that held intelligence and patience mixed with hunger. He had looked into those eyes, and for a moment, he'd understood what Thomas must have felt. The certainty that something ancient and powerful was real. The desire to bridge the gap between their world and this one.

And then Thomas had convulsed, and the Napiyaw had withdrawn, and Takoda had been left with the familiar hollow feeling of failure.

"What if we're wrong?" The words came out before Takoda could stop them. "What if there is no vessel? What if we keep searching forever, keep testing people, and none of them—"

"Then we continue anyway." Maskwa paused in his work, his massive hands full of earth. He looked at Takoda with an expression that was almost pitying. "We keep the ceremonies alive. We honor the old ways. We maintain the connection, even if we never achieve a full transformation again."

"Even if it means more deaths?"

"Thomas volunteered. They all volunteer." Maskwa returned to filling the grave. "When Ayâs senses potential, she asks. She doesn't force. Thomas chose to drink the pure nature's milk. He knew the risk."

Takoda thought about the distinction. The pure nature's milk—undiluted, powerful, dangerous—was reserved only for transformation attempts. That's what had killed Thomas. That's what had killed the others before him.

But the ceremonial tea they served to new members like Marcus Webb—that was different. Weaker. Nature's milk diluted with other herbs, designed not to transform but to open minds, create spiritual experiences, bond people to the community. It made them suggestible, receptive. Over time, willing.

"Marcus is different though," Takoda said, following his own thoughts aloud. "We brought him here. He didn't come seeking."

"We invited him." Maskwa's voice held a warning. "There's a difference."

"He didn't know what he was accepting."

"No one ever does." Maskwa stood, the grave filled and mounded now. "But Marcus fits here. You saw it when you met him on the trail—he had the right energy, the right... openness. He was alone, searching for something even if he didn't know what. We offered him community. Purpose."

"And the tea."

"The tea helps," Maskwa acknowledged. "But it doesn't force. Marcus drinks it willingly at our gatherings. It shows him the truth—that this life has meaning his old life lacked. Some people need help seeing what's already inside them."

Takoda wrapped his arms tighter around himself. "We're not going to try to transform him, though. That's not why we brought him here."

"No." Maskwa shook his head firmly. "Marcus is meant to be part of the community, not a vessel. We need members, Takoda. People to hunt, to build, to maintain what we've created here. Not everyone has to be tested for transformation. Most don't. Most are like you—believers who support the ceremonies but aren't candidates themselves."

The words should have been reassuring, but Takoda heard the implication underneath: *You're useful, but you're not special. Not the way Thomas was. Not the way this mysterious woman will be.*

"When this woman comes," Takoda said slowly, "will she be like Thomas? A volunteer? Or like Marcus—someone we invite and then… encourage?"

Maskwa placed his hand on Takoda's shoulder, a gesture of reassurance. "Ayâs will know when she sees her. If she's truly the vessel, she'll sense it herself. Feel the pull. She'll come willingly to the ceremony when the time is right."

"And if she doesn't?"

Maskwa's expression darkened slightly. "Then we help her understand what she already knows deep down. We give her the tea at gatherings, let her see what we see, feel what we feel. By the time Ayâs asks her to drink the pure nature's milk and attempt transformation, she'll want it. She'll understand it's her purpose."

From the forest around them came a sound—a low rumble, felt more than heard. Not quite a growl, not quite speech. The trees seemed to lean inward, listening.

Takoda's skin prickled. They were still here. Still watching. Still waiting.

Maskwa knelt at the head of the grave, pressing his palm into the freshly turned earth. "Rest well, Thomas Whitehorse. You walked the old path with honor. May you find the Napiyaw in the next world, since you could not become their vessel in this one."

Takoda knelt beside him, adding his own hand to the earth. "You were brother to us. We carry your memory."

They remained that way for a long moment, two men kneeling in the forest, honoring a third who had given everything for a vision that had eluded him.

Finally, Maskwa rose. "The woman is coming. Soon. Days, maybe. Weeks at most."

"How do you know?"

Maskwa gestured toward the forest, toward the darkness where amber eyes had watched the ceremony. "Because they know. The Napiyaw are restless because they sense her. When they know something, we must believe them."

He started back toward camp, his massive frame moving silently through the undergrowth. Takoda followed, casting one last look at Thomas's grave. The mounded earth looked dark and fresh in the moonlight. By morning, moss would begin to claim it. By next summer, it would be indistinguishable from a dozen other graves scattered through these woods.

The Wapiti kept no markers, no monuments. The forest remembered for them.

As they neared the camp, the last embers of the ceremonial fire glowed like distant stars. Most of the lodges were dark now, their occupants sleeping or pretending to sleep. Tomorrow they would hunt, gather, repair shelters, live the life they had chosen or been drawn into. Tomorrow, the rhythms of the camp would continue as they always had.

But underneath it all, the waiting. Always the waiting.

Maskwa paused at the edge of the clearing. "When she comes—the woman Ayâs has sensed—you'll need to find her. Approach her carefully. Make her curious, make her interested. Bring her to us in a way that feels like her choice."

"The way I did with Marcus?"

"Yes. But this woman is different. She's not meant to join the community as a member. She's meant to transform it—to transform everything." Maskwa's voice carried absolute conviction. "Approach her with respect. With reverence. She may not know what she is yet, but we do."

"And when she's here? When she's drinking the tea at our gatherings, participating in ceremonies?"

"We watch her. We teach her. We let Ayâs guide her toward readiness." Maskwa turned to face Takoda directly. "And when the time comes, Ayâs will offer her the pure nature's milk. The real thing. And she will drink it willingly, knowing it might kill her, because by then she'll understand—this is why she came to these mountains. This is her purpose."

From somewhere deep in the trees, a howl rose—long, mournful, ending in that almost-human note that never failed to send chills down Takoda's spine. The Napiyaw were singing their own song for Thomas. Or perhaps they were calling for the woman who was coming.

Either way, the sound carried a promise and a warning.

They were waiting. They were always waiting.

And when she arrived—whoever she was—everything would change.

Takoda just hoped it would change in the right direction.

Maskwa walked toward his lodge, leaving Takoda alone at the forest's edge. The howl faded into the night, but the feeling of being watched remained. The Napiyaw hadn't truly left. They never did anymore. They lingered at the boundaries, patient and eternal, waiting for the one who could finally bridge the worlds.

Takoda looked back toward the burial site, though it was hidden now by trees and darkness. Twelve attempts. Twelve failures. And now they would try again with a woman none of them had even met yet.

He closed his eyes and sent a silent thought toward Thomas's grave: *I hope she's worth it, brother. I hope this time it works.*

From the forest, no answer came.

Only the eternal patience of things far older than doubt.

CHAPTER 4

FIRST CONNECTIONS

The black Escalade glided through the mountain highway like a shark through deep water, its tinted windows reflecting the impossible beauty of the Canadian Rockies. Inside, Elaine Whitmore-Calhoun pressed her forehead against the cool glass, watching the peaks slide past in a procession of granite and ice.

Her phone buzzed for the sixteenth time since leaving Calgary International. She didn't need to look to know it was Bradford. The first three texts she'd read had been enough:

This is incredibly immature.
Mother is asking questions I can't answer.
You're embarrassing both families.

She'd stopped reading after that, but the buzzing continued at regular intervals, each vibration a little stab of obligation she was three thousand miles from fulfilling. *Let him buzz. Let his mother ask questions. Let the Junior League wonder where Mrs. Bradford Calhoun III had disappeared to.*

The answer was simple: she was running.

"That's Cascade Mountain ahead," said a cheerful voice from the passenger seat next to her. "And if you look to the left—just there—you can see Ha Ling Peak. The local Stoney Nakoda people have names for all of them, of course. Much older names than the ones on our maps."

Elaine forced her attention to the woman beside her—Maureen something, a professor who'd been waiting for a ride at the airport with an apologetic smile and an overstuffed backpack. Elaine had offered to share her car service partly out of politeness, partly because even fleeing her life, certain social protocols remained ingrained.

"The Sleeping Buffalo is coming up," Maureen continued, her enthusiasm undimmed by Elaine's silence. "It was a landmark for centuries—Indigenous peoples, fur trappers, early explorers. They'd look for that distinctive silhouette to know they were approaching the Banff valley."

Elaine's phone buzzed again. This time she couldn't help but glance.

I've already had to make excuses at the Vanderbilt dinner. You're making me look like a fool.

She powered the phone off completely and dropped it in her purse.

"I don't see a buffalo," she said, hearing the edge in her own voice and not quite managing to soften it.

"No, not from this angle. You'll see it when we swing around to the west." Maureen pointed ahead with undisguised excitement. "I studied the local geography before coming. The cultural history here is fascinating. Indigenous peoples have occupied this valley for over ten thousand years. Can you imagine? Ten thousand years of stories, all embedded in this landscape."

Elaine tried to imagine it and failed. Ten thousand years was a number without meaning, like trying to picture infinity. What she could picture was Bradford at the Vanderbilt dinner, making excuses for her absence, his jaw tight with controlled anger.

Good. Let him be angry.

She'd been angry for three years.

"Thank you again for the ride," Maureen said, apparently taking Elaine's silence as her cue to fill it. "You saved me a hundred-dollar fare from Calgary. That's a significant expense on a professor's salary."

"Of course," Elaine replied automatically. "What was I going to do with all this empty space?" She gestured at the SUV's cavernous interior, ordered by her assistant without her input because Bradford thought sedans were "inappropriate for rough terrain." Never mind that she'd be on a major highway.

One hundred dollars, she thought. *Who cares about that? It's barely one lunch in the city.*

The thought made her uncomfortable, though she couldn't say why. Maureen's gratitude over something so trivial felt like a mirror held up to show Elaine something she'd rather not see. The difference between their worlds, maybe. The difference between someone who had to count costs and someone who'd never been taught how.

"So you're a realtor in New Jersey?" Maureen asked.

Elaine suppressed a grimace, turning it into something resembling a smile. "We own real estate. New Jersey, New York, New Hampshire. Several office buildings, apartment complexes. One college campus."

She watched Maureen's expression shift from polite interest to surprise. "How do you own a college campus?

I thought those were government institutions or nonprofit endowments."

"They usually are today. But two hundred years ago, they were all private affairs. My family still has one." Elaine heard how it sounded—casually mentioning her family's ownership of an entire institution of higher learning—but she'd never learned another way to say it. Facts were facts.

"Like Harvard?"

Elaine allowed herself a small laugh. "Yes, like Harvard. On a smaller scale." She didn't mention that smaller didn't mean cheaper. Whitmore College's tuition exceeded most Ivy League schools, but that was the point. Students—and, more importantly, their parents—paid premium prices to be part of the right social circles, to have their names in the right alumni directories.

"That's quite different from Virginia Commonwealth University, where I teach," Maureen said, her freckled face brightening with academic pride. "But VCU has a fantastic faculty studying ancient theology. We're known globally in the field. That's what drew me there."

Elaine made an appreciative sound, though she'd never heard of VCU and hadn't known ancient theology was even a field of study. She glanced at Maureen more carefully—really looked at her for the first time. Midforties probably, with the kind of body that suggested fitness was practical rather than ornamental. Long red hair pulled back in a careless ponytail. Clothes from outdoor outfitters rather than boutiques. The eager enthusiasm of someone who still found joy in her work.

A flutter of something—envy? longing?—stirred in Elaine's chest. When was the last time she'd been enthusiastic about anything? When had her life become a series of obligations performed for an invisible audience that never stopped judging?

"If you don't mind my asking," Maureen ventured, her tone carefully gentle, "why are you on this vacation? It's not exactly elegant luxury."

The question was more perceptive than Elaine expected. She felt her defenses rise automatically, then forced them down. What did it matter what this stranger thought? She'd never see her again after this week.

"I'm not here for the luxury," Elaine heard herself say. "I get enough of that on other trips. I wanted something different. Beautiful scenery. Physical challenge. No one watching." She paused, then added with more honesty than she'd intended, "No one who knows me."

Maureen's expression softened with understanding. "Well, this is the place. I don't know you, and we're already friends, aren't we?" She smiled warmly. "In fact, you're probably a better runner than I am. Certainly thirty pounds lighter and several inches taller."

Elaine felt herself relax slightly. Compliments on her appearance were familiar territory. "Thank you. But I'm sure you're more practiced at trail running."

The SUV slowed, and their driver spoke for the first time since Calgary. "Excuse me, ladies. This is the hotel. If you wait a moment, I'll get your door and your bags."

He stepped out briskly and circled to the curb. Elaine watched him open Maureen's door first, helping her out with professional courtesy. When he came to her side, she extended her hand, and he took it to assist her exit. As she stood, she pressed a folded hundred-dollar bill into his palm.

"How gentlemanly," Maureen observed, not having seen the transaction.

"Yes, he is," Elaine agreed, smoothing her linen pants. The money had changed hands so smoothly it might never have happened—a habit so ingrained she barely registered it anymore. That's what money was for, wasn't it? Making interactions smooth, keeping everything pleasant, ensuring people treated you well.

Bradford's voice echoed in her memory: *You buy people, Elaine. You don't befriend them.*

She pushed the thought away as a petite woman bounded toward them from the hotel entrance.

"Ladies! You're just in time. I'm Zuri Davies, your event director."

The British accent was as cheerful in person as it had been on the video calls, and Zuri's energy was immediately infectious. She couldn't have been more than five-four, but she radiated the kind of presence that filled a space. Brown eyes sparkled with genuine warmth, and her smile seemed to engage her entire face.

"Zuri! It's wonderful to meet you in person." Maureen extended her hand, but Zuri pulled her into a quick, firm hug instead.

"We're huggers at Global Runners Travel," Zuri announced. "It might seem forward now, but you're about to make some of your best friends this week. I've seen it happen a hundred times."

Maureen beamed at the embrace. Elaine accepted her own hug with what she hoped was grace, though she couldn't help trying to end it quickly. Physical affection from strangers wasn't something her upbringing had prepared her for.

"Dinner begins in an hour," Zuri said, producing two key cards with a flourish. "Drop your bags in your rooms and come down to the banquet hall. We'll have drinks and appetizers while everyone arrives, then a proper welcome dinner. You'll want to fuel up—tomorrow we hit the trails hard."

Elaine took both keys and turned immediately to their driver. "If you wouldn't mind?"

"Of course, ma'am."

"Perfect. Let's go straight through then, shall we? I'm ready for a drink." Elaine strode toward the hotel entrance, heels clicking on the pavement. Behind her, Maureen hurried to keep pace, and Zuri's laugh followed them through the automatic doors.

CHAPTER 5

BASECAMP

Louise Mountain Lodge was exactly what its name suggested—rustic charm meeting contemporary luxury in a carefully curated space. Reclaimed wood beams crossed the high ceiling, while modern furniture in earth tones clustered around a massive stone fireplace. Floor-to-ceiling windows framed views of the mountains that made Elaine pause despite herself.

"Gorgeous, isn't it?" Maureen stopped beside her, both women momentarily silenced by the vista. Three

Sisters peaks stood guard to the east, their snow-covered summits catching the late afternoon sun.

The lobby was moderately busy—other guests checking in, families returning from day hikes, a few people in business casual who looked distinctly out of place in this athletic setting. Near the bar, a wall-mounted television played a local hockey game at low volume.

"Excuse me, I've got to greet another arrival," Zuri said, heading to the front door.

While Zuri returned to her duties, Elaine found herself drawn to a display case near the windows. It held Indigenous artifacts—beaded moccasins, a small dreamcatcher, photographs of early inhabitants. Her eyes skipped over most of it until landing on a hand-drawn map labeled "Traditional Territories of the Stoney Nakota First Nations."

"Fascinating, isn't it?" Maureen had materialized beside her. The woman moved quietly for someone so enthusiastic. "The Stoney Nakota have three distinct bands—Bearspaw, Chiniki, and Goodstoney. They've occupied this area since before European contact."

"How do you know all this?"

"Research." Maureen smiled sheepishly. "I always study the culture and history before traveling somewhere new. It's part of being a religious studies scholar. Every place has a spiritual history, and this region is particularly rich. The Indigenous peoples here have creation stories, sacred sites, ceremonial practices that go back millennia."

Elaine studied the map more closely. The territory covered vast areas of what was now Banff National Park and beyond. She thought about her family's property holdings in New Jersey—land her great-great-grandfather had acquired through business deals she'd never questioned. Had there been people there first, too? People whose names weren't on the deeds?

"—still searching for Marcus Webb," the television said, pulling Elaine's attention. She turned to see a news anchor with an expression of professional concern. Behind him, a photo showed a man in his early forties with sandy brown hair and a casual smile, wearing a North Face jacket and holding hiking poles.

"That's concerning," said a voice near the TV. Elaine glanced over to see an older couple, both in their sixties, watching the broadcast with worried frowns.

"Marcus Webb, 42, was last seen three months ago near the Spray Valley trails," the anchor continued. "Webb, a photographer from Portland, had posted on several hiking forums about seeking authentic Indigenous cultural experiences in the Canadian Rockies. Park rangers conducted extensive searches but found no evidence of foul play. Officials remind visitors that while Banff's trails are generally safe, the wilderness can be unpredictable."

The screen showed search and rescue teams combing through the forest, then cut to an interview with a park ranger. "We always advise hikers to travel in groups, carry proper safety equipment, and register their routes with someone. The mountains are beautiful, but they demand respect."

"They always say that," the woman near the TV murmured to her husband. "No evidence of foul play. But people don't just vanish."

Her husband squeezed her shoulder. "Come on, dear. We're scheduled for a guided hike. We'll be perfectly safe."

They moved away, but Elaine still stared at the television. The screen had shifted to show another photo—this one older, more dated. A professional headshot of a man who looked to be in his forties, with high cheekbones and copper skin that suggested Indigenous heritage, though his features held European influences too.

"Thomas Whitehorse was last seen in 1997," the anchor said, his tone suggesting this was a colder case being revisited. "The 35-year-old Microsoft engineer came to Banff seeking connections to his Stoney Nakota heritage and simply disappeared. His case remains one of the area's most persistent mysteries."

"Twenty-eight years," someone murmured nearby. "Poor man's probably dead somewhere in a ravine."

"Happens more often than you'd think," said a new voice. Elaine turned to find a tall man with close-cropped grey hair standing nearby. He wore a hotel uniform with a name tag that read "James - Concierge." His expression was sympathetic but not alarmed. "Not the disappearances specifically, but the accidents. Broken ankles, hypothermia, people getting lost. The mountains are less forgiving than tourists expect."

"Should we be worried?" Maureen asked, though her tone suggested intellectual curiosity more than actual fear.

"Not if you're with Global Runners," James assured them. "Zuri's outfit is one of the best. They have an excellent safety record. But it's good to remember that this isn't a theme park. The wilderness is real out there." He paused, glancing at the television. "The Webb case is unusual, though. Most lost hikers are found within days—either alive or… well, found. Three months with no trace? That's rare."

He smiled professionally and moved away to help another guest, leaving Elaine staring at the two photos now displayed side by side on the screen: Marcus Webb's recent portrait and Thomas Whitehorse's decades-old headshot.

What would it be like to simply vanish? To walk into the trees and never come back? To have your photo on the news while strangers speculated about what happened?

"All sorted!" Zuri reappeared, her energy deliberately bright, clearly trying to redirect attention from the grim television report. "Would either of you like a drink?"

"Gin and tonic?" Maureen answered questioningly. "I'm officially starting my vacation—now."

"Wonderful. What about you, Elaine?"

Elaine realized both women were looking at her expectantly. "Yes, of course. I'll have the same." She hadn't even noticed what Maureen had ordered.

"Perfect. Oh, and Elaine?" Zuri's voice dropped slightly, becoming more personal. "I'm so glad you're here. You can let the weight of the world go for a few days. Many people come on these trips to get away from the pressures that chase them. Here, you can literally run away from all of that. Sometimes you need to run toward something new before you know what you're running from."

The observation was startlingly perceptive, and Elaine felt suddenly exposed. She managed a tight smile. "Thank you. I'll remember that." Still pondering Zuri's words, she added, "I think I will need some time in my room after all."

Then she turned and headed for the elevators, forgetting her drink, and aware of Maureen's concerned gaze following her. The image from the television was frozen in her mind—two faces that left this world and walked into mysterious oblivion.

CHAPTER 6

WELCOME DINNER

Room 318 was comfortable but unremarkable—the kind of mid-tier mountain lodge aesthetic Elaine recognized from ski resorts that catered to the upper-middle class rather than true luxury. Exposed beams from reclaimed timber, a gas fireplace with visible controls, a bed with a duvet in predictable earth tones, and those floor-to-ceiling windows that were nice but showed signs of being builder-grade rather than custom. It was impressive to most people. Perfectly adequate. Just not what she was used to. Bradford would have taken one look and insisted they upgrade, probably to some private chalet in Banff proper where the real money stayed. But that was exactly why she'd chosen this—it was beneath his standards, which meant it would annoy him.

She dropped her bag on the luggage rack and moved to the window. The late afternoon sun painted the mountains in shades of amber and rose. Three Sisters stood sentinel to the east, their peaks still holding winter's snow despite the summer warmth in the valley. It was beautiful in a way that made her chest tight—too vast, too indifferent, too far from anything she understood.

Her phone sat silent in her purse. She should charge it. Check messages. Let Bradford know she'd arrived safely, even if she wasn't ready to actually speak to him.

Instead, she unpacked with mechanical precision, hanging her carefully selected athletic wear in the closet. Each outfit had been chosen by a personal shopper who specialized in "adventure tourism chic"—technical fabrics in flattering cuts, designer labels that wouldn't look out of place in a fitness magazine spread. Nothing she owned would actually keep her warm if she were genuinely lost in these mountains, but that wasn't the point. The point was looking like someone who belonged on an adventure, even if she'd never had one.

Forty-five minutes later, she stood before the mirror, reassessing. Hair smoothed into a sleek ponytail. Minimal makeup that looked like no makeup. Tom Ford leggings that cost more than some people's monthly grocery budget, paired with a cashmere pullover in dove gray. Diamond studs that Bradford's mother had given her as a wedding present, small enough to be tasteful but expensive enough to signal status.

She looked perfect. She always looked perfect. That was the problem.

The elevator ride down felt like descending into uncertainty. The doors opened to reveal the lobby transformed—the fireplace now flanked by high-top tables, a portable bar set up near the windows, and clusters of people already gathering with drinks in hand. The energy was palpably different from an hour ago. Where the lobby had been quiet and transitional, now it hummed with anticipation and the particular brand of nervous excitement that came from strangers about to become temporary companions.

Zuri spotted her immediately and waved her over with the kind of enthusiasm that suggested she'd been watching for arrivals. "Elaine! Perfect timing. Come get a drink. We're starting with a local specialty."

At the bar, a cheerful server with a name tag reading "Sophie" was mixing drinks with visible flourish. "Bloody Caesar?" she offered before Elaine could ask what was available.

"I—what's in it?"

"Calgary's gift to the cocktail world," Sophie said with civic pride. "Vodka, Clamato juice, hot sauce, Worcestershire, celery salt on the rim. Think of it as Canada's answer to the Bloody Mary, but better."

"Clamato juice?" Elaine couldn't keep the doubt from her voice.

"Clam and tomato," Zuri interjected. "I know it sounds mad, but trust me—it's brilliant. The clam adds a savory depth. You'll love it or hate it, but you've got to try it at least once."

Sophie was already preparing one, her movements efficient and smooth. She rimmed a tall glass with celery salt, added ice, poured vodka with a sharp eye for measurement rather than bothering with a jigger, then filled it with the thick red juice. Three dashes of hot sauce, a splash of Worcestershire, a vigorous stir, and she garnished it with a celery stick that stood at attention like a flag.

"There you are. Welcome to Alberta."

Elaine accepted the glass and took a cautious sip. The flavor was complex—savory, spicy, oddly satisfying. She'd expected to hate it, had been prepared to smile politely and set it aside. Instead, she found herself taking another sip.

"Good, right?" Zuri grinned. "That's your first real Canadian experience. Now come on, let me introduce you around."

The crowd near the fireplace had grown to about a dozen people, and Elaine did an automatic assessment of their clothing—a habit bred from years of charity galas where you could calculate someone's net worth from their accessories. What she saw surprised her. These people weren't wearing the designer technical wear she'd packed. They wore regular athletic brands—Nike, Adidas, some North Face, a few pieces that looked like they'd come from discount outdoor retailers. Functional gear, well-used, in some cases slightly worn. A few people even had visible brand logos, something Elaine's personal shopper had specifically told her to avoid—logos are for people who need to prove something—she had said. She glanced down at her own outfit—the leggings, the cashmere pullover, the diamond studs. She looked expensive. They looked like actual athletes. For the first time, she wondered if she'd dressed wrong, if her attempt to look like she belonged on an adventure had only succeeded in broadcasting that she didn't.

"Everyone!" Zuri's voice cut through the conversations. "This is Elaine. She's joining us from New Jersey. Elaine, this is—well, actually, let's go around. Names, home cities, and why you picked this particular adventure. I'll start. Zuri Davies, originally from Wales but based in Colorado now, and I picked this adventure because it's my job." She laughed at her own joke. "But truly, the Canadian Rockies in summer might be my favorite place on Earth to run trails."

"I'm Dana Mitchell, from Savannah, Georgia." A petite blonde woman with a Southern accent and an immediately warm smile stepped forward. She was holding her phone at an angle that made Elaine realize she was probably filming. "I'm here because my followers have been asking for adventure content, and I wanted to push myself outside my comfort zone. Y'all, I'll be sharing everything this week!"

An athletic-looking couple stepped forward together. The man was tall and blonde, with the kind of casual confidence that suggested a former athlete. The woman beside him was lean and intense, with dark hair pulled back severely and green eyes that seemed to assess everything.

"Dave Thornton," the man said. "Phoenix, Arizona. Real estate agent, recreational runner, and this is my third Global Runners trip. First one was Iceland two years ago." He glanced at his companion with obvious affection. "Where I met Stella."

"Stella Garrison," the woman added. "Also Arizona, also recreational running, though I do ultras. Leadership coach by day. This is my—" she paused to count on her fingers, "—eleventh trip with Global Runners. I'm basically addicted."

"Eleven trips?" Elaine couldn't hide her surprise. "That's—"

"A lot, I know." Stella's smile softened her angular features. "But once you do one, you understand. It's not just running. It's this perfect combination of challenge, beauty, and getting away from everything that normally drains you. I'm already planning my twelfth."

"And I'm trying to keep up with her," Dave added with good humor. "This is only my third, but I'm learning. The trails are better than basketball courts, it turns out."

Maureen appeared at Elaine's elbow, holding what looked like the same Caesar. "Isn't this fascinating? Everyone's from somewhere different, but we're all here for the same reason."

"Which is?" Elaine asked.

"To run," Maureen said simply. "But also, to be somewhere we're not. To do something that doesn't fit in our regular lives." She gestured around the group. "Dana probably never runs trails in Georgia. Stella probably has a whole life in Arizona she's taking a break from. Same with Dave. Same with you, I'd wager."

It was more perceptive than Elaine was comfortable with, so she took another sip of her Caesar instead of responding.

A broad-shouldered man in his fifties approached with a grin that suggested he was perpetually about to tell a joke. "Rogerio Santos," he announced with a slight Brazilian accent. "São Paulo originally, but I've been all over. Software developer, which means I sit at a desk all day staring at screens, which means I need to do this—" he gestured at the mountains beyond the windows, "—to remember I have a body. This is my fourth Global Runners trip. Ecuador, the Azores, South Africa, and now Canada."

"What happened in the Azores?" Dave asked, something in his tone suggesting he already knew the story.

"What always happens to Rogerio," someone called from across the group, triggering laughter.

Rogerio clutched his chest in mock offense. "I have terrible luck! It's not my fault. In Ecuador, I got altitude sickness. In the Azores, aggressive geese chased me. South Africa—"

"Don't forget getting lost in Costa Rica," a woman added helpfully.

"That was Stella, not me," Rogerio corrected. "But yes, in South Africa, I had a minor incident with a baboon who stole my energy bars. I'm basically a disaster magnet. Zuri has learned to keep extra first aid supplies specifically for me."

"It's true," Zuri confirmed. "But you're also one of my favorite repeat customers because you have the best attitude about it. Most people would get discouraged. You turn it into comedy."

"What else can you do?" Rogerio shrugged philosophically. "The universe has decided I'm the comic relief. I've accepted my role."

The introductions continued—Ben, a software engineer from Seattle; a teacher from Toronto; Sarah and Luke—a couple from Austin celebrating their twentieth anniversary. Elaine tried to keep track of names and faces, but they blurred together in a way that felt familiar from countless charity galas and society dinners. The difference was that here, no one seemed to care about what she did for a living or who her family was. They cared about whether she could keep up on the trails.

"Alright, everyone!" Zuri clapped her hands, pulling attention back to her. "The dining room is ready for us. Let's head in, and I'll have you seated at tables of six. You'll rotate seats each meal, so by the end of the week, you'll have gotten to know everyone."

The dining room had been set up banquet-style, with four round tables arranged in a circle so everyone could see each other. The centerpieces were simple—pine branches and river stones—but the overall effect was warm and inviting. Elaine found herself seated between Maureen and Dave, with Stella across from her, Dana to Stella's left, and Rogerio completing their table of six.

At the head of the room, a man in chef's whites was waiting to address the group. Zuri introduced him with a flourish: "Everyone, this is Chef Henry, who's prepared something special for your first night in Alberta."

Chef Henry stepped forward with the confident bearing of someone who knew his craft. He was perhaps sixty, with silver-streaked black hair and the kind of compact, efficient build that came from decades of kitchen work.

"Welcome to Canada," he said, his accent placing him as locally raised. "Since it's your first night here, I wanted to fuel you properly with some of Alberta's best. I can see many of you have already started with our Bloody Caesar—invented in Calgary by a bartender named Walter Chell in 1969. He was looking for a drink to pair with spaghetti, if you can believe it."

This triggered appreciative laughter from those who'd been skeptical of the clam juice.

"At your place settings," Chef Henry continued, "you'll find green onion cakes with dipping sauce. The cakes are made like a pancake—crispy on the outside, tender and layered inside. The dipping sauce is soy, rice wine vinegar, sesame oil, and just a pinch of sugar. This is an Edmonton invention, our sister city to the north. The Chinese community there created these, and now you can't have a gathering in this area without them."

Elaine looked down at the small plate before her. The green onion cake was golden and crispy, cut into wedges. She tried a piece with the dipping sauce and was surprised by how the savory, slightly sweet sauce complemented the crispy, scallion-rich pancake. Around the table, others were making similar appreciative sounds.

"And for your main course—" Chef Henry moved to the buffet line, lifting lids as he walked, "—we have braised bison short ribs. Bison is leaner than beef and more flavorful. These have been cooking since this morning, slow-braised until the meat falls off the bone. Beef roast in rich gravy for those who prefer something more traditional. Roasted potatoes, mashed potatoes, fried potatoes— we take our starches seriously in Canada. They keep us warm through the winters. And roasted vegetables—carrots, squash, sweet potatoes, and Brussels sprouts."

He moved to the dessert table with visible pride. "And for dessert, saskatoon berry pie with whipped cream and ice cream. Saskatoons are similar to blueberries but with a slight tartness, almost like cherries. They're native to the prairies, and we consider them a treasure. Bon appétit!"

The group actually applauded, and the buffet line formed immediately. Elaine waited, uncomfortable with the scramble even though she was genuinely hungry. Maureen seemed to have no such hesitation, joining the line with enthusiasm.

When Elaine finally made her way through, she loaded her plate more than she'd intended—the bison ribs, roasted vegetables, a modest portion of mashed potatoes. Back at the table, she found the others already eating with the focused intensity of athletes who understood food as fuel.

"This is incredible," Dave said around a mouthful of bison. "I've had beef ribs, but these are better."

"Leaner but still flavorful," Stella agreed. "Higher protein, lower fat. Perfect trail food."

"Everything in Canada tastes better than it should," Rogerio announced. "I don't know what they do differently, but even their vegetables are better."

Dana had her phone propped against a water glass, clearly filming her plate. "Y'all, this is what high-altitude trail running fuel looks like. Look at that bison—falling off the bone. And these vegetables? Roasted to perfection. I'm going to need extra miles tomorrow to work this off."

"You'll get them," Zuri called from the next table. "Tomorrow, we tackle Jewell Pass. Fifteen kilometers with six hundred meters of elevation gain. You'll earn every calorie."

This information seemed to relax the table rather than worry them. These were people who'd paid to be challenged, who measured their vacations in vertical feet and trail miles rather than spa treatments and poolside lounging.

For several minutes, conversation paused as everyone focused on eating. Elaine genuinely enjoyed the food—the bison was rich and savory, the vegetables roasted with just enough char, the potatoes rich and indulgent. She couldn't remember the last time she'd eaten mashed potatoes. Bradford's mother had strong opinions about carbohydrates.

"So," Dave said eventually, leaning back with satisfaction, "anyone else see that news report in the lobby? About the missing hikers?"

The table's energy shifted immediately. Dana's phone remained propped up, still filming.

"I saw it," Maureen said. "Two men. One disappeared decades ago; one just three months ago. It's unsettling."

"Mountains are dangerous," Stella said pragmatically. "People underestimate them. They come from sea level, hike at altitude without proper acclimatization, go off trail, don't bring enough water. It happens."

"But no bodies," Rogerio pointed out. "That's the weird part. Usually they find something—equipment, remains, something. These guys just vanished."

"The older one, Thomas Whitehorse," Maureen said thoughtfully, "the news said he came here seeking connections to his Indigenous heritage. That detail stuck with me."

"Why?" Elaine asked.

"Because seeking spiritual connection is different from recreation. It suggests a different mindset, a different risk-taking, perhaps. Someone looking for meaning might go places recreational hikers wouldn't."

"Or he might have found what he was looking for," Dave suggested. "Maybe he connected with some community and decided to stay. It's not technically 'missing' if you choose not to go back."

"For twenty-eight years without telling anyone?" Stella's skepticism was evident. "That seems unlikely."

"People do disappear on purpose," Dave insisted. "Start new lives. Especially after divorces or career crises. The news said he was going through both."

"The recent one, though," Dana interjected. "Marcus Webb. Three months isn't twenty-eight years. His case is active. I saw posers in town. They're still expecting to find him."

"They said he was looking for 'authentic Indigenous experiences,'" Maureen recalled. "That's interesting phrasing. Suggests he was going off the tourist trail too."

"Or getting himself lost in the wilderness," Stella countered. "There's a fine line between authentic experience and reckless behavior."

Rogerio leaned forward conspiratorially. "You know what I think? Sasquatch."

The table groaned in unison.

"I'm serious!" Rogerio continued, clearly enjoying himself. "These mountains are perfect Bigfoot territory. Dense forests, remote areas, plenty of game animals for them to hunt. Maybe these missing hikers got too close to a Sasquatch family and—" he made a dramatic gesture of being snatched away.

"You can't be serious," Stella said.

"Why not? Indigenous peoples have legends about giant forest creatures. The Stoney Nakota call them Napiyaw. Every culture has stories about things in the woods that don't quite fit our understanding of nature."

"Stories," Stella emphasized. "Mythology. Not actual apex predators snatching hikers."

"But what if the stories are based on something real?" Rogerio was warming to his theme. "What if there really is something in these mountains that local people have known about for generations, but Western science dismisses because we can't categorize it?"

"Now you're sounding like a cryptozoologist," Dave laughed.

"I'm just saying—two men vanish without a trace in mountains where Indigenous peoples have centuries-old stories about mysterious forest creatures. Maybe everyone's looking for a rational explanation when the real one is something we don't want to believe."

"On that note," Zuri called from the next table, clearly having overheard, "let's keep the Sasquatch speculation to a minimum, shall we? The last thing I need is everyone jumping at shadows on the trail tomorrow."

CHAPTER 7

SASKATOON

The conversation had shifted the energy at the table. What had been comfortable camaraderie now carried an undercurrent of unease, especially for those who'd seen the news report.

"I have a question," Dana said, addressing Zuri across the room. "What's the scariest thing in these mountains? Like, actually dangerous, not Rogerio's Bigfoot fantasies."

Zuri seemed to consider the question carefully. "Honestly? The weather. It can change in minutes up at elevation. You start a hike in sunshine and end up in sleet. That's what gets people—they're not prepared for how quickly conditions deteriorate."

"What about animals?" Someone from another table called out.

"Bears, obviously. Grizzlies and black bears both. But they're generally more scared of you than you are of them. Make noise on the trail, don't surprise them, and you'll likely never see one. Cougars are more elusive but more dangerous if you do encounter them. Elk during the rutting season can be aggressive. Basically, everything out there is wild. That's what makes it beautiful, but it also means respecting boundaries."

"Has anyone on your trips ever been seriously hurt?" Dave asked.

Zuri's expression became more serious. "I've had close calls. We had a runner separate from the group during a trail run. She took a wrong turn, ended up lost for four hours. We found her eventually—she'd followed a stream down like we'd taught her, found a local village. But those four hours were the worst of my professional life."

"Was that you?" Dave looked at Stella with sudden realization.

Stella's face colored slightly. "Costa Rica. And it was three hours, not four. And I found my own way back, thank you very much."

"After we'd already organized search parties," Zuri added gently. "The point is, these adventures are as safe as I can make them, but I can't make them completely safe. The wilderness doesn't work that way. What I can promise is that we have protocols, we have safety equipment, we have emergency contacts, and I've been doing this long enough to know how to manage risk. But you all need to promise me something in return."

She stood up, making sure she had everyone's attention.

"Stay with the group. Follow instructions. If you feel uncomfortable or unsafe, speak up. Don't be the person who thinks they can handle something alone because they don't want to slow everyone down. There's no shame in struggling—there's only shame in hiding it until it becomes an actual emergency. Understood?"

A chorus of agreement rippled through the room.

"Good. Now who's ready for saskatoon berry pie?"

The tension broke as people rose and made their way to the dessert table. Elaine remained seated, watching the group dynamics. Dana was filming the pie, narrating its appearance for her social media followers. Rogerio was still making Bigfoot jokes to anyone who would listen. Stella and Dave moved together with the easy comfort of a long-term couple, finishing each other's sentences.

And Maureen was in her element, talking animatedly with the software engineer from Seattle about traditional Stoney Nakota spiritual practices, her academic enthusiasm infectious even as it made Elaine slightly uncomfortable. There was something almost desperate in how Maureen pursued these conversations, as if she were mining for something valuable.

"Not getting dessert?" Dave had returned to the table with a generous slice of pie.

"In a moment," Elaine said. "I'm still processing dinner."

"That's fair. They really load you up." He took a bite and made an appreciative sound. "Though you should definitely try this. The saskatoon berries are wild—they taste like blueberries and cherries had a baby."

Despite herself, Elaine smiled. "That's quite the description."

"I'm a real estate agent. I'm professionally good at making things sound appealing." He paused, studying her with more perception than she'd expected. "You seem a little overwhelmed. First Global Runners trip?"

"Is it that obvious?"

"Only because I remember my first one. I showed up in Iceland thinking I knew what I was getting into because I ran marathons. Then I realized trail running in volcanic terrain with a group of strangers was completely different from jogging around my Phoenix desert. Took me about two days to relax and just enjoy it."

"What made you relax?"

"Honestly? Screwing something up. I tried to keep pace with a real Boston competitor on day two, completely bonked after three miles, had to walk the rest of the route back. Everyone was incredibly nice about it. That's when I realized these trips aren't about performance—they're about the experience. Nobody's judging you. We're all just here to run in beautiful places and eat too much at dinner."

It was more reassuring than Elaine wanted to admit. "Thank you. That helps."

"Anytime. Now seriously, get some pie before Rogerio eats it all. The man has no self-control when it comes to dessert."

Elaine made her way to the dessert table, where Chef Henry was serving slices with visible pride. The pie was rustic and beautiful—the saskatoon berries dark purple beneath a lattice crust, whipped cream melting into the warm filling.

"First time trying saskatoon?" Chef Henry asked as he served her.

"First time I've even heard of it."

"Then you're in for a treat. My grandmother used to pick these on the prairies. They're a pain to harvest—the bushes are thorny and the berries are small—but the flavor is worth it. Nothing else quite like them."

Back at the table, Elaine tried a bite. The berries were indeed unlike anything she'd tasted—simultaneously tart and sweet, with an almost winey depth. The crust was buttery and flaky; the whipped cream rich without being cloying.

"Told you," Dave said, watching her reaction with satisfaction.

Around the dining room, the energy had shifted from nervous anticipation to genuine warmth. People were laughing, sharing stories, moving between tables to introduce themselves to people they hadn't met yet. Dana was showing Maureen something on her phone—probably her social media channels. Rogerio was demonstrating his baboon encounter to an increasingly amused audience. Stella was deep in conversation with one of the other women about ultramarathon training strategies.

Zuri moved through the room like a conductor managing an orchestra, facilitating introductions, making sure no one felt isolated, maintaining the delicate social chemistry that would determine whether this group gelled or fractured over the coming days.

"Can I have everyone's attention?" Zuri called out as people were finishing their pie. "Just a few more details about tomorrow before you head up to bed. We meet in the lobby at six-thirty. Yes, that's early. Yes, it's necessary—we want to beat the crowds and the heat. Breakfast will be available starting at six. Pack your running gear, bring water, wear layers because it'll be cool at the start but warm up quickly. We're driving to Jewell Pass, running the loop, then a picnic lunch. This afternoon we have an even bigger adventure planned, but I'm not spoiling that surprise yet."

"Is it the Via Ferrata?" someone called out.

"Maybe," Zuri said with a mysterious smile. "You'll find out tomorrow. For now, get some sleep. You'll want to be rested. And one more thing—"

She paused for effect.

"Welcome to the adventure. I'm so glad you're all here. This week is going to be extraordinary. I can already tell you're an excellent group, and I promise you'll leave here with stories you'll be telling for years and friendships that will last even longer. Now get some rest. Tomorrow, we run."

The room broke into applause, and people began drifting toward the exits, saying goodnight, making plans to meet for breakfast. Elaine found herself caught in the flow, moving toward the elevators with Maureen beside her.

"That was lovely," Maureen said contentedly. "Exactly what I needed. Good food, interesting people, and tomorrow we get to run through some of the most beautiful mountains in the world. What more could you want?"

Elaine thought about her phone, still dead in her purse. About Bradford's angry texts and his mother's questions and the Vanderbilt dinner she'd missed. About the life she'd left behind in New Jersey—the life that looked perfect from the outside but felt suffocating from within.

"Nothing," she heard herself say. "This is exactly what I needed too."

And for the first time since boarding the plane in Newark, she meant it.

FERRATA AND FALLS

FIRST TRAIL

The alarm pierced Elaine's dreamless sleep at 5:45 AM. Her body's internal clock had been trained by years of early morning Pilates sessions and charity breakfast meetings. She lay in the unfamiliar bed for a moment, disoriented by the quality of darkness. In New Jersey, even before dawn, there was always ambient light—street lamps, neighboring houses, the perpetual glow of the city bleeding into the suburbs. Here, the darkness was absolute, pressing against the windows like something with weight.

She reached for her phone out of habit, then remembered the dead battery she'd declined to charge. The temptation to plug it in, to check messages, to see what disaster Bradford claimed she'd caused by her absence—it was almost instinctual. Instead, she threw back the covers and headed for the shower.

Thirty minutes later, dressed in her carefully curated running gear, she made her way down to the breakfast room. The hotel was eerily quiet at this hour, as if she'd woken in an abandoned building. But the breakfast room glowed with warmth and energy, already half-full of Global Runners fueling up for the day ahead.

"Morning!" Zuri's voice was inexplicably cheerful for 6:15 AM. She was stationed near the coffee urns like a benevolent caffeine guardian, waving Elaine over. "Sleep well? First night in a new place is always rough. I've learned to bring my own pillow on these trips—sounds mad, I know, but it makes all the difference."

"I slept fine, actually." Elaine was surprised to realize it was true. No dreams, no midnight anxiety, just deep, black sleep.

"Brilliant. Get some food in you—we've got a proper climb ahead. The Jewell Pass isn't technically difficult, but it's steady elevation gain for the first hour. Your legs will remember it tomorrow." Zuri handed her a coffee without asking if she wanted one, somehow knowing she did. "Milk's over there, sugar if you need it."

Elaine accepted the coffee and moved toward the breakfast buffet. It was simpler than last night's dinner—oatmeal, yogurt, fresh fruit, toast, hard-boiled eggs, some breakfast meats. She loaded a plate with what seemed sensible: yogurt, granola, some melon, an egg. Around her, other runners were doing the same, though their portions were considerably larger.

Maureen appeared at her elbow, her red hair still damp from a shower, her freckled face flushed with excitement. "Good morning! I've been awake since five—couldn't sleep. I kept thinking about the route. Did you know Jewell Pass has been used as a travel corridor for thousands of years? The Stoney Nakota used it to move between valleys. There are probably archaeological sites all along the trail that haven't been documented yet."

It was too early for this level of enthusiasm, but Elaine found herself charmed despite her fatigue. "Have you always been a morning person?"

"God, no. But adventure makes me one. When I'm home, I hit snooze three times and drag myself to campus. Put me in a place with actual history and I'm up before dawn." Maureen grabbed a plate and began loading it with the efficiency of someone who knew exactly how many calories she'd be burning. "I brought my field notebook. I know we're running, not conducting research, but if I see anything interesting—rock formations, unusual plants, signs of historical use—I want to document it."

"You're going to run with a notebook?"

"Small one. Fits in my pocket." Maureen patted her running vest. "You'd be amazed what you can miss if you don't write it down immediately. The brain edits memories, fills in gaps with what it thinks should have been there rather than what was actually there. Contemporary documentation is crucial."

They found seats at a table where Dave and Stella were already eating with focused intensity. Dave looked considerably more awake than Elaine felt, while Stella had the alert, coiled energy of someone who'd probably already done a warm-up run.

"Morning," Dave offered around a mouthful of oatmeal. "Everyone ready for this?"

"Been ready since yesterday," Stella said. She was wearing a GPS watch that looked more complicated than most smartphones, and she was studying it with the concentration of a pilot checking instruments. "I've run the route virtually about six times. The elevation profile is steady but manageable. We gain most of the altitude in the first five kilometers, then it levels out for the middle section before a gentle descent back. Total distance is fifteen kilometers."

"You've run it virtually?" Elaine asked.

"Well, mentally, on trail running apps. You can preview routes, see elevation profiles, get a sense of what you're in for. I always scout digitally before a physical run." Stella finally looked up from her watch. "It's probably overkill, but I don't like surprises."

"After Costa Rica, can you blame her?" Dave said with affectionate humor.

"That was one time. One wrong turn in three years of trail running."

"That we know of," he teased.

Stella swatted his arm, but she was smiling. The easy intimacy between them made Elaine think of Bradford—how they never teased, never showed affection that wasn't choreographed for an audience. When had that happened? When had their relationship become a performance rather than a partnership?

"Right, everyone!" Zuri's voice cut through the breakfast chatter. "Buses load in ten minutes. Make sure you've got your water, your layers, your snacks. It's cool now but it'll warm up by midday, so dress in layers you can shed. And please, for the love of God, use the toilets now. There aren't any facilities on the trail, and nobody wants to be the person asking the group to stop twenty minutes in."

This triggered a small exodus toward the restrooms. Elaine used the opportunity to refill her water bottle, check her small running pack one more time. She had water, a lightweight jacket, some energy gels she'd been told to bring even though she'd never used them before. Everything felt simultaneously too much and not enough.

Outside, two luxury coach buses waited in the dim pre-dawn light, their engines running, exhaust visible in the cold air. The temperature had dropped overnight—Elaine could see her breath—and she was suddenly grateful for the extra layer she'd debated bringing.

"These aren't the usual transport," Maureen observed as they boarded. "Most adventure companies use old school buses or vans. These are quite nice."

"Zuri doesn't cut corners," said a voice behind them. Rogerio had appeared, looking simultaneously exhausted and excited. "On my Ecuador trip, we had luxury buses even though we were in remote areas. She says if you're going to ask people to push themselves physically, the least you can do is give them comfortable transport."

They found seats about midway back. Through the windows, Elaine watched the other runners boarding—Dana with her phone already recording, a couple from Austin she'd met briefly at dinner—Sarah and something, the software engineer from Seattle. Everyone looked prepared, experienced, like they belonged here. She felt like an impostor playing dress-up.

The buses pulled out of the hotel lot, heading west into darkness that was just beginning to lighten at the edges. Inside, the mood was subdued—people were waking up, drinking coffee from travel mugs, looking out windows at the emerging landscape.

Zuri stood at the front of the bus with a handheld microphone, her petite frame somehow commanding attention. "Morning, everyone. Proper morning to those of you who are actually awake, and sympathetic understanding to those of you who are just pretending." This got some laughs. "We're about twenty minutes from the trailhead. I want to go over a few things whilst we drive.

"First, the route. We're running Jewell Pass, which is considered moderate difficulty. The trail is well-maintained, but it's still wilderness—roots, rocks, some narrow sections. The first hour is steady climbing through aspen forest. Then we break out above the tree line and you'll see why we got up at stupid o'clock—the views are absolutely brilliant when you catch them early. We'll reach the pass itself around the four-mile mark. That's our high point, and then it's a lovely rolling descent back to the trailhead.

"Second, pacing. This isn't a race. We'll have three groups—fast, moderate, and scenic pace. I don't care which group you choose, but be honest with yourselves. If you're feeling tired, drop back to the next group. If you need to walk, walk. There's no shame in it, and you'll enjoy the experience more if you're not suffering the whole time.

"Third, safety. We have support vehicles at the trailhead and at the midpoint where a service road crosses our trail. If anyone needs to stop, we can get you picked up. We have cellphones. We have first aid. We have emergency protocols. But the best safety measure is staying together and speaking up if something's wrong. Don't be a hero. Don't push through pain. Don't wander off trail too far for photos."

She paused, her brown eyes scanning the bus. "And finally, enjoy this. Look up from your feet occasionally. Yes, the trail requires attention, but you're running through some of the most beautiful landscape on Earth. This is why we're here."

The buses slowed, turning onto a gravel road that led to a small parking area. Through the windows, Elaine could see the trailhead—a wooden sign, some information boards, and beyond that, forest climbing up into the mountains.

"Alright," Zuri said as the bus came to a stop. "Let's go have an adventure."

The cold hit immediately when Elaine stepped off the bus—sharp, clean, carrying the scent of pine and something else she couldn't identify. Stone? Snow from the high peaks? The air itself tasted different here, thin and pure in a way that made her realize how much she'd been breathing recycled atmosphere in New Jersey.

"Brilliant morning for it," Zuri announced, her breath visible in the dawn light. She was doing some kind of dynamic stretching, pulling her knee to her chest, then swinging it side to side. Around her, other runners were doing the same—loosening cold muscles, preparing bodies for effort.

Elaine attempted to mimic their movements, feeling awkward and uncoordinated. Maureen, beside her, was bent nearly in half, her palms flat on the ground despite no apparent warm-up. *How was everyone so flexible?*

"Right, listen up!" Zuri called. "Fast group, you're with me. We'll set a pace of about six minutes per kilometer on the climbs, faster on the flats and descents. That's a nine-forty in American miles. Moderate group, you're with James—that's seven-minute pace on climbs. Scenic group, you're with Sophie—no pace targets, just steady movement and stopping for views when you want them. Choose your group now, and remember, no shame in starting moderate or scenic. You can always push harder tomorrow when your legs know what they're in for."

The group divided, people making quick decisions based on their own assessments. Dave and Stella moved immediately to the fast group. Rogerio hesitated, then joined the moderate. Dana headed for scenic, her phone already recording.

Maureen was studying the fast group with obvious longing, but then she looked at Elaine. "Which one are you thinking?"

"Moderate?" Elaine said it like a question.

"Perfect. Me too." But Maureen's expression suggested she'd chosen moderate only because Elaine had, which made Elaine feel grateful and not at all guilty.

The moderate group ended up being the largest—about ten runners including them. James, their leader, was the concierge from the hotel, now wearing technical running gear that revealed he was considerably more athletic than his hotel uniform had suggested.

"Alright, moderate crew," he said with a warm smile. "We're going to have a brilliant time. The pace will be conversational on the climbs—if you can't talk, we're going too fast. We'll regroup at several viewpoints to make sure nobody falls behind. Questions?"

Someone asked about bathroom protocols, which James answered with pragmatic efficiency: "Find a spot off trail, go at least ten meters from the path and any water sources, pack out your toilet paper if you brought it. Wilderness rules."

And then they were moving, the trail opening before them like an invitation.

ASPEN CONNECTIONS

The first section was as Zuri had promised—steady climbing through aspen forest. The trail was wide and well-maintained, carpeted with the previous autumn's leaves. On either side, the aspen trunks rose like white pillars, their bark scarred with the black marks that made them look ancient despite being relatively young trees.

"Did you know," Maureen said from beside her, breathing hard but still able to talk, "that aspens are actually one of the largest living organisms on Earth? These trees all around us—they're likely all connected by a single root system. They're essentially clones of each other, all part of one massive underground network."

"Really?" Elaine's own breathing was labored enough that conversation required effort.

"Really. Some aspen groves in Utah are estimated to be thousands of years old—not the individual trees, but the root system itself. They've been here since before recorded history, just continuously sending up new trunks while the old ones die back."

It was impossible to look at the forest the same way after that. What had seemed like individual trees now revealed itself as something else—a single, vast organism that had witnessed everything that happened in this valley for millennia. The thought was both comforting and unsettling.

The trail switchbacked up the mountainside, the grade steep enough that Elaine could feel it in her calves and quads. Around her, the other moderate runners had fallen into a rhythm—breathing synchronized, footfalls finding the most stable parts of the trail, nobody talking much anymore as the effort increased.

Ahead, James moved with easy efficiency, occasionally calling back encouragement. "You're doing brilliant! Another twenty minutes and we break out of the trees—the views are worth every step."

Elaine wasn't sure she believed him. Her legs were burning, her lungs working harder than they had in any boutique fitness class. This was real effort, sustained effort, the kind of physical challenge she'd successfully avoided her entire adult life. *Why had she thought she could do this? Why had she signed up for four days of this when she could barely handle an hour?*

"You all right?" Maureen had dropped back beside her, her face flushed but her breathing surprisingly steady.

"Fine," Elaine managed, which was obviously a lie.

"First climb is always the hardest. Your body doesn't know what you're asking it to do yet. By day three, this will feel easy."

"Day three sounds very far away right now."

Maureen laughed. "Fair enough. But look." She gestured ahead where the trail was beginning to level out, the trees thinning. "We're almost there."

And then they broke out above the tree line, and Elaine forgot about her burning legs entirely.

The view was impossible. That was the only word for it. The trail emerged onto an open ridge, and spread before them was a panorama that made her understand why people used words like "breathtaking" and "awesome" despite those words being insufficient.

Mountains stretched in every direction—layers of peaks receding into the blue distance, their summits still holding winter snow despite the summer warmth below. The valley they'd climbed from was a patchwork of dark forest and lighter meadows, threaded with the silver line of a river. And behind them, to the east, the sun was just clearing the horizon, painting everything in shades of gold and rose.

The moderate group had stopped automatically, everyone needing this moment. Even James, who must have seen this view dozens of times, was smiling with genuine appreciation.

"This is Yates Mountain," he said, gesturing to the peak to their right. "And over there, that's Heart Mountain, Grotto Mountain, and the Three Sisters in the distance. On a clear day like this, you can see fifty kilometers easy."

Phones came out—everyone wanted to capture this, to have proof that places like this existed. Dana was filming, narrating for her followers. "Y'all, I cannot even explain this. The pictures won't do it justice. You have to see this with your own eyes."

Maureen pulled out her small field notebook and was sketching something, her hand moving quickly. "The way the valley opens to the north," she murmured to herself. "The sight lines to the peaks. This would have been significant."

"Significant how?" Elaine asked, grateful for the excuse to keep standing still.

"For Indigenous peoples. This is a natural vantage point—you can see for miles in every direction. You'd see game animals, weather patterns, other groups traveling through the valley. This was probably a hunting lookout, maybe a vision quest site. Somewhere important."

She was looking around with an intensity that went beyond tourism or even academic interest. She was reading the landscape like a text, seeing meanings Elaine couldn't appreciate.

"There's power in high places," Maureen continued, almost to herself. "Every culture recognizes it. Mountains are where you go to meet gods, to have revelations, to see clearly. You're literally closer to the heavens, farther from the ordinary world. Standing here, you can understand why."

"Right, everyone!" James called. "Five more minutes, then we need to keep moving. We want to reach the pass before the heat gets up."

The group reluctantly began preparing to move on, taking final photos, capping water bottles. Elaine wished she could stay here, in this moment, with this view, regardless of whatever came next.

As they set off again, the trail now traversing the open ridge, Maureen fell into step beside her. "Thank you, by the way."

"For what?"

"For being here. For being my default running partner. I know we just met yesterday, but already you're making this trip better. I tend to get too into my own head on these things, too focused on research. It's nice to have someone to share it with."

The words were kind, but they made Elaine uncomfortable in a way she couldn't quite articulate. She was being thanked for existing, for basic human proximity, as if that were some kind of gift she was bestowing rather than something she was receiving. It highlighted the transactional nature of everything in her life—even kindness came with expectations, with obligations.

"Of course," she said, because that was the expected response.

The trail descended back into forest, but this time the trees were different—Douglas fir and lodgepole pine instead of aspen, their dark needles creating shade that was almost gloomy after the bright openness of the ridge. The temperature dropped noticeably, and Elaine donned her extra layer.

They'd been running for nearly an hour now, though "running" was perhaps generous—it was more like an aggressive hike with occasional jogging sections. Her legs had moved beyond burning into a kind of numb acceptance. This was her life now. She would be climbing this mountain forever, or at least until lunch.

Ahead, James stopped at a junction where another trail intersected theirs. "Quick water break, everyone. Drink even if you're not thirsty—altitude dehydrates you faster than you realize."

The group clustered at the junction, pulling out water bottles, stretching calves and quads. Elaine collapsed onto a convenient log, wondering if she'd be able to stand up again.

"First big trail run?" asked a voice. She looked up to see the software engineer from Seattle—she thought his name was Ben, but she wasn't certain.

"That obvious?"

"Only because I remember my first one. I signed up for a trail marathon thinking, 'How different can it be from road running?' and then wanted to die around mile three." He laughed. "You're doing great, though. Keeping up with the moderate group on your first day is impressive."

The encouragement was kind, even if it felt undeserved. Around her, the other runners were chatting, comparing notes on the trail, sharing snacks. There was a camaraderie developing that Elaine was eager to be part of.

"Alright, crew," James called. "Another hour to the pass itself, then we'll stop for proper snacks before the descent. Everyone good to continue?"

A chorus of affirmatives, and they were moving again. The trail narrowed here, becoming more technical—rocks and roots requiring attention, each step deliberate. Conversation died as everyone focused on not twisting an ankle.

Maureen had moved ahead, her attention caught by something off trail. She'd stopped and was studying a rock formation, her notebook already out.

"Maureen," James called back. "Stay on trail, please."

"Just one second." She was examining something carved into the stone—or at least, she seemed to think it was carved rather than natural. "This looks like it might be a marker of some kind."

"It's probably just erosion," James said, but he'd backtracked to look. "Oh. Huh. That's… yeah, that could be intentional. Good eye."

The group had stopped again, curious. Elaine moved closer and saw what had caught Maureen's attention—a series of marks on a flat rock face, weathered but still visible. They looked like deliberately made lines and curves rather than random natural patterns.

"This could be a trail marker," Maureen said, her voice vibrating with excitement. "Indigenous peoples would mark important routes. This pass is a natural travel corridor—it makes sense there would be markers."

"Or it's just someone with a knife and time to kill," offered Rogerio, who'd rejoined them from the moderate group. "Don't get me wrong—I hope you're right because that's cooler. But I've seen a lot of 'ancient carvings' that turned out to be 'bored teenager in 1987."

"The weathering patterns are wrong for recent carving," Maureen insisted, running her finger near but not touching the marks. "This is old. A century at minimum, possibly much older."

"Either way," James said gently, "we need to keep moving."

Maureen reluctantly stepped back onto the trail, but Elaine could see she was still thinking about the marks, her academic wheels turning. She pulled out her phone and took a quick photo before following the group.

They climbed higher, the forest around them thinning again. The air was noticeably thinner here—Elaine could feel it in her lungs, the way each breath seemed to contain less oxygen than it should. Her heart was working harder, her legs screaming protests with each step.

And then, finally, they reached the pass itself.

CHAPTER 10

JEWEL IN THE WILDERNESS

Jewell Pass was a saddle between two peaks, a relatively flat area where the trail achieved its high point before descending the other side. Someone had built a small cairn—a stack of stones—marking the summit, and runners from all three groups were gathering around it, adding stones of their own to the pile.

"Tradition," James explained. "Everyone who reaches the pass adds a stone. There're probably hundreds of years of stones in that pile, layer upon layer."

The fast group had arrived at least twenty minutes earlier—Stella and Dave were sitting on rocks, looking annoyingly fresh despite having run considerably faster. Zuri was moving among all the groups, checking in with everyone, her energy undiminished.

"Well done, everyone!" she called. "The hard part's over. From here, it's all downhill. Metaphorically and literally." She was handing out energy bars, making sure everyone was drinking water, her attention moving from person to person.

When she reached Elaine, her assessment was immediate and accurate. "You're knackered, aren't you? First big elevation gain?"

"Is it that obvious?"

"Only to someone who's watching. You're doing brilliantly—you kept up with the moderate group your entire first day. That's harder than it sounds." Zuri pressed an energy bar into her hand. "Eat this. Your body needs fuel. And drink at least half your water. We've got another hour to the finish."

"An hour sounds like an eternity right now."

"It's downhill. Your legs will remember how to work. Trust me." Zuri's brown eyes were warm with genuine concern, not the performative sympathy Elaine was used to from Bradford's social circle. "You're doing great. I mean that. Half the people on their first trail run would have dropped back to the scenic group by now."

The encouragement was simple and sincere, and it made something in Elaine's chest tighten. When was the last time someone had noticed her struggling and offered help without judgment? When was the last time someone had seen her as a person rather than a performance?

"Thank you," she managed.

"That's what I'm here for." Zuri squeezed her shoulder and moved on to check the next person, her attention already shifting to whoever needed it.

Maureen had wandered to the edge of the pass, looking down into the valley beyond. Elaine forced herself to stand and join her, curious about what had caught her attention.

The view was different on this side—wilder and more remote. The valley below was narrower, the forest darker, the mountains beyond more jagged and imposing. It felt less like territory that welcomed visitors and more like somewhere that could break them.

"This is the traditional boundary," Maureen said quietly. "The pass marks the transition between territories. On the other side, we were in commonly traveled areas. This side would have been more contested, more dangerous. You'd need permission to cross."

"Permission from whom?"

"Whichever band controlled this valley. Or from the spirits of the place, depending on your belief system."

Maureen pulled out her notebook again, sketching the view. "Every culture has liminal spaces—thresholds between one realm and another. Passes like this are classic examples. You're neither in one valley nor the other. You're between, which is always a powerful and dangerous position."

"You sound like you believe in that. The spirits and danger."

Maureen looked up from her notebook, her expression thoughtful. "I'm a scholar of religion, which means I've spent my career studying why people believe what they believe. After a while, you realize that belief creates its own reality. Whether the spirits are objectively real or not, if the people who live here have believed in them for thousands of years, that belief has power. It shapes behavior, creates meaning, establishes boundaries. In that sense, the spirits are absolutely real."

Before Elaine could respond, a figure appeared on the trail ahead—a hiker coming from the opposite direction, moving upward toward the pass. He emerged from the treeline about fifty meters away, and something about him immediately drew attention.

He was tall and lean, dressed in worn outdoor gear that looked well used rather than newly purchased for a vacation. Dark hair, weathered features, and an ease of movement that suggested he spent considerably more time in the wilderness than in cities. He carried a large pack but moved with it as if it weighed nothing.

As he approached the pass, his eyes swept across the gathered runners with obvious curiosity. When he spotted their group, his trajectory shifted slightly, bringing him closer to where they stood.

"Good morning, runners," he said, his voice carrying a clear Canadian accent. "You're all clearly an organized group. Global Runners Travel, maybe?"

"That's us," Zuri confirmed, stepping forward with her professional, friendly demeanor. "And you are?"

"Takoda." He smiled easily. "I'm local. Well, local-ish. I've got a camp near here. Just out for the morning to gather some mushrooms before they wither in the sun." He gestured to his pack, which did indeed have several small fabric bags tied to the outside.

"Takoda," Maureen repeated, moving closer with obvious interest. "That's a Stoney Nakota name, isn't it?"

His eyebrows rose, impressed. "It is. Not many tourists know that. You've done your homework."

"I'm a professor of ancient theology. I study religious practices around the world, including Indigenous spiritual traditions. I always research the cultural before traveling somewhere new."

"Well then, you'd know that this—" he gestured around the pass, "—has been significant to my people for a very long time. This is old territory. Sacred to my ancestors."

The other runners gathered around, curious about the conversation. Dave and Stella drifted over, as did Rogerio and several others. Their new visitor had an authenticity that made him stand out among the athletic tourists in their technical gear.

"Are you camping up here alone?" Stella asked, her tone carrying a hint of suspicion.

"Oh, no. I'm not camping—I'm in a permanent camp. Well, permanent for the season. I'm part of an Indigenous peoples' group—we're a small band that's broken off from the Stoney Nakota nation. We spend summers up here maintaining traditional practices. My grandparents' grandparents were some of the original founders. We're kind of the Indigenous equivalent of a tribal church group, if that makes sense."

Maureen's entire body language changed—she went from interested to absolutely riveted. "A traditional band? That's fascinating. What kind of practices do you maintain?"

"Ceremonies mostly. Connection to the land. The old ways of living that the modern world has mostly forgotten. We keep them alive—partly for ourselves, partly for anyone who's interested in learning."

"Would I have heard of your group? I've studied several Stoney Nakota bands in my research."

Takoda pulled at his chin thoughtfully. "Probably not. We keep a low profile. Our name is difficult to pronounce in English — most people just call us the Wapiti band, after the valley we occupy. We don't seek attention. As long as we stay unobtrusive, the government doesn't bother us anymore."

"I'd love to know more," Maureen said, her academic hunger obvious. "Would it be possible to talk sometime? I can be very discreet — no need to reveal specific locations or sensitive practices."

Elaine watched Maureen with growing concern. The professor's eagerness was palpable, almost desperate. This was more than scholarly curiosity — it looked like someone who'd spotted an opportunity and was afraid it might slip away.

Takoda considered the request, his expression thoughtful. "You know, we occasionally invite visitors to join us for evening meals. It's a community affair — everyone together, some simple ceremonies afterward. I think you might be welcome."

"Really? That would be incredible." Maureen was practically vibrating with excitement.

"Maureen," Stella interjected, her voice cautious. "We have plans. Lunch after this run, then the Via Ferrata this afternoon. Group dinner tonight."

"Oh, right." Maureen's face fell with obvious disappointment. "Of course. We do have a schedule."

Takoda smiled easily. "No pressure. If it works out, it works out. I can meet you at the end of the Via

Ferrata—everyone knows where that is. Six o'clock? You can tell me then if you're able to come. If not, no worries." His eyes scanned the group quickly and came to rest on Elaine. For a brief moment he studied her face before returning his attention to Maureen.

"Six o'clock," Maureen confirmed immediately. "I'll be there. I mean, I'll let you know then if I can make it."

But everyone could hear in her voice that she'd already decided. She was going, schedule or no schedule.

Zuri's expression suggested she was thinking the same thing, and she wasn't pleased about it. But before she could say anything, Takoda had given them all a friendly wave and continued up toward the summit cairn, moving with that same effortless efficiency.

"Well," Dave said after a moment. "That was interesting."

"That was a fantastic opportunity," Maureen corrected, her eyes still following Takoda's retreating form. "Do you understand what it means to make contact with an unrecorded traditional band? If they're practicing ceremonies that haven't been documented in academic literature—this could be significant. This could be important."

"Or it could be dangerous," Stella said bluntly. "Meeting a stranger in the woods who invites you to his camp? That's literally the beginning of every horror story."

"It's not like that. He's Indigenous, maintaining traditional practices. This is cultural preservation, not—" Maureen stopped, frustration evident in her voice. "You wouldn't understand. This is my field. My life's work. I know how to assess these situations."

"Right, everyone," Zuri called, her voice carefully neutral but her eyes sharp as she looked at Maureen. "Time to start our descent. We've still got an hour to the bottom, and I'd like to get there before the afternoon heat."

The groups began reforming, preparing for the downhill run. As they did, Elaine noticed Zuri pulling Stella aside for a quick, quiet conversation. Both women glanced toward Maureen, their expressions concerned.

But Maureen seemed oblivious to their worry, still watching the direction Takoda had gone, her field notebook clutched in her hands like a talisman.

Elaine had a sudden, sharp feeling that the easy camaraderie of the morning had acquired an edge of tension.

"Come on," Maureen said, finally turning back toward the trail. Her smile was bright, but her eyes held an intensity that hadn't been there before. "Let's finish this run. I've got a date to keep."

And as they began their descent, Elaine couldn't shake the feeling that Maureen had just made a decision that would affect them all, whether they'd agreed to it or not.

CHAPTER 11

THE IRON ROAD

After a lavish picnic lunch, the buses delivered them to a parking area at the base of Mount Norquay for their afternoon adventure. There, a collection of people in climbing gear were preparing equipment and checking harnesses. The Via Ferrata setup was more elaborate than Elaine had expected—racks of helmets and harnesses, multiple guides conferring over clipboards, and most impressively, the route itself visible on the cliff face above them: a thin line of steel cable ascending the mountain like a scar.

"Welcome to the Iron Road of Banff!" Their guide for the afternoon stepped forward with the kind of rugged handsomeness that seemed almost too perfect—dirty blonde hair, chiseled features, an Italian accent that made even safety instructions sound romantic. "I'm Andre. The Via Ferrata is Italian for 'iron road,' and today you will climb this mountain using the path we've built for you. With proper equipment and following my instructions, it's completely safe. Without proper equipment or ignoring my instructions—" he paused dramatically, "—you are at risk of death."

Elaine's stomach dropped. Several people laughed nervously.

"Andre," Zuri interjected quickly, "you're joking, right? Just joking?"

"Oh, no, I never joke about safety," Andre replied with absolute seriousness. Several people, including Elaine, began removing their harnesses. "But with this equipment, the climb is as safe as walking along a path in the woods. At the very worst, you might skin your knee."

"Much better," Zuri said firmly, giving Andre a look that suggested they'd had this conversation before. She turned to the group. "Everyone alright? Better?"

"I'll stay," Elaine announced, pulling her harness back up around her waist. Around her, others did the same, though a few people looked distinctly uncertain.

Andre continued with undiminished enthusiasm. "Excellent! So follow me, and we will get everyone clipped onto the rock. This is thrilling, yes?"

"Yes!" Stella confirmed with genuine excitement.

"Yes?" Rogerio echoed weakly, making it sound more like a question than an agreement.

They spent the next twenty minutes learning the clipping system—two carabiners attached to their harnesses via lanyards, always keeping at least one clipped to the steel cable at all times. As they practiced on a test section, Andre moved among them, correcting grips and demonstrating proper technique.

"The cable is your friend," he said. "Always stay connected. When you reach an anchor point—see here, where the cable attaches to the rock—you unclip one carabiner, move it past the anchor, then unclip the second and move it past. This way, you are never without connection. Never."

The practice section was a simple bridge across a small ravine, close enough to the ground that falling would result in nothing worse than embarrassment. Within minutes, everyone had mastered the basic movements, and the initial nervousness was giving way to confidence.

"Right then," Andre announced. "Now we begin the real climb. Follow me, stay clipped in, and remember—if you can do what we just practiced, you can do this entire route. It is only your fear that makes it difficult, not the actual climbing."

The group formed a line and began to ascend.

The first section was easy—almost disappointingly so. They walked across a solid bridge, practicing their clipping technique as they moved from anchor point to anchor point. The ravine below was perhaps twenty feet deep, dramatic enough to be interesting but not enough to trigger fear or vertigo.

Dave, ahead of Elaine in line, deliberately stepped off the bridge entirely.

"Go ahead—try to fall—I dare you," Stella had said from behind him, her tone playful and challenging.

He'd taken her literally. With a grin, he stepped both feet off the bridge and dropped through empty air.

Stella's scream was immediate and genuine—pure terror condensed into sound. "DAVE!"

But his plummet lasted less than a second. The safety cables caught him immediately, the carabiners locked, and he hung suspended between them, turning slowly in the breeze. He smiled up at Stella with mischievous delight. "See? Completely safe, just as Andre promised."

Stella moved up to his position and swatted him on the helmet. "Don't EVER do that again! My heart can't take it!" But even as she scolded him, Elaine could see she was shaking slightly beneath her jacket.

Dave climbed back onto the bridge and pulled Stella into a quick hug. "Sorry. I thought—well, I thought it would be funny. I didn't realize it would actually scare you."

"You dangling over a cliff didn't scare me?" Stella's voice was sharp, but she was already forgiving him. "What exactly did you think would happen?"

"Fair point." He kissed her helmet where her forehead would be. "I'm sorry. Really. No more stunts."

Andre had witnessed the entire scene from his position at the front of the line. In America, this behavior would have drawn a stern lecture about safety and possibly removal from the tour. But Andre merely shrugged with Italian pragmatism. "The system works, no? This is what the safety cables are for. Now please, everyone, let us continue with less drama."

The line moved forward, but the incident had broken the ice in an unexpected way. People were laughing about it, the tension of the initial climb released through Dave's demonstration that they were actually safe.

"Well," Rogerio called from several positions back, "at least we know one of us won't die today. Dave already used up our group's near-death experience."

"Don't tempt fate," Maureen warned, but she was smiling.

The route changed after the practice bridge. The cable now led them along the face of the cliff, a sheer wall of rock on their left and nothing but empty air on their right. The steel cable became their lifeline—both literally and psychologically—as they traversed the mountain face.

"Holy shit," Rogerio muttered ahead of Maureen. "This is kind of wicked."

The left-side safety cable was bolted directly into the rock face. The right-side cable had disappeared entirely. Beneath their feet, the trail had been replaced by U-shaped rebar steps hammered into the stone at regular intervals. Each step protruded perhaps eight inches from the face—enough to stand on comfortably, but narrow enough that you were constantly aware of the three-hundred-foot drop behind you.

"This section is just as safe as the bridges we already crossed," Andre called back. "It just feels more dangerous because there's nothing behind you. Your mind creates fear where there is no actual danger. Just keep stepping from one rebar to the next. The cables will not let you fall."

Despite Andre's reassurance, Elaine's heart was hammering. She kept her eyes fixed on Maureen's back ahead of her, refusing to look down, refusing to acknowledge the vast emptiness pressing against her spine. This was insane. This was absolutely insane. Why had she thought this was a good idea?

Behind her, she could hear someone breathing hard—quick, shallow breaths that suggested panic barely contained. She didn't turn to look, didn't want to see her own fear reflected in someone else's face.

Maureen seemed to sense her distress and turned carefully, keeping both hands on the cable. "You alright?"

"Fine," Elaine managed, which was obviously untrue.

"First traverse is always the hardest. Your body doesn't trust what your mind knows—that you're completely safe. By the third or fourth section like this, it'll feel routine." Maureen's voice was steady, reassuring. "But look—really look. Not down, but out. At the view."

Against her better judgment, Elaine lifted her eyes from Maureen's back and looked.

The valley spread below them, a patchwork of dark forest and bright meadows, threaded with rivers that caught the afternoon sun like silver ribbons. Mountains marched away in layers of blue and purple, each range more distant and dreamlike than the last. And above, the sky was so blue it almost hurt to look at, the kind of saturated color that seemed impossible, like someone had adjusted reality's contrast settings.

"It's extraordinary, isn't it?" Maureen said softly. "I feel like an eagle up here. Free from gravity. No boundaries. Just floating in all this space."

And somehow, impossibly, Elaine found herself agreeing. The fear was still there, but alongside it was something else—a kind of wild exhilaration. She was clinging to the side of a mountain hundreds of feet above the ground, and she was doing it. Her body was doing what it needed to do. She was capable of this.

"Thank you," she said to Maureen, and meant it.

"Any time. I can't wait to see what comes next."

The group progressed along the cliff face, each person finding their rhythm. Some moved quickly, confidence growing with each step. Others went slowly, carefully, but everyone kept moving. The line strung out along the mountain like beads on a wire, and from Andre's position at the front, he called back encouragement.

"You are all doing brilliantly! Another fifty meters and we reach the ladder section—that will be even more fun!"

Opinions varied on whether "more fun" sounded appealing or terrifying.

They'd been on the cliff face for perhaps twenty minutes when it happened.

Ahead of Elaine, Maureen had reached another anchor point and was smoothly transitioning her carabiners. Beyond her, Rogerio was doing the same. And then—

A sharp metallic snap.

"Yikes! Urgh!" The words barely escaped Rogerio's mouth before his body slammed into the rock face with a sickening thud.

He hung there, suspended by his safety cables, completely still.

The line behind him froze. Several people gasped. Someone—Dana, maybe—made a small sound of distress.

Then Rogerio took a deep, shuddering breath. "I'm okay. I think. I slipped off the step."

"Hang on!" Dave was already moving, carefully but quickly traversing toward him. "Take my hand. I'll help you back onto the step."

But when Dave reached him, both men stopped and stared down at Rogerio's feet. The rebar step he'd been standing on was twisted downward at an angle, one side still attached to the rock but the other clearly broken away.

"It broke," Rogerio said, his voice small and shocked. "I was standing on it and then it just—it broke."

Andre was already moving toward them with the same monkey-like agility he'd shown on the practice section, somehow climbing across the rock face and past several people with impossible speed. When he reached Rogerio, he examined the broken step with intense focus.

"This should be impossible," Andre muttered, his accent thickening with concern. "These steps hold over

500 pounds. You are not even 200 pounds." He looked closer at the break point, his eyes narrowing. Then his expression changed—just slightly, just for a moment—to something that might have been alarm before his professional mask returned.

"It is just bad luck," he announced to the group, his voice carefully neutral. "This step was damaged somehow—rust, erosion inside the rock. It happens, though rarely. This is exactly why we have the safety cables, yes? The system worked perfectly. Rogerio is completely safe."

But Zuri, from her position, could see what Andre had seen. The break was too clean, too straight. That wasn't erosion. That was a cut—deliberate and precise, made with something sharp enough to slice through steel.

Someone had sabotaged the step.

Andre helped Dave pull Rogerio back onto solid footing, both men working carefully to get him positioned on the next step up. Rogerio's face was pale beneath his helmet, his hands shaking as he re-gripped the cable.

"You good?" Dave asked, his voice low and serious.

"Yeah. Yeah, I think so. Just—give me a second." Rogerio closed his eyes, breathing deeply. "Okay. Okay, I'm good. That was terrifying. Can we please never do that again?"

"Agreed," Dave said firmly. "No more broken steps, no more testing the safety system. We've had enough excitement for one afternoon."

Andre was already moving back to the front of the line, stomping firmly on each rebar step as he passed, testing them audibly for the group's reassurance. "I check every step now. No more surprises. We have only a few more sections like this, then we reach solid trail for the descent. Everyone stay calm, stay clipped in, and we will all arrive safely."

The line began moving again, but the easy camaraderie had evaporated. People were moving more carefully now, testing each step before committing their full weight, hyperaware of the empty space behind them.

Zuri thought about the cut step. Who would do that? And why? The Via Ferrata was used by dozens of people every day—sabotaging a step could have killed anyone. It was random sabotage, senseless destruction.

Unless it wasn't random. Unless someone had known exactly when this group would be here.

But that was paranoid thinking. She was shaken from the scare, that was all. Reading malice into what was probably just structural failure that Andre was covering up to avoid liability issues.

Still, as they continued along the cliff face, she checked each step more carefully than before, trusting the safety cables more than the apparently solid steel beneath her feet.

BREAKING AWAY

The rest of the route passed without incident, though it took longer than planned. By the time they descended the final section back to solid ground, everyone was exhausted in a different way than they'd been after the morning's run. This exhaustion was psychological as much as physical—the sustained tension of being suspended over empty space, the aftermath of Rogerio's near-fall, the awareness that they'd been somewhere genuinely dangerous even if the safety systems had worked.

"Well," Rogerio announced as he removed his helmet, "that was either the best or worst experience of my life. I'm still trying to decide."

"Best," Dave said firmly. "Any time you walk away is the best experience."

"Even when your heart rate was over 160 for twenty minutes straight?" Stella touched her watch. "Because mine was. That step breaking—I thought—" She stopped, shook her head. "I thought we were about to watch you fall."

"But I didn't fall. The cables and harnesses worked. That's literally what they're designed for." Rogerio's color was returning, and with it, his characteristic humor. "Although I have to say, when I told you all that I'm a disaster magnet, I didn't expect to prove it quite so quickly."

"Ecuador, Azores, South Africa, and now Canada," Dave counted on his fingers. "You really can't go anywhere without something trying to kill you, can you?"

"It's a gift," Rogerio said solemnly. "The universe looks at me and thinks, 'How can I make this man's life more interesting?' And then it sends aggressive geese. Or breaks the steel steps beneath my feet. It keeps me on my toes."

Despite the lingering tension, people laughed. Rogerio's ability to defuse his own terror with humor was reassuring—if he could joke about it, maybe it really had been just bad luck rather than something more concerning.

But Elaine noticed Zuri wasn't laughing. The trip director was standing apart from the group, talking quietly with Andre. Both of them kept glancing at the cliff face, and Andre was shaking his head firmly, his expression serious. Whatever they were discussing, it wasn't the casual post-activity debrief.

After a few minutes, Zuri returned to the group, her professional smile back in place, though her eyes remained worried. "Right, everyone. Brilliant job up there. You all handled that beautifully, especially you, Rogerio—well done keeping your head. We're a bit behind schedule, so we'll head straight back to the hotel. You've got about ninety minutes of free time before dinner. Rest, shower, whatever you need. We'll meet in the dining room at seven-thirty."

As people began moving toward the buses, Maureen pulled Zuri aside. Elaine was close enough to overhear.

"The thing is," Maureen was saying, "I really would like to meet with Takoda. It's six now—he said he'd be here at six to see if I could join them for dinner."

Zuri's expression hardened slightly. "Maureen, we've just had a rather serious incident. Rogerio could have been badly hurt. I'm not comfortable with anyone wandering off alone right now."

"But it was just a mechanical failure. Andre said so himself—just bad luck with a damaged step. That has nothing to do with Takoda or his community."

"We don't know that. We don't know what we're dealing with." Zuri lowered her voice. "Look, I called the sheriff's office this morning like I promised. Sheriff Adaire confirmed that the group exists, that they've been coming to the area for years, and that there've been no reports of trouble. But that doesn't mean I'm thrilled about you going into the woods alone to visit them."

"I'm not going alone—I'm going with Takoda. He'll guide me there and back. And it's not like they're criminals. They're Indigenous peoples maintaining traditional practices. This could be incredibly valuable for my research."

"Your research isn't worth risking your safety."

"I appreciate your concern, but I'm an adult. I've spent time with isolated communities all over the world—remote villages in Peru, tribal groups in Africa, indigenous populations in Southeast Asia. This is what I do. I know how to watch out for myself, and I know when an opportunity is knocking."

Zuri studied her for a long moment. "If you're going, then I want you to turn on location tracking on your phone and send me a link. At least I'll be able to see where you are."

"Done." Maureen was already pulling out her phone, her fingers moving quickly. "There—you should have access now. And Takoda said they're not far from Banff, so even if something went wrong—which it won't—you could reach me quickly."

"How quickly is 'not far'?"

"He said an hour's hike. But again, nothing's going to go wrong. They're just a small community maintaining their cultural heritage. They're not dangerous."

"Fine." Zuri's voice was tight. "But you check in with me tonight when you get back. Text me when you arrive at their camp, text me when you leave, and text me when you're safely back at the hotel. If I don't hear from you by midnight, I'm calling the sheriff."

"That's more than fair. Thank you, Zuri." Maureen squeezed her arm. "I really appreciate you understanding how important this is."

She hurried away toward the gear shack, leaving Zuri standing with Stella, who'd drifted over during the conversation.

"You don't like this," Stella observed.

"No, I bloody well don't." Zuri watched Maureen disappear around the building. "But she's right that she's an adult, and I can't stop her. I just have a bad feeling about it."

"Want me to go with her?" Stella offered. "I could say I'm interested in Indigenous cultures too. Safety in numbers."

"And lose track of two of you? No, that wouldn't be better. Sorry."

Just then, Maureen reappeared with Takoda beside her. The young man looked exactly as he had that morning—calm, friendly, completely unthreatening. He waved at the cluster of runners near the buses.

"Thank you for letting Maureen join us," Takoda called to Zuri. "I promise we'll take good care of her. She'll be back before you know it, full of stories about our history and probably with a notebook full of research details."

"I'm holding you to that," Zuri replied, her tone pleasant but with an edge. "She's my responsibility, and I take that seriously."

"As you should. You're a good shepherd." Takoda smiled warmly. "Come on, Maureen. We should get going—dinner preparation starts soon, and you'll want to see how we make our fry bread."

Maureen gave the group a quick wave, her face bright with academic excitement, and followed Takoda toward the tree line. Within moments, they'd disappeared into the forest, and she was gone.

"I still don't like it," Zuri muttered.

"Me neither," Stella agreed. "But what can we do?"

"Nothing. Right now, nothing." Zuri pulled out her phone, checking that she could see Maureen's location. A small blue dot appeared on her screen, moving slowly away from the parking area. "But I'm watching that dot all night. If it stops moving or goes somewhere unexpected, I'm not waiting until midnight to call for help."

Elaine, standing nearby and pretending not to eavesdrop, thought about her own phone. Should she enable tracking? Should she be preparing for something to go wrong?

But that was paranoid thinking. Maureen was fine. She was with a local guide going to visit an Indigenous community. It was a cultural experience, nothing more.

"Right," Zuri called to the group, forcibly brightening her tone. "Everyone on the buses. Let's get back to the hotel. You've earned your dinner tonight, and Chef Henry has promised something special. Let's not keep him waiting."

As they boarded the buses, Elaine took one last look at the tree line where Maureen had disappeared. She was already missing her new friend. The forest looked darker now, the shadows between the trees deeper and more impenetrable than they'd seemed that morning.

And somewhere in those shadows, Maureen was walking deeper into the wilderness, following a man she'd met just hours ago, drawn by the promise of something she wanted desperately enough to ignore every reasonable warning.

The buses pulled away, and the parking area emptied, and the forest kept whatever secrets it held.

CHAPTER 13

AMONG THE WAPITI

The hike to the Wapiti camp took longer than Maureen expected—nearly ninety minutes of steady hiking through dense forest that showed no signs of human presence. No trail markers, no worn paths, just Takoda moving through the wilderness with the confidence of someone who knew every tree and stone.

"How do you find your way back here?" Maureen asked, slightly breathless from the pace. "There's no trail."

"There are trails," Takoda said over his shoulder. "You just have to know how to read them. See that cluster of three birches? And the way the moss grows thicker on the north side of that boulder? The land tells you where to go if you're willing to listen."

Maureen pulled out her notebook, jotting down the observation even as she walked. *Traditional way-finding through natural landmarks. Environmental literacy vs. technological dependence.* Her academic mind was already cataloging, analyzing, preparing to write about this experience in journals that would never fully capture what it felt like to walk through wilderness that felt utterly untouched by modernity.

The forest changed as they climbed—the trees grew older, thicker, their trunks massive and gnarled. The undergrowth thinned out, as if the forest floor itself had been carefully maintained. And then, quite suddenly, they emerged into a clearing.

The Wapiti camp spread before her like something from another century.

A dozen structures dotted the clearing—a mix of traditional teepees with painted hides and more permanent log lodges with sod roofs. Smoke rose from multiple fire pits, carrying the scent of burning cedar and cooking meat. People moved between the structures exhibiting casual purposefulness—some tending fires, others working hides stretched on frames, a group of children playing a game with carved wooden pieces near one of the lodges.

"Oh my God," Maureen breathed, her hand already reaching for her phone camera before she remembered to ask permission. "This is incredible. How long has this camp been here?"

"We've used this location for decades. But we've had camps in these mountains for over a century and a half. We move when we need to—when the authorities get too pushy, when the game moves to different ranges, when the spirits tell us it's time." Takoda smiled at her obvious excitement. "Come. I'll introduce you to some of the elders. They'll want to meet you."

Maureen spent the next hour in a state of academic euphoria, her notebook filling with observations and interviews. An elderly man named Gunther—who spoke with a slight German accent beneath his careful English—told her about joining the Wapiti thirty years ago after "the modern world stopped making sense." A woman named Rebecca, perhaps in her forties, described discovering the band during a college field trip. She'd returned to school with so many questions, so many urges to learn more, to experience more. At the end of the term, she'd returned and been welcomed with open arms. Since then, she'd learned a new set of skills from the elders and the land itself.

"Don't you miss the outside world?" Maureen asked Rebecca as they sat outside one of the lodges, Rebecca's hands working efficiently at scraping a deer hide. "Modern conveniences? Technology? Connection to other people?"

"I have connection," Rebecca said simply. "Just not to your world. I'm connected to this land, to our people, to the old ways that sustained humans for thousands of years before electricity and the internet and all the things that make people feel connected while they're actually alone." She smiled, her expression gentle rather than judgmental. "You feel it, don't you? How quiet it is here? How much you can hear when the modern noise stops?"

Maureen realized Rebecca was right. The camp was quiet—no engines, no electronics, no constant background hum she'd grown so accustomed to that she only noticed it in its absence. Just wind in the trees, distant bird calls, the crackle of fires, and the sounds of people actually doing things with their hands.

"I do feel it," Maureen admitted. "It's unsettling and peaceful at the same time."

"That's the beginning of understanding." Rebecca set aside her scraping tool and looked at Maureen directly. "Most visitors never get past the romantic idea of living simply. They see us as quaint or primitive or tragic—people stuck in the past because we can't handle the present. But we're not stuck. We chose this. Every person here chose to leave your world for this one."

"Why?" It was the question Maureen had been asking all afternoon, in different ways, to different people. "What made you choose this?"

Rebecca was quiet for a long moment, her eyes distant. "I saw what was coming. In the world out there. The emptiness of it. People connected to everything and understanding nothing. I wanted to be connected to something real, something ancient, something that mattered beyond quarterly profits and social media likes." She returned her attention to the hide. "I wanted to serve something greater than myself. Here, I can do that."

Maureen wrote it all down, her hand cramping from the constant note-taking. But underneath the academic documentation, something else was happening—a resonance, a recognition. These weren't crazy people or deluded cultists. They were searchers who'd found something most people spent their whole lives looking for.

As the sun began its descent toward the mountains, Takoda found Maureen still conducting interviews, this time with a young man who'd lived his entire life with the Wapiti.

"Come," Takoda said gently. "Ayâs wants to meet you before the evening meal."

Maureen followed him to the largest of the log lodges. Inside, the space was dim and heavy with the scent of dried herbs hanging from the rafters. Furs covered the floor, and a small fire burned in a central pit, its smoke rising through a hole in the roof.

Ayâs sat beside the fire, so still she might have been carved from wood. When she turned her head to look at Maureen, the firelight caught the tattoo on her forehead—that crude, powerful face that seemed to shift in the flickering light. Then Maureen realized it wasn't a tattoo, but a raised scar—a brand?

"The scholar has come," Ayâs said, her voice carrying surprising strength for someone so ancient. "Sit, child. Let me look at you."

Maureen sat across the fire, acutely aware that this moment mattered in ways she didn't fully understand yet. Ayâs studied her with eyes that saw through flesh to what lay beneath.

"You seek knowledge," Ayâs finally said. "But not the knowledge your universities value. You seek truth."

"I—yes." Maureen fumbled for her professional composure. "I'm an anthropologist of religion. I study spiritual practices, belief systems, how communities maintain traditional—"

"Words." Ayâs waved a dismissive hand. "You hide behind words. But I see what you really seek. You want to know if there's something more. Something beyond the material world your education tells you is all that exists."

Maureen's throat tightened. *How did this woman know that?*

"The answer is yes," Ayâs continued. "There is more. Much more. And you are open enough to perceive it, if you're brave enough to look."

Ayâs turned to Takoda, who'd remained standing near the entrance. "This one has the gift of sight, though she doesn't know it yet. She'll make a fine witness."

Takoda nodded. "Should we—"

"Tonight. Let her experience the ceremony. Give her food and root tea with everyone. We'll see how she responds."

Maureen wanted to ask what they meant, what they expected her to see, but Ayâs had already turned her attention to the fire, clearly ending the conversation. Takoda guided her back outside into the golden light of dusk.

"What did she mean?" Maureen asked. "About me being a witness?"

"You'll understand tonight," Takoda said. "For now, help us prepare the meal. Everyone contributes here."

ROOT TEA

Dinner was a communal affair, the entire band gathering around the central fire as darkness settled over the camp. The meal was simple but substantial—venison stew thick with wild roots and herbs, flatbread cooked on hot stones, dried berries mixed with rendered fat.

Maureen ate hungrily, the physical exertion of the day making everything taste better than it had any right to. Around her, the Wapiti talked and laughed, told stories, teased each other. It felt less like a cult gathering and more like a large, functional family.

After the meal, wooden cups were passed around, filled with a pale liquid that steamed in the cooling air.

"This is the tea we drink before ceremonies," Takoda explained, handing Maureen a cup. "Traditional herbs and roots. It helps open perception, lets you see more clearly."

Maureen hesitated, her academic training warring with her desire to participate. She thought about Zuri's concern, about the warnings she'd ignored to be here.

"What's in it?" she asked.

"Yarrow, sage, cedar, and other plants. Nothing harmful—we've been drinking it for generations. But if you're uncomfortable, you don't have to."

Around her, everyone else was drinking without hesitation. Children too, though their cups held less. If it were dangerous, surely they wouldn't give it to children?

"I'm here to understand your practices," Maureen said, making her decision. "To truly understand this, I need to participate."

She drank.

The tea was bitter and earthy, with an underlying sweetness that made it almost pleasant. She felt it warm her from the inside, spreading through her chest and limbs. Nothing dramatic happened—no immediate visions or dizziness, just a gentle loosening, as if tension she'd been carrying for years was finally releasing.

Alcohol? Caffeine? Maureen thought the effect was similar to both, but not exactly like either of those.

The drumming started slowly. Three men with traditional drums made from hide stretched over wooden frames began a steady rhythm that seemed to match her heartbeat. Then the chanting began — voices in that old language Takoda had used at the Via Ferrata, rising and falling in patterns that felt so very ancient.

Maureen swayed slightly, caught in the rhythm. The firelight seemed brighter, the stars overhead more numerous. The forest around the clearing felt closer, more present, as if it was leaning in to listen.

This is what I've been searching for, she thought with sudden clarity. *This connection. This sense of something larger.*

She'd spent years studying religion from the outside, analyzing belief systems as cultural artifacts, maintaining a scholarly distance. But here, now, she understood what her research subjects had been trying to tell her all along — faith wasn't something you could understand from the outside. You had to step into it, let it change you, allow yourself to be vulnerable to transformation.

The chanting grew louder, more insistent. Maureen closed her eyes and let the sound wash over her. In the darkness behind her eyelids, she saw — or felt, or somehow perceived — shapes moving through the forest beyond the firelight. Massive shapes. Ancient and patient and impossibly old.

Her eyes snapped open. "Did you see—"

But Takoda was watching her with a knowing smile. "You're beginning to see what's really here. What's always been here."

The ceremony continued for hours. At some point, people began dancing around the fire—not the structured, performative dancing of powwows Maureen had attended in the past, but something more primal, more genuine. Bodies moving in response to the drums and the darkness and whatever they perceived in the forest's depths.

Maureen didn't dance, but she watched with an anthropologist's eye that was slowly transforming into a believer's awe. This wasn't performance. This was communion with something much bigger.

When the ceremony finally wound down, the camp settling into quiet conversations around smaller fires, Ayâs appeared beside Maureen like a ghost materializing from smoke.

"Come," the old woman said. "We need to talk."

They walked to Ayâs's lodge, leaving the fires and voices behind. Inside, the priestess poured two cups of liquid from a clay vessel—not the tea from earlier, but something different. The liquid was whiter, thicker and slightly luminescent in the lamplight.

"This is nature's milk," Ayâs said. "Just a little stronger version of what you had earlier. This is what we give to those ready for true sight."

Maureen's heart raced. "I don't understand. Why me?"

Ayâs studied Maureen across the fire. "You feel it, don't you? The call of something greater than your books and theories."

Maureen nodded, unable to speak. The visions were still swirling—she'd sensed the creatures in the forest, felt their ancient presence, understood in her bones that these weren't legends but truths the modern world had forgotten.

"But you're not the one we've been waiting for," Ayâs said gently. "You're the hunter. The one who will bring her to us."

"Her?" Maureen's voice was barely a whisper. "Who?"

"Drink," Ayâs commanded, holding out the cup. "And you'll understand your purpose. You'll see what we need you to do."

Maureen took the cup with trembling hands. This was the moment—the threshold between academic study and willing participation. Some rational part of her brain screamed warnings about going too far, about unknown substances, about cults and manipulation, about all the cautionary stories she'd heard.

But a deeper part—a part that had been awakened by the ceremony, by the forest, by everything she'd experienced today—knew this was the right direction. This was necessary.

She drank.

The world exploded into vision.

Not hallucinogenic chaos, but clarity so intense it hurt. Maureen saw the forest around the camp, but not as it appeared in physical reality. She saw it as it truly was—alive, conscious, ancient beyond human comprehension. Trees that were beings. Rocks that held memory. Rivers that carried intention.

And moving through it all, a huge and ancient creature—the Napiyaw.

They were everywhere and nowhere, existing in the liminal space between the physical and spiritual. Massive figures covered in dark fur, walking upright like humans but possessing something humans had lost—a complete integration with the land, a presence so rooted in this place that they were simultaneously creatures and the forest itself.

They're real, Maureen thought with wonder and terror. *They're actually real.*

She saw their history—millennia of existing in these mountains, watching as the glaciers retreated, as humans arrived, as the modern world encroached. She felt their slow fading as human activity expanded, as belief in them dwindled, and the boundary between two worlds thickened and hardened.

And she understood the Wapiti's purpose with devastating clarity. They were the bridge keepers, maintaining the ceremonies that kept the Napiyaw from dissolving entirely into myth. Every generation, they found someone who could serve as a vessel—a person rare and special enough to exist in both worlds, to anchor the Ancient Ones in physical reality.

Then the vision shifted.

She saw a woman—elegant, lost, searching for something she couldn't name. Dazzling hair, sparkling eyes. Expensive clothes that meant nothing. A life of privilege that felt like a prison. The woman stood at a crossroads she didn't recognize, about to choose a path that would change her future.

"Who is she?" Maureen asked aloud, though her voice seemed to come from very far away.

"The one we've been waiting for," Ayâs's voice came through the vision like an anchor to reality. "The one who can become what we need. A bridge. A priestess. A mother to the Ancient Ones."

"But how will I—" Maureen couldn't finish the question. The vision was showing her.

She saw herself back with the running group. Saw the woman among them. Saw the path forward—not forced, not coerced, but guided. Opportunities created. Choices presented. The woman's own longing and emptiness leading her exactly where she needed to be.

"You'll know her when you see her," Ayâs said. "Your spirit will recognize hers. And you'll help her find her way to us."

The visions faded, reality reasserting itself slowly. Maureen found herself still in Ayâs's lodge, still holding the empty cup, but with a new perspective on the world. She wasn't the same person who'd drunk from it.

She understood now. This wasn't academic research. This was a mission, a destiny she was meant to perform.

Maureen sat outside Ayâs's lodge, wrapped in a borrowed blanket, watching the camp go to sleep. Her notebook lay open beside her, but she hadn't written anything since the meeting with Ayâs. How could words capture what she'd experienced? How could academic language contain the truths she'd seen?

Takoda emerged from one of the lodges and came to sit beside her. He didn't speak, just sat in companionable silence as the camp settled for the night.

Finally, Maureen found her voice. "I need to go back. To the running group."

"Yes," Takoda agreed. "They'll be worried. And you have work to do."

"She's with them. Isn't she? The woman from my vision."

"Ayâs believes so. And Ayâs is never wrong about these things." Takoda stood, offering his hand to help her up. "You'll guide her to us. Not by force—that never works. But by showing her possibilities. By helping her see what she's been missing in her old life."

"What if she doesn't come? What if I fail?"

"You won't fail. This is what you were meant for, Maureen. Why you came to these mountains, why you found us. The land brought you here to serve this purpose." Takoda smiled. "Trust in that."

They walked back through the forest, following those invisible trails only Takoda could see. Maureen's mind was still reeling from the visions, from the clarity of purpose she now carried. She thought about her academic career, her research, her plans for tenure. All of it seemed trivial now, meaningless compared to what the Wapiti needed from her.

"What happens after?" she asked as they neared civilization. "After I bring her to you? What's my role then?"

"Whatever you choose," Takoda said. "Some return to their old lives, carrying the knowledge of what's real. Others stay with us, become part of the band. Ayâs will help you when the time comes to choose which path is yours."

They emerged from the forest at the edge of town, the hotel visible in the distance. Maureen checked her phone—12:47 AM. She texted Zuri quickly: *Back at hotel soon. Thank you for worrying. Safe and sound. The experience was amazing.*

"Thank you," she said to Takoda. "For everything."

"Thank the land," Takoda replied. "And thank yourself for being open enough to hear its call."

He melted back into the forest, leaving Maureen alone at civilization's edge. She looked back at the wilderness, seeing it now with new eyes. The Napiyaw were there, watching, waiting. Always watching, always waiting for the bridge that would anchor them back in the physical world.

And she would help them find it.

Maureen walked to her hotel room with purpose crystallizing in her chest. She knew what she had to do. Tomorrow, she would find the woman from her vision. And she would help that woman discover her true destiny, even if the woman didn't realize she was being guided.

This was real. All of it was real. And Maureen O'Sullivan, academic and skeptic, had become a true believer.

She lay in her bed, exhausted but unable to sleep, her mind still alive with visions of ancient forests and creatures just as ancient. By morning, she knew, the intensity would fade somewhat. The visions would become memories rather than immediate realities. But the conviction would remain.

She had seen the truth. And having seen it, she could never go back to pretending the modern world was all that existed.

Tomorrow, she would begin her mission.

BANFF ON THE WATER

MORNING DOUBTS

Zuri hadn't slept well. She'd lain awake watching the blue dot on her phone's tracking app, following Maureen's progress through the wilderness like tracking a ship at sea. The dot had stopped moving around 7:30 PM—presumably arriving at the Wapiti camp. It had remained stationary for hours, which should have been reassuring but somehow wasn't. And then, around 11:45 PM, it had started moving again, slowly making its way back toward the hotel.

The final text had come at 12:47 AM: *Back at hotel soon. Safe and sound. Thank you for worrying. The experience was amazing.*

Zuri had stared at that message for a long time. The words were Maureen's, but she was too casual? Too cheerful for someone who'd just completed a several-hour night hike? Or was Zuri reading too much into it?

She'd finally fallen asleep around 2 AM, her phone still clutched in her hand.

Now, standing in the breakfast room at 6:15 AM with her second coffee already half-gone, Zuri felt the exhaustion pulling at her like gravity. Around her, the Global Runners were arriving in their usual pre-run states—some bright and energetic, others moving like zombies toward the coffee urns.

But no Maureen.

"She's probably just running late," Stella said, appearing at Zuri's elbow with her own coffee. "After getting back past midnight, I'd sleep through my alarm too."

"She's never late." Zuri checked her phone again—6:17 AM. The buses would leave at 6:45. "In four years of leading these trips, Maureen has never been late for a single activity. She's always the first one down, the most eager to get started."

"Want me to go knock on her door?"

Before Zuri could answer, the elevator doors opened and Maureen stepped out.

At first glance, she looked alert and ready to go—running gear, ponytail, her usual running vest with its many pockets. But as she moved through the breakfast room toward them, Zuri noticed subtle differences. Maureen's movements were slower, more deliberate, as if she were navigating through water rather than air. Her expression was too placid—not quite happy, not quite neutral, but somewhere in between. Peaceful, maybe. Serene.

It was unsettling.

"Good morning!" Maureen's voice was bright, but it had a dreamy quality, like someone speaking from the edge of sleep. "Sorry, I'm running a bit behind. I was up quite late."

"So, I gathered from your text," Zuri said carefully. "How was it? The visit to the Wapiti camp?"

"Oh, Zuri." Maureen's face transformed with an expression that was almost beatific. "It was extraordinary. Absolutely extraordinary. Everything I'd hoped for and more." She moved toward the breakfast buffet, loading her plate with the same efficiency as always.

Stella and Zuri exchanged glances.

"Tell us about it," Stella prompted, following Maureen to a table. "What were the ceremonies like?"

Maureen set down her plate and considered the question carefully, as if translating from another language. "They were… ancient. Rooted. The kind of spiritual practice that's been lost in the modern world. They have this connection to the land, to the old ways, that's just—" she paused, searching for words, "—it's indescribable. You have to experience it to understand."

"What kind of ceremonies specifically?" Zuri asked, her trip director instincts moving into interview mode. "Chanting? Dancing? What did you actually see?"

"Drumming and singing around the fire. Stories in their traditional language—Takoda translated some of it for me. They have this drink they make from roots and herbs. They call it 'nature's milk.' It opens your perception, helps you see things more clearly. The boundaries between the physical and spiritual worlds become… thinner." Maureen took a bite of her scrambled eggs, chewing slowly. "I took so many notes. This could be groundbreaking for my research."

"This drink," Stella said, her voice careful and controlled. "What was in it?"

"Oh, I don't know exactly. Traditional herbs and roots. Nothing dangerous—they've been drinking it for generations. It's part of their ceremonial practice." Maureen smiled, with the same serene expression. "Kind of earthy and bitter. No sugar like everything we drink. They said it would help me understand what they were doing. The connection between their people and the land. They claim you can sense the old spirits that still inhabit these mountains."

Zuri felt ice forming in her stomach. "Maureen, did they pressure you to drink this? Did you feel like you could refuse?"

"Pressure me? No, not at all. They offered, I accepted. It would have been rude to refuse." Maureen looked genuinely puzzled by the question. "Why would I refuse? I was there to learn about their practices. Participating is part of understanding."

"As a researcher, you're supposed to observe, not necessarily participate," Stella pointed out. "Especially when it comes to substances you don't know the composition of. It could have been alcohol, hallucinogens, or something more dangerous."

Maureen blinked as she accepted the logic of this. "You're right, I did take a chance with the drink. But I don't think it had much effect, no hallucinations, no hangover. I'm an anthropologist of religion, not a lab scientist. Participant observation is a fundamental methodology. How can I write about their spiritual experiences without having some version of those experiences myself?" Maureen's voice became more firm.

"I'm not questioning your expertise," Zuri said, keeping her voice gentle. "I'm just concerned about your safety. You went into the woods with people we don't know, drank something you couldn't identify, and got back to the hotel past midnight. Can you understand why that might worry me?"

Maureen's expression softened again, the irritation fading back into that unsettling calm. "Yes. I'm sorry I worried you. But I'm fine. Better than fine, actually. I feel… clear. Purposeful." She reached across the table and squeezed Zuri's hand. "Thank you for caring. But truly, I'm perfectly safe. They're good people. Like the sheriff said. Traditional people. They have rituals that I don't think have been documented before. This could be a big find for me."

Other runners were starting to listen in, and Zuri didn't want to continue this conversation in front of them. "We'll talk more later, alright? For now, just—please stick with the group for the rest of the trip. And if they invite you again, maybe you save that for your work time—and bring other people with you."

"Of course." Maureen's agreement came too easily, too quickly. "Whatever you think is best."

That was wrong too. The old Maureen would have argued, would have defended her academic autonomy, would have pushed back against being managed. This acquiescence, this easy compliance—it was as concerning as the serene expression and the dreamy voice.

Elaine had arrived during the conversation and taken a seat at their table, her own plate loaded with what was clearly more food than she was used to eating for breakfast. She was listening with obvious concern.

"Are you alright?" Elaine asked Maureen directly. "You seem… distracted."

"Do I?" Maureen considered this. "I suppose I feel different. But in a good way. Clearer. More focused. I know what I'm supposed to be doing now."

"Which is?" Elaine pressed.

"Learning. Documenting. Understanding what the Wapiti are preserving before it's lost forever." Maureen smiled at her. "You should come with me next time. They'd welcome you. They welcome everyone who's genuinely interested in their old ways."

"Maybe," Elaine said noncommittally, though her expression suggested she'd rather eat broken glass.

Dave and Rogerio had joined the table, both men looking considerably more awake than Zuri felt.

"Morning, everyone!" Dave's cheerfulness was genuine and infectious. "Ready for Chester Lake? I've been looking forward to this one—the photos online are spectacular."

"How are you doing, Rogerio?" Zuri asked, grateful for the subject change. "Any soreness from yesterday's incident?"

"Just bruises on my pride and my ribcage." Rogerio patted his side. "But I've decided it's a badge of honor. I survived the Via Ferrata collapse of 2025. Future tour groups will speak of it in hushed, reverent tones."

"Or they'll use you as a cautionary tale," Dave suggested. "Check your footing, don't wander off, and for God's sake, don't be Rogerio."

"That's hurtful but fair," Rogerio acknowledged. "Although in my defense, I didn't exactly choose to have the step break under me. That was the universe's decision."

"The universe has it out for you," Stella agreed. "We've established this. The question is whether it's done with you for this trip or if it's saving something special for later."

"Please don't tempt fate," Rogerio said, making an elaborate warding gesture. "We still have three days left. That's three more opportunities for me to nearly die in increasingly creative ways."

The table laughed, and the mood lightened. Only Maureen seemed detached from the conversation, eating her breakfast with mechanical precision, her expression distant.

Zuri watched her carefully. Something had happened at that camp. Something more than just a cultural experience and some herbal tea. The question was whether Maureen would shake it off—jet lag and strange herbs wearing off by midday—or whether this change was something deeper.

And if it was deeper, what exactly had the Wapiti done to her?

CHESTER LAKE

The drive to Chester Lake took them deeper into Spray Valley Provincial Park, the landscape becoming increasingly dramatic as they climbed. The morning sun painted the mountains in shades of gold and copper, and despite her exhaustion and worry, Zuri felt her spirits lift. This was why she did this job—not just to enjoy moments like this, but to facilitate moments like this for others. To help people step outside their ordinary lives and remember that the world was vast and beautiful and full of wonders.

"Right, everyone," she announced as the buses slowed near the trailhead. "Chester Lake is about seven and a half kilometers round trip, moderate elevation gain. The lake itself is stunning—proper alpine setting, surrounded by peaks. We'll be running at altitude, so pace yourselves. The air's thinner up here than what most of you are used to."

The group disembarked with the now-familiar routine—adjusting packs, checking water bottles, forming into their speed groups. Maureen moved through these preparations with the same automatic efficiency, but Zuri noticed she kept drifting toward the tree line, her gaze drawn to the forest as if looking for something.

Or waiting for someone.

"Maureen," Zuri called. "You're with the moderate group again today, yeah?"

"Hmm? Oh, yes. Moderate is fine." Maureen returned her attention to the group, but that distant quality remained.

They set off with James leading the moderate group, the trail climbing steadily through subalpine forest. The air was crisp and thin, each breath feeling slightly insufficient, and Zuri was working harder than usual to maintain the pace. Altitude was always deceptive—you felt fine until suddenly you didn't.

Around her, the runners were settling into rhythm, some chatting quietly, others focused on their breathing.

The trail was well-maintained but rocky, requiring attention to foot placement. On either side, the forest was dense and dark, the kind of old-growth wilderness that felt primeval, untouched.

After about forty minutes of steady climbing, the trail leveled out, and the forest thinned. Ahead, Zuri could see the bright blue of alpine water through the trees—Chester Lake, exactly as promised.

They emerged into an open basin, and even the most jaded runners stopped to take in the view. The lake was a perfect jewel of turquoise water, its surface so still it reflected the surrounding peaks with mirror precision. Larches ringed the shoreline—deciduous conifers that would turn brilliant gold in autumn but were now vivid green. Beyond the lake, mountains rose in layers of gray and white, their snowfields permanent even in summer.

"This is ridiculous," Dave said, pulling out his phone. "This can't be real. This is what desktop wallpapers look like."

"And yet here we are," Stella said, already taking photos in multiple directions. "This is why we do this. This exact moment right here."

Dana was filming, naturally, narrating for her followers. "Y'all, I don't even know what to say. The pictures don't do it justice. You're literally standing in a postcard.

This is what heaven looks like if heaven is cold and requires hiking to reach."

The moderate group arrived and spread out along the lakeshore, everyone finding their own perfect vantage point. Some were taking photos, some were just sitting in silence, absorbing the beauty. It was one of those rare moments when even the most talkative people had nothing to say because no words were adequate.

Maureen wandered to the far edge of the group, close to where the forest met the shore. She was looking across the lake with intense focus, and Zuri followed her gaze.

On the opposite shore, perhaps three hundred meters away, there were figures. Three of them, standing at the water's edge. From this distance, details were hard to make out, but they appeared to be dressed in dark, rough clothing—not the bright technical fabrics of tourists.

"What are they doing?" Rogerio had noticed them too. "Just standing there?"

"Fishing, maybe?" Dave suggested.

But they didn't appear to be fishing. They were simply standing, facing the lake—or perhaps facing the Global Runners across the water.

One of the figures moved to the water's edge, wading in knee-deep. Even from this distance, Zuri could see he was holding something—a bundle of some kind that he lit. Smoke rose, pale gray against the dark forest behind.

"Is that… is that a ceremony?" Elaine asked quietly.

Maureen's entire body had gone still, her attention locked on the distant figures. "Yes," she breathed. "Yes, it is."

The figure in the water began moving his arms in deliberate patterns, the smoke trailing around him. Though no sound carried across the lake, there was something unmistakably ritualistic about his movements—slow, precise, meaningful.

The second figure joined him in the water, and together they appeared to be chanting or singing, their heads tilted back, arms raised. The third figure remained on shore, tending what must have been a small fire given the amount of smoke now rising.

"Are they people from your camp?" Rogerio asked, glancing at Maureen. "Looks like rough clothing. Traditional style."

"It could be them," Maureen agreed, her voice distant. "The Wapiti range throughout this area. They go where the ceremonies need to be performed."

"What kind of ceremony requires standing in a freezing alpine lake?" Stella asked skeptically.

"Purification, probably. Connection to water spirits. Blessing the land." Maureen's hand had moved to her pocket, where Zuri knew she kept her field notebook. In moments she was capturing details of the scene in both words and sketches. She just stood there, watching with a hypnotic intensity.

The ceremony—if that's what it was—continued for perhaps ten minutes. The two figures in the water performed their synchronized movements while the third tended the fire, occasionally adding what looked like bundles of herbs that created thick, aromatic smoke. Even from across the lake, Zuri thought she could smell it—something sweet and earthy and slightly acrid.

Then, as abruptly as it had begun, the ceremony ended. The three figures gathered together briefly, then melted back into the forest, disappearing so quickly and completely it was almost as if they'd never been there. Only the smoke remained, dissipating slowly in the still air.

"Well," Dave said after a long silence. "That was unexpected."

"Unexpected but fascinating," Maureen said. "A reminder that we're not alone out here. These mountains hold more than just geology and wildlife. They have a long history."

Her tone made Zuri deeply uncomfortable. It was reverent in a way that went beyond academic interest. It sounded devotional.

"Right," Zuri said, injecting false brightness into her voice. "We should probably start heading back. We've got a full afternoon planned, and I don't want us running late."

Reluctantly, the group began preparing to leave, taking final photos, capping water bottles. But Maureen remained at the edge, staring at the spot where the three figures had disappeared.

"Maureen," Zuri called. "Time to go."

"They were calling something," Maureen said, still not moving. "The ceremony wasn't just purification. I think they were calling to something in the forest. Inviting it to witness something."

"Calling what?" Elaine asked, though she sounded like she wasn't sure she wanted the answer.

"The old ones. The first people of these mountains. The Napiyaw." Maureen finally turned to look at them, and her eyes were bright with something between excitement and fear. "They believe the past is just sleeping, waiting to be reawakened."

"That's a bit dramatic, don't you think?" Stella said, though her voice lacked its usual certainty.

"That's what I gathered from last night." Maureen gestured at the surrounding forest. "We're in one of the most remote wilderness areas in North America. Indigenous peoples have lived here for ten thousand years. They have stories about these mountains, about the things that live in them. Things that existed before humans. They believe those stories might be based on something real."

"Because Bigfoot isn't real," Rogerio said, trying to inject humor into the suddenly tense conversation. "I know I joked about it at dinner the other night, but I was joking. Cryptids aren't actually real."

"No, they're not, are they?" Maureen smiled, but it wasn't her usual warm expression. It was peaceful and distant.

Zuri had heard enough. "Everyone, gather up. We're leaving now." She used her trip director voice—the one that allowed no argument, the one that had successfully moved groups through airports and border crossings and difficult trails.

Maureen blinked, and the distraction faded. "Right. Yes, of course. Sorry, I was just… the ceremony was fascinating. From an anthropological perspective."

But as they began the hike back to the trailhead, Zuri kept Maureen in her peripheral vision. The professor ran normally enough, kept pace with the group, even made occasional comments about the landscape. But every so often, she'd stare into the trees as if she were looking for something that wasn't there.

THE FOREST WATCHERS

What the Global Runners didn't see—what they couldn't see from their position across the lake—was the fourth figure.

He stood deep in the tree line, perhaps thirty meters behind where Takoda, Maskwa, and another Wapiti member had performed their ceremony. At over seven feet tall, with a lean, powerful build covered in dark, shaggy fur, he would have been impossible to miss if he'd chosen to be seen. But he had not chosen, and so he remained invisible—a shadow among shadows, perfectly still, perfectly silent.

The First Walker watched the ceremony with ancient eyes, understanding its purpose completely. The Wapiti were calling to him, to his kind, requesting their attention, their blessing, their participation in whatever the band was planning. He'd seen such ceremonies countless times over the centuries, performed by generation after generation of humans who remembered—or thought they remembered—the old agreements between his people and theirs.

But this ceremony was different. The focus of the calling wasn't the land itself, or the general spirits of the wilderness. It was directed at something—or someone—specific.

His gaze followed Takoda's line of sight across the lake to where the running group had gathered. Even at this distance, the First Walker could smell them—the peculiar scent of modern humans, overlaid with the chemical odors of their clothing and equipment. Sweat and fear and excitement and exhaustion, all mixed together in a bouquet that told stories about each individual.

Most of them smelled ordinary. Unremarkable. The kind of humans who passed through the wilderness without leaving much impression beyond footprints and discarded energy bar wrappers.

But two of them were different.

One—the smaller woman with red hair who kept looking back at where the ceremony had taken place—carried a new scent. Something he recognized from long experience: the Wapiti's ceremonial drink, the mixture of roots and herbs that opened human perception to things normally hidden. She'd been dosed, and recently. The scent still clung to her breath, her skin, her hair. She was more alert, able to see what the earth held.

And the other—the tall woman with blonde hair who seemed uncomfortable in her expensive gear—she smelled of potential. Not the potential the red-haired woman carried, which was created and directed by the Wapiti. This was something innate, something the woman herself didn't recognize. A capacity for bridging worlds. A spiritual sensitivity buried beneath layers of modern living but still present, still accessible.

The First Walker had learned over centuries to recognize such individuals. They were rare, growing rarer as human societies moved further from the land, further from the old ways. But they still appeared occasionally—people who could, with the right circumstances or the right catalyst, perceive beyond the purely physical world.

The Wapiti had sensed this too, clearly. Their ceremony was directed at the entire group, not certain of who held the potential. The question was what the band intended to do with them.

Behind the First Walker, three more Napiyaw waited in deeper shadow—members of his band, his responsibility. They were younger, less patient, and one of them made a soft sound of inquiry.

Should we reveal ourselves?

The First Walker made a subtle gesture: *No. We watch only.*

The balance was delicate. The Wapiti needed the ceremonies to maintain their connection to the old ways, to justify their existence as a separate band. And the Napiyaw needed the Wapiti to maintain the bridges between worlds, to remember the old agreements, to keep alive the knowledge of what had existed before modern civilization erased it.

But the Wapiti's methods had grown aggressive over recent years, their priestess Ayâs becoming more desperate as she aged without finding a successor. The band had taken too many people, kept too many who came seeking the ceremonies but never intended to stay. The missing hikers were no accident—they were converts, willing or otherwise.

And now the Wapiti had their sights set on these runners. The First Walker could smell the intention in the smoke from the ceremony, could read it in the way Takoda had looked across the water. The band had decided. Plans were in motion.

The question was whether the Napiyaw would allow it.

Across the lake, the running group was preparing to leave, gathering their belongings and beginning the run back to wherever they'd come from. The red-haired woman lingered longest, staring back at the forest with eyes that saw more than they had a day ago. The blonde woman urged her to move, concern evident in her body language.

The First Walker watched them go, committing their scents and sounds to memory. His kind would know them if they encountered them again—would recognize them in daylight or darkness.

And they would encounter them again. The Wapiti's ceremony guaranteed it.

As the runners disappeared back into the forest, heading away from the lake, Takoda and Maskwa watched from the tree line where they'd hidden after the ceremony.

"They saw us," Takoda said in his own language, the old dialect that predated English. "The woman who came to camp—she recognized the ceremony."

"Ayâs believes someone in that group is the one," Maskwa added, his deep voice respectful but excited. "The one who can bridge the worlds fully, who can become what Ayâs is. If we can bring her to the ceremony, give her the milk, guide her transformation—the Napiyaw could walk in the physical world again, fully manifested, as they were in the old times."

"You assume much," Takoda said, emphasizing his words with the gesture language known only to the oldest

Wapiti families. "You assume she will choose this. You assume we will collect her."

"Don't you?" Maskwa's question was genuine, confused. "Isn't that what we've been waiting for? Someone who can perform the ceremonies properly, who can call Napiyaw into full presence rather than these half-glimpsed shadows?"

The First Walker listened from its secret place in the trees. It considered the question. *Did he want full manifestation? The ability to walk openly, to be seen and acknowledged, to exist completely in the physical world again rather than in this liminal state between matter and spirit?*

Perhaps. Once. Centuries ago, when his kind numbered in the thousands and the land was theirs without question.

But now? In this modern age? With so few of them remaining, their territory shrinking every year, their existence denied by the very species that had once known them well?

Full manifestation might mean full discovery. And discovery meant hunters, strangers, governments. It meant becoming specimens rather than spirits, subjects rather than sacred.

Sometimes sleeping things should remain sleeping, he thought.

"Yes, of course I do," Takoda said. "Ayâs is dying. She knows it. We all know it. She needs a successor before she passes, or everything dies with her—the ceremonies, the knowledge, the connection to Napiyaw. She'll do whatever it takes to ensure continuation."

"She believes it will save all of us," Maskwa stated flatly.

The First Walker listened to the exchange. *Let the Wapiti believe what they want. We have our own destiny in this world.*

He would watch. When the band made their move—and they would make their move soon, with the group across the river—he would be there. Toward what end, he hadn't yet decided.

The runners were gone now, their scent fading on the wind. The lake returned to its pristine silence, the mountains to their eternal watch. And in the shadows between the trees, the ancient things that humans had forgotten watched back, patient as stone, old as the peaks themselves.

Waiting to see what choices the destructive creatures called humans would make.

Waiting to see if those choices would finally wake the sleepers.

Or if the sleepers would decide to wake themselves.

CHAPTER 18

DOWN THE RIVER

The afternoon had warmed considerably by the time the buses delivered them to the Bow River put-in point. Elaine could feel the sun on her shoulders, pleasant and almost drowsy after the morning's exertion. Her legs were protesting the idea of more activity—two trail runs in two days was more exercise than she'd done in the past year—but the promise of canoeing sounded blissfully low impact.

"I hope you're recharged from lunch and some downtime," Zuri announced as people gathered near the water's edge, "because we have an afternoon canoe trip planned for you."

The setting was idyllic—a gentle curve in the Bow River where the water ran clear and relatively calm, willows trailing their branches along the banks, and mountains rising in every direction like a cathedral of stone. Along the shore, several large canoes waited, their fiberglass hulls painted with Indigenous designs—stylized animals, geometric patterns, and symbols Elaine didn't recognize but found beautiful, nonetheless.

A tall man with weathered features and an easy smile stepped forward. "I'm Steven Waters, your guide for this afternoon. My family has been here for so many generations that we've lost count. They were literally part of the First Nations before the Europeans showed up. Like most of my nation, I have two names. Within modern communities, I'm Steven Waters, which is easy to say and record in documents. But for tribal groups, I'm Mni Zha, which means Water Eagle. It's appropriate for my profession."

He moved among the canoes as he spoke, his hand trailing along their sides with obvious affection. "We'll be taking these canoes down the Bow River—a very special place to all the original tribes in this area. The Stoney Nakoda name for this river is Ijathibe Wapta, which means 'a place where people made bows out of Saskatoon saplings.'"

Elaine found herself unexpectedly interested. "The same saskatoon that's in the pies?"

Steven's face lit up with pleasure. "Exactly! I'm glad you've had a chance to try it. The wood for bows was probably more important to the ancient tribes—the bow and arrow were central to life here because the primary food source was buffalo. But being able to eat the berries makes the saskatoon tree doubly valuable."

"What about fishing?" Dave asked. "We saw people at Chester Lake this morning who seemed to be performing some kind of fishing ceremony."

Steven's expression became more thoughtful. "Fishing has an interesting history in this region. There were, and are, multiple nations in this area, and they all had slightly different practices. For reasons long lost to history, the Stoney Nakoda were the only nation who fished as a primary source of food. The others—like the Blackfoot and Siksika—were almost entirely focused on hunting buffalo."

He gestured at the surrounding landscape. "You've seen the terrain here? A popular hunting method was to drive the buffalo into a valley and then over cliffs. They would fall and break legs or worse. Then the hunters could move among them, dispatching them with spears or arrows." He noted the grimaces on several faces and added apologetically, "Sorry for the gruesome details. It was their equivalent of a modern slaughterhouse. It produced more meat in a day than chasing animals across the plains trying to drop them with crude weapons."

"But the ceremony we saw wasn't about fishing," Maureen interjected, her voice carrying that same dreamy quality it had held all day. "It was about connection. About honoring the water spirits and the old agreements between people and the land."

Steven looked at her with a mixture of surprise and respect. "You know something about traditional practices."

"I'm learning," Maureen said simply. "There's so much knowledge that's been lost. But it's still here if you know where to look."

An uncomfortable silence followed this statement, broken by Zuri's deliberately cheerful voice. "Right then! Steven, should we get everyone sorted into canoes?"

"Absolutely." Steven moved to the first canoe. "Each of these will hold eight people comfortably. They're stable and forgiving—perfect for beginners and experienced paddlers alike. The river will do most of the work since we're going downstream. Your job is mainly steering and enjoying the scenery. Everyone, choose your canoe and let's get you on the water."

The group divided naturally—some by friendship, some by athletic ability, some simply by proximity. Elaine found herself in a canoe with Maureen, Dana, Rogerio, and four others, including the quiet couple from Austin and Ben, the software engineer from Seattle.

"This should be relaxing," Dana said, adjusting her phone mount on the canoe's side. "After two days of climbing, I'm ready for something that doesn't require vertical movement."

"Speak for yourself," Rogerio said, already testing his paddle. "I'm planning to turn this into a race. Gotta redeem myself after yesterday's Via Ferrata incident."

"Please don't race," Ben said mildly. "Some of us would like to arrive at the destination without capsizing."

Steven moved among the canoes, making final adjustments and providing basic paddling instruction. "The person at the front sets the pace. The person at the back steers. Everyone else, just match the rhythm and don't paddle against each other. Sounds simple because it is — until someone gets excited and throws off the timing. Then you'll go in circles."

He pushed their canoe into the current, and suddenly they were moving, the shore sliding away with surprising speed. The sensation was both exhilarating and slightly unnerving—losing control and being carried by water, while the land receded with each passing moment.

"I thought canoeing would be harder than this," Elaine said as they found their rhythm.

Maureen turned on her seat, her paddle resting across her knees. "It would be if we were alone. But there are eight of us sharing the work in this boat. Also, the river is giving us a vigorous boost. We're traveling downstream, which means we don't have to fight the current. Luckily, this is a one-way trip, so we don't have to paddle back to the starting point, against the river."

From another canoe—a bright red one about thirty feet ahead—Dave's voice carried across the water. "Hey slackers! We'll race you to that next bend!"

Before anyone in Elaine's canoe could respond, Rogerio accepted the challenge without consulting his crew. "You're on! I hope you can paddle as hard as you run, gazelle!"

Then, turning to the rest of them with a grin: "Let's show that red canoe what we can do."

After a moment of surprised hesitation, the entire crew agreed, and they fell into an aggressive rhythm. Water churned beside the hull as eight paddles bit into the river in synchronized strokes. The canoe surged forward with surprising speed.

Ahead, the red canoe with Dave, Stella, and their crew was also accelerating, paddles flashing in the sunlight. The race was on—impromptu and absurd and exactly the kind of thing that made these trips memorable.

But not everyone took part in the competition. Behind the racing canoes, the third vessel moved at a gentler pace, its occupants choosing leisure over speed.

"Should we join the race?" someone in the slower canoe asked.

"Absolutely not," came the firm reply. "I already put in my run for the day. This is supposed to be the relaxing portion of our afternoon."

"Agreed. Let them tire themselves out. We'll just enjoy the scenery."

And the scenery was spectacular. The Bow River wound through a landscape of almost impossible beauty—dense forest alternating with open meadows, mountains rising in every direction, and the water itself so clear you could see smooth stones on the bottom. Eagles circled overhead, and occasionally they'd spot deer drinking at the water's edge, lifting their heads to watch the canoes pass before returning to the business of simple living.

In the racing canoe, Elaine had found a rhythm she hadn't expected—the repetitive motion of paddling, the cool spray of water on her face, the satisfaction of working in unison with seven other people toward a common goal. Her shoulders burned and her forearms ached, but it was good pain, earned pain, the kind that came from actually using her body rather than maintaining it.

They rounded the bend neck-and-neck with the red canoe, and both crews erupted in competitive cheers and good-natured trash talk.

"Is that all you've got?" Stella called across the water.

"We're just getting started!" Rogerio shot back.

But as the immediate excitement of the race faded, and they settled back into a more sustainable pace, Elaine became aware that Maureen had stopped paddling. The professor sat with her paddle across her lap, staring at the riverbank with intense focus.

"Maureen?" Elaine touched her shoulder. "Are you alright?"

"Do you hear that?" Maureen asked softly.

"Hear what?"

"Drumming. Singing. Coming from the forest." Maureen's head tilted, as if tracking a sound that moved just below the threshold of hearing. "They're calling to their past."

Elaine listened carefully. She heard the splash of paddles, the rush of water, birdsong, and the wind in the trees. But no drumming. No singing. Nothing that suggested a human presence in the surrounding wilderness.

"I don't hear anything," she said carefully.

"You will," Maureen replied with certainty. "Once you open yourself to it, you'll hear everything. The land speaks if you listen."

This was becoming genuinely concerning. Maureen's comments were crossing from enthusiastic academic interest into something that sounded almost delusional. Elaine glanced toward the front of the canoe where Dana was filming and wondered if she should say something to Zuri when they reached the end point.

The canoes continued downriver, the racing pairs continuing at a more leisurely pace as the initial competitive energy burned off. The landscape changed subtly—the forest growing denser, the mountains closer, the river narrower. They were moving deeper into the wilderness, further from the roads and towns that represented civilization.

After perhaps forty-five minutes on the water, Dana noticed something concerning. "Um, guys? Is it just me, or is there water in the boat?"

Everyone looked down. The bottom of the canoe, which had been dry when they launched, now held a thin layer of water that sloshed with each paddle stroke.

"There's definitely water," Ben confirmed, tapping his foot to show the splash. "Are we leaking?"

"Maybe we picked up something on the bottom?" Rogerio suggested. "Hit a submerged rock or log?"

The water level was rising slowly but steadily—not catastrophically, but enough to be noticeable. And concerning.

"What should we do?" someone asked. "Everyone else is way ahead. Should we call for help?"

Rogerio pulled out his phone, hoping for cell service. The screen showed no bars, no connection to the outside world. "I don't have any signal. Does anyone else?"

Everyone checked their phones in a choreographed dance of the digitally dependent. Seven hands raised seven phones toward the sky, searching for that elusive connection to civilization. Elaine sat silently, remembering her phone on the bedside table back in the room. Every voice confirmed what Rogerio already knew:

"Nothing."

"No service."

"Not even one bar."

"We're in a dead zone."

"So, we're stranded?" The question came from Sarah of the Austin couple, her voice carrying the first real edge of fear they'd heard all day.

"Not stranded," Maureen said calmly, finally returning her attention to the immediate situation. "We're exploring. We just need to get to shore before the water gets too deep. Look—there's a point of land jutting into the river ahead. We can beach the canoe there."

It was sensible advice, and everyone immediately began paddling toward the indicated spot—a small peninsula where rock and sand met the water, backed by forest but accessible from the river. As they crossed the current to reach it, the water inside the canoe rose more quickly, now covering their feet.

"Stroke, stroke!" Maureen called out, taking charge with surprising authority. "We're racing the leak. Steady rhythm, everyone together."

They reached the peninsula just as the water was deep enough to be truly uncomfortable. The canoe's bow scraped against sand and rock with a sound of relief—they'd made it.

"Alright, water dogs," Maureen announced. "This is the end of the line. Wade out onto shore."

Everyone disembarked through the shallow water, stepping carefully on the rocky bottom until they stood on dry land. Eight people, thoroughly damp from the knees down, stared at a canoe that was clearly taking on water from some breach they couldn't immediately identify.

"No injuries," Dana said, checking everyone automatically. "We're safe and sound."

"And lost," Elaine added, looking around at the unfamiliar wilderness.

"Not lost," Maureen corrected, her voice carrying the same unsettling certainty it had held all day. "We know exactly where we are—on the Bow River, in the heart of territory where the Stoney Nakota used to fish and hunt buffalo. This land has been home to people for ten thousand years. We're not lost. We're just temporarily separated from our group."

The distinction didn't make Elaine feel better, but before she could say so, Ben held his phone up triumphantly. "I've got one bar! Just one, but maybe enough to—" The bar disappeared. "Never mind. It's gone."

"We should wait here," suggested Luke, the second of the Austin couple, a practical-minded man who looked like he'd done outdoor recreation before. "The other canoes will realize we're missing when they reach the endpoint. They'll come back looking for us."

"Yes, that's right," Maureen agreed. "Zuri and Steven won't abandon us. They can't miss us on this peninsula. They'll come back, see the canoe, see us, and voilà — we're rescued."

"How long will that take?" Dana asked, glancing at the sun, which had begun its afternoon descent.

"Could be an hour. Maybe two if they're ahead of us by a lot. They have to reach the endpoint, realize we're gone, organize a search, and paddle back upstream." Ben was thinking it through logically. "But we're fine here. It's warm, we have water bottles, and there's plenty of daylight left."

"Someone should stay with the canoe," Dana suggested. "In case the rescue party arrives before we all get back."

"Back? Back from where?" Elaine asked, though she suspected she already knew the answer.

Maureen was standing with Dana, looking into the forest with that focused intensity again. "There's a trail." She pointed into the trees where, indeed, a narrow but clearly maintained path wound away from the peninsula into the wilderness. "This spot is obviously a place where people come on purpose. Let's see where the trail goes. Maybe it leads to a road or a ranger station."

"Or maybe it leads deeper into nowhere," Elaine countered, her unease growing.

"Only one way to find out." Maureen was already walking toward the trail entrance. "I'm going to explore. Anyone who wants to come with me is welcome. Anyone who wants to stay with the canoe should feel free to do that."

It was phrased as a choice, but there was something in Maureen's tone that suggested she'd be going regardless of whether anyone joined her. And the thought of splitting up—some people staying with the canoe, others disappearing into the forest—felt like the beginning of a horror movie Elaine didn't want to be in.

"I'll come," she heard herself say, surprising herself. Better to keep everyone together than to fragment further.

"Me too," Dana added. "I'm not splitting the party. That's how people die in movies."

One by one, the others agreed—some enthusiastically, some reluctantly. Only Ben volunteered to stay behind.

"Someone should be here when help arrives," he said reasonably. "I'll stay with the canoe. If you're not back in an hour, I'll try hiking downriver to find the others."

"An hour," Maureen agreed. "We won't go far. Just far enough to see what's ahead. There might be a road or a building—something that explains why there's a maintained trail here."

She led the way into the forest, and the others followed—seven people leaving the safety of the river for the uncertainty of the wilderness. As they walked, Elaine looked back over her shoulder, watching Ben grow smaller beside the damaged canoe until the forest swallowed him from view.

CHAPTER 19

THE TRAIL

The trail was well-worn, which should have been reassuring but somehow wasn't. Someone—or many someones—used this path regularly, walking from the river deep into the forest toward... what?

The temperature dropped noticeably once they entered the trees. The sun, so warm and pleasant on the river, couldn't penetrate the dense canopy. It was a darker wilderness. Shadows clustered between the trunks, and the forest floor was carpeted with needles that muffled their footsteps.

"This is actually really beautiful," Dana said, filming as she walked. "Very Hansel and Gretel. Hopefully without the child-eating witch at the end."

"Germanic fairy tales don't really apply to the Canadian wilderness," Rogerio pointed out. "If anything, we should worry about bears or—" He lowered his voice dramatically. "—Sasquatch."

"You need to let the Sasquatch thing go," Sarah said, though she was smiling. "It's not real."

"But what if it is?" Rogerio was enjoying himself despite their predicament. "What if we're about to stumble onto the cryptozoological discovery of the century? I'd like to be on record as having predicted it."

"Noted," Dana said, training her camera on him. "When we find Bigfoot, you get full credit."

But Maureen wasn't taking part in the light banter. She walked at the front of the group with focused intent, her attention shifting between the trail ahead and the forest on either side. Several times she paused, listening to something the rest of them couldn't hear, then continued forward with renewed purpose.

"Maureen," Elaine called softly, catching up to walk beside her. "Are you sure we should be going this far? We said an hour. We should probably turn back soon."

"We're almost there," Maureen replied, though there was no obvious landmark to support this claim.

"Almost where?"

"Where we're supposed to be." Maureen smiled, and there was something unsettling about the expression— too knowing, too certain, like she was privy to information the rest of them lacked. "Can't you feel it? This trail is taking us exactly where we need to go."

Before Elaine could respond, the forest opened ahead of them into a cleared area. Not a natural clearing—this was deliberate, maintained, human-shaped.

They had found the Wapiti camp.

It was larger than Elaine had imagined from Maureen's description. Multiple structures clustered around a central fire pit—some were teepees covered in hide, others were rough log cabins that looked decades old. Smoke rose from several locations, carrying the smell of cooking food and something herbal and slightly sweet.

And there were people. Perhaps thirty or forty individuals of various ages, all dressed in a mixture of traditional animal-skin clothing and modern outdoor gear. They moved through the camp tending fires, preparing food, working on various crafts and tools.

When the Global Runners emerged from the trail, several heads turned toward them. But rather than surprise or alarm at the appearance of strangers, the Wapiti seemed almost… expectant. As if visitors arriving from the forest was a normal, anticipated occurrence.

An older woman emerged from the largest cabin. She was small and stooped, her weathered face framed by wild braids, and she wore elaborately beaded animal skins that marked her as someone important. When she saw the group, her face broke into a smile that was both welcoming and strangely triumphant.

"Maureen!" The old woman's voice was surprisingly strong. "You've returned. And you've brought friends. How wonderful."

Maureen moved forward as if drawn by invisible threads, her expression bright with something between joy and relief. "Ayâs. I didn't know—we didn't mean to—our canoe had a leak, we followed the trail and—"

"And here you are." Ayâs stepped closer, her dark eyes scanning the group with obvious interest. "Exactly as it should be. The river brought you. The land guided you. There are no accidents, child. Only paths we were meant to walk."

The other Wapiti members had stopped their work and were gathering around, studying the newcomers with varied expressions—some curious, some pleased, some unreadable. Elaine felt increasingly uncomfortable under their collective gaze, like a specimen being evaluated.

Takoda emerged from the crowd, and his smile was warm and genuine. "What a pleasant surprise! When

Maureen came to visit yesterday, I hoped more of you might find your way here, eventually. Welcome to our camp."

"We're not staying," Elaine said quickly, perhaps too quickly. "Our canoe had a leak. We just followed the trail to see if it led to help. We should probably head back—our friend is waiting with the canoe, and our group will be looking for us."

"Of course, of course," Ayâs said, though her tone suggested she had different ideas. "But you've walked so far, and the day grows cold. Please, sit. Rest. Have some water and food. We wouldn't send you back onto the trail without refreshment. That would be poor hospitality."

It was phrased as an offer, but something in the way the Wapiti had arranged themselves—casually, seemingly without coordination, but effectively blocking the trail back the way they'd come—made it feel less like an invitation and more like a requirement.

"Just for a few minutes," Maureen said, already moving toward the central fire pit where rough wooden benches waited. "We can't be rude. And I'd like you all to experience what I did yesterday. These people are preserving something precious. Something the modern world has forgotten."

One by one, the Global Runners moved toward the fire, drawn by Maureen's enthusiasm and the Wapiti's insistent hospitality. Elaine was sitting on a log bench, accepting a cup of water from a young woman who smiled but didn't speak.

Around them, the Wapiti resumed their activities, but Elaine noticed they'd shifted positions subtly. Where before they'd been scattered throughout the camp, now they formed a loose perimeter around the visitors. Not threatening, not obvious, but definitely present.

Definitely watching.

Ayâs stood before the fire, her ancient face illuminated by flames that danced to their own rhythm. She looked at each of the visitors in turn, her gaze lingering longest on Elaine.

"Welcome," she said softly, and the word carried weight beyond its simple meaning. "Welcome to the old ways. Welcome to truth. Welcome home."

And despite the fire, despite being surrounded by dozens of people, Elaine felt suddenly, profoundly cold.

They had walked into something. Something planned. Something waiting.

And she had no idea how to walk back out.

CHAPTER 20

FOUND

The red canoe reached the takeout point first, as Dave had predicted with competitive satisfaction. He and Stella helped pull it onto the sandy bank, then stood catching their breath while waiting for the other canoes to arrive.

"Good run," Stella said, checking her watch. "We made excellent time."

"I told you we'd beat them." Dave grinned, scanning the river upstream for signs of the other canoes. "Although I expected them to be closer behind us. We weren't that much faster."

Within ten minutes, two more canoes appeared around the bend, their crews paddling with the leisurely confidence of people who'd given up on racing and settled into enjoying the scenery. Steven Waters was in one of them, and he beached his canoe quickly before helping the others.

"Everyone accounted for?" he called out cheerfully.

"Not yet," Zuri replied, her tone already carrying an edge of concern. "We're still missing one canoe. The one with Maureen, Elaine, and some others."

"They probably stopped to look at something," Steven said, though he was already scanning the river with more attention. "Happens all the time. Someone spots an eagle or an interesting rock formation, and before you know it, they're twenty minutes behind."

But twenty minutes passed, then thirty, and the missing canoe didn't appear. The remaining runners had gathered on the bank, their earlier good humor fading into worry.

"This isn't right," Zuri said, pulling out her phone. No signal, as expected—they were still too remote. "They should be here by now. Even if they stopped to look at something, they should be here."

"Could they have capsized?" Dave asked.

"Not on this river," Steven assured him. "The current is gentle, there aren't any rapids or obstacles. And those canoes are incredibly stable. You'd have to try pretty hard to tip one."

"Could they have gotten lost?" Stella suggested. "Taken a wrong channel or something?"

"There are no channels to take wrong. The river runs straight from where we launched to here." Steven was looking genuinely concerned now. "But they might have had equipment trouble. A broken paddle, maybe, or someone got injured and they had to stop."

"We need to go back," Zuri said firmly. "Now. We need to find them."

"Agreed." Steven was already moving toward his canoe. "I'll take my boat back upstream. Zuri, you should come with me—you know your people best. We'll paddle back along the route and look for them."

"I'm coming too," Dave said immediately.

"And me," Stella added.

"Fine. Four of us in my canoe—we'll move faster with more paddlers, anyway." Steven looked at the remaining runners on the bank. "The rest of you, stay here. If they show up while we're searching, someone needs to be here to meet them. And if we're not back in two hours, call for help." He handed a satellite phone to one of the other trip leaders. "This has signal anywhere. Emergency services is on speed dial."

They launched quickly, Steven's canoe cutting back upstream with powerful strokes from four motivated paddlers. The river that had seemed so pleasant and lazy during the descent now felt agonizingly slow as they fought against the current.

"There!" Stella pointed ahead where the river curved. "Is that them?"

A canoe was visible, beached on a small peninsula. But as they drew closer, it was clear the vessel was abandoned—tilted on its side, water pooling in its hull, and no sign of its crew.

"That's definitely one of ours," Steven said grimly, recognizing the painted design on the hull.

They beached beside it, and Zuri immediately spotted a figure sitting on a rock nearby. "Ben! Thank God—are you alright? Where are the others?"

Ben stood, relief evident on his face. "You came back. I was starting to worry. Everyone else is fine—they went down that trail about an hour ago, maybe more. The canoe was leaking, we had to beach it, and Maureen wanted to explore that path to see if it led to help."

"An hour ago?" Zuri's concern ratcheted higher. "They should have been back by now. Or at least, one of them should have come back to tell you what they found."

"I know." Ben looked at the trail entrance, his expression troubled. "I was about to head down myself to look for them. I'm glad you're here."

"Show us where they went," Dave said, already moving toward the tree line.

The four of them—Zuri, Dave, Stella, and Ben—entered the forest with Steven staying behind to secure the canoes and wait in case the missing group returned from a different direction. The trail was obvious, well-worn by countless feet, winding through dense forest that blocked most of the afternoon light.

They moved quickly, calling out names occasionally, listening for responses that never came. The forest was eerily quiet—no birds singing, no small animals rustling in the undergrowth. Just the sound of their own footsteps and breathing.

"This trail goes somewhere specific," Stella observed. "It's too maintained to be random. Someone uses this path regularly."

"But who?" Dave asked. "We're miles from any road or building."

Zuri didn't answer, but her mind was racing through possibilities, none of them good. A maintained trail in remote wilderness, Maureen's changed behavior after visiting the Wapiti camp, the convenient leak in the canoe that forced them to shore at this exact spot…

"I think I know where this leads," she said quietly.

They rounded a bend, and the forest opened into a clearing. What Zuri saw confirmed her worst fears.

The Wapiti camp spread before them—multiple structures, smoking fires, and dozens of people moving through the space with purposeful activity. And there, sitting on log benches around the central fire pit, were the missing members of their group.

Maureen sat closest to the fire, her posture relaxed and comfortable as if she'd been there for hours. Elaine was beside her, looking considerably less comfortable, her body language broadcasting discomfort. Dana, Rogerio, and the others were scattered on nearby benches, all holding cups of something and looking varying degrees of uncomfortable.

An old woman in elaborate animal skins stood before the fire, clearly in the middle of speaking. She stopped when she noticed the new arrivals, and her weathered face broke into a smile.

"More guests!" Her voice was strong despite her apparent age. "How wonderful. The river brings exactly who needs to be here."

Takoda appeared from the crowd, his expression welcoming. "Zuri! I didn't expect to see you so soon. Please, come join us. Your friends have been enjoying our hospitality."

Zuri's professional instincts were screaming warnings, but she kept her voice calm and polite. "Thank you, but we need to collect our group and get back to the river. It's getting late, and we have a schedule to keep."

"Nonsense," the old woman—this must be Ayâs—said dismissively. "You've walked so far. You must rest, have food and drink. We're preparing dinner now. You'll join us."

"That's very kind," Zuri said, her tone still pleasant but firm, "but we really must be going. Our group is expected back at the hotel, and people will worry if we're late."

"Just a quick meal," Ayâs insisted, gesturing to the benches. "Surely you can spare thirty minutes for hospitality. It would be rude to refuse."

Zuri moved toward her group, assessing each person quickly. Maureen looked almost drugged—her eyes unfocused, her movements slow. Elaine's relief at seeing Zuri was palpable. The others looked confused and uncomfortable but unharmed.

"Everyone up," Zuri said in her trip director voice—the one that brooked no argument. "We're leaving now. Thank you for your hospitality," she added to Ayâs, "but we need to return to the river before dark."

As her group stood, Wapiti members moved subtly to block the trail. Not obviously, not threateningly, but they were suddenly there—between the Global Runners and the exit, their bodies creating a human barrier.

"Please," Ayâs said, her voice hardening slightly. "Sit. Eat. There's no rush."

"There is a rush," Zuri countered, her own voice losing its polite veneer. "It's already late afternoon. We have a several-hour journey back to our hotel. We need to leave. Now."

Stella had moved closer to the fire, her attention caught by someone in the crowd. A man in his forties, wearing a mixture of modern hiking clothes and traditional items, his face vaguely familiar…

"Oh my God," Stella breathed. "Dave, look at him. Third person from the left. Isn't that—"

Dave followed her gaze and his eyes widened. "The missing hiker. From the posters. Marcus Webb, I think."

The man noticed their attention and met Stella's eyes. For a moment, something flickered in his expression—recognition? Concern? But then it smoothed into calm acceptance, and he smiled slightly before looking away.

"You're keeping people here," Stella said, her voice rising with anger and fear. "That man is supposed to be missing. His family is looking for him. And you're just— what? Holding him prisoner?"

"Prisoner?" Takoda looked genuinely puzzled. "No one here is a prisoner. Marcus came to us seeking a new kind of life. He found it and chose to stay. Just as Maureen chose to visit us, and your friends chose to follow the trail here. These are all choices freely made."

"Maureen," Zuri said sharply, turning to the professor. "Tell me honestly—did they force you to come here yesterday? Did they give you something without your consent?"

Maureen's gaze was distant, serene. "No one forced me. I came because I wanted to learn. They shared their knowledge. Their ceremonies. Their drinks that open the mind." She smiled. "I'm exactly where I'm supposed to be."

"That's the drugs talking," Dave said bluntly. "You've been drugged. They've done something to you."

"Enlightened," Maureen corrected gently. "Not drugged. Enlightened. There's a difference."

The sun was sinking lower, shadows lengthening across the camp. Zuri felt time slipping away, felt the situation deteriorating by the second. Around them, more Wapiti members had gathered, forming a tighter perimeter. The pretense of hospitality was wearing thin.

"We're leaving," Zuri announced, putting steel in her voice. She grabbed Maureen's arm and pulled her to her feet. "Everyone, back to the canoes. We're walking out of here right now. If anyone tries to stop us, that's kidnapping, and we will involve the police."

"The police." Ayâs laughed, a sound like dry leaves scraping stone. "By the time the police arrive, if they arrive, you'll be long gone from here. This camp moves. We move. We've been moving for over a century, staying ahead of authorities who don't understand what we preserve."

"So, you admit you're holding us," Stella said.

"I admit nothing. I simply state facts." Ayâs moved closer to the fire, the flames casting her face into sharp relief—ancient, determined, and utterly uncompromising. "You came here. The land brought you. And now you'll stay until the ceremony is complete."

"What ceremony?" Zuri demanded.

"The one we've been preparing. The one that will restore the old ways. The one that requires"—Ayâs's gaze settled on Elaine with predatory focus—"very specific participants."

Dave had been assessing the situation tactically. "There's about thirty of them and twelve of us. If we rush the trail all together—"

"You'll be stopped," Maskwa said, his massive form stepping forward from the crowd. At six-foot-four and heavily muscled, he was larger than anyone in the Global Runners group. "Please don't make this difficult. We don't want violence. We want understanding. Cooperation. But we will have what we need."

"We need to leave," Zuri repeated, her voice shaking slightly now—not with fear, but with barely controlled anger. "We have jobs, families, responsibilities. We're expected back at our hotel. People are already looking for us. You can't just keep us here like—like some kind of cult compound."

"Cult." Ayâs tasted the word. "Such a modern term. We are not a cult. We are the keepers of the knowledge your world tried to destroy. We are the last connection to powers your civilization forgot. And yes, we will keep you here. Not forever. Just until the ceremony is complete. Until one of you"—again that focused stare at Elaine—"steps into her true purpose."

The temperature seemed to drop despite the fire. Around them, the Wapiti had formed a complete circle, and the way back to the trail was now blocked by at least a dozen people.

"Let me be absolutely clear," Zuri said, her British accent becoming more pronounced as her stress rose. "If you keep us here against our will, that is illegal. That is kidnapping. And when—not if, but when—we get out of here, there will be consequences. Legal consequences. You cannot do this."

"But we can," Ayâs said simply. "And we are. The sun is setting. You have nowhere to go. Your canoes are miles away. The forest is thick and easy to get lost in. You'll stay tonight. You'll share our food. You'll witness our ceremony. And by morning, perhaps you'll understand what you've been offered—a chance to be part of something ancient, something meaningful, something far more important than whatever small lives you left behind."

She gestured, and Wapiti members began moving closer, herding the Global Runners toward a large structure—one of the animal-skin teepees. Not violently, not with weapons, but with inexorable physical presence.

"No," Zuri said, planting her feet. "We're not going anywhere. We're not—"

Maskwa moved behind her, his hand gentle but unyielding on her shoulder. "Please don't make this harder than it needs to be. We don't want to hurt anyone. But we will do what's necessary."

Dave tensed, ready to fight, but Stella grabbed his arm. "There's too many of them. And look—" She nodded toward the crowd where several Wapiti men had moved their hands to their belts, where Stella could see the handles of knives. "They're armed. We're not. Fighting now will just get someone hurt."

"So, we just go along with being kidnapped?" Dave's voice was incredulous.

"We stay calm," Zuri said, though her own voice shook. "We cooperate for now. We look for opportunities. And we remember that eventually, they'll have to let their guard down. When they do, we run."

Around them, the Wapiti tightened their circle, and the last rays of sunlight disappeared behind the mountains. In the growing darkness, the fire became the only source of light, and Ayâs's shadow stretched long and distorted across the ground.

"Come," the old woman said, her voice almost gentle now. "Let's get you settled. Dinner will be ready soon. And after dinner… after dinner, you'll see something remarkable. Something your world thought was only a legend."

She smiled, and in the firelight, her teeth looked very sharp.

"You'll see the old gods wake."

CHAPTER 21

THE CAPTURE

Maureen stepped forward before Zuri could say anything more, placing a gentle hand on her trip director's arm. "It's alright, Zuri, really. You're frightened because you don't understand yet. But once you experience what they're offering, you'll see. This is a gift, not a threat."

Zuri stared at her, searching Maureen's face for any sign of the sharp-minded professor she'd known just two days ago. "Maureen, listen to me. They've drugged you. Whatever they gave you yesterday—that 'nature's milk'— it's altered your thinking. This isn't you talking."

"This is more me than I've ever been." Maureen's smile was serene, untouched by Zuri's distress. "I was lost before. Searching for meaning in dusty books and academic journals, chasing tenure and recognition like they mattered. But this—" she gestured at the camp, the fire, the gathered Wapiti, "—this is real. Ancient. True. They're preserving knowledge that could transform how we understand spirituality, consciousness, our relationship with the land."

"They're keeping us prisoner," Stella said bluntly.

"They're keeping you safe," Maureen corrected. "The forest at night is dangerous. You don't know the trails. You'd get lost, hurt, or worse. Stay tonight. Share their food. Witness the ceremony. In the morning, you'll be free to leave—if you still want to."

The way she said that last part—if you still want to—sent ice down Elaine's spine.

"Everyone, please." Takoda stepped forward, his expression earnest and apologetic. "I understand this is frightening. You feel trapped. But truly, we mean you no harm. We simply want to share something extraordinary with you. Our ceremonies, our connection to the old powers—these things are dying out. Young people leave for the cities. The government tries to suppress traditional practices. We're fighting to keep alive knowledge that's sustained our people for thousands of years."

"By kidnapping tourists?" Dave's voice dripped with sarcasm.

"By offering opportunities to those the land brings to us." Takoda's tone remained patient. "You think it's a coincidence that your canoe leaked at exactly the right spot? That the trail led you here? The land guided you. The spirits arranged it. We're simply honoring what was meant to be."

"That's insane," Ben said, speaking for the first time since they'd arrived at the camp. "You're talking about mystical destiny when what actually happened is you sabotaged our canoe."

A flicker of something—annoyance? acknowledgment?—crossed Takoda's face before the pleasant mask returned. "Believe what you need to believe. But you're here now. Fighting it will only make tonight more difficult for everyone. Accept what's offered. Rest. Eat. Watch. Learn. That's all we ask."

Ayâs had been watching this exchange with obvious amusement. Now she stepped forward again, and her presence commanded immediate attention despite her small, stooped frame. "Enough debate. The sun is almost gone. We have preparations to make. Maskwa, Takoda— show our guests to the lodge. Make them comfortable."

"Comfortable," Zuri repeated bitterly. "Is that what we're calling imprisonment now?"

"Comfortable." Ayâs's eyes were ancient and unmoved. "The ceremony happens tonight regardless of your labels for it. You can participate willingly or unwillingly, but you will be present. The choice of attitude is yours."

Maskwa moved behind the group, his massive presence making resistance seem futile. Other Wapiti members flanked them on all sides, creating a human corridor toward a teepee perhaps twenty feet in diameter, its hide covering painted with symbols that shifted in the flickering firelight.

"Inside," Maskwa said, his deep voice leaving no room for argument.

One by one, the Global Runners filed into the structure. The interior was dim, lit only by what firelight penetrated the hide walls and a small oil lamp hanging on the center pole. The floor was covered with fur pelts and woven blankets, and the air smelled of smoke, leather, and something herbal Elaine couldn't identify.

"Sit," Maskwa instructed from the entrance. "Food will be brought. Don't try to leave. There are people watching this lodge. If you attempt to escape before the ceremony is complete, you will be stopped. Am I clear?"

"Crystal," Zuri said through gritted teeth.

Maskwa nodded and stepped outside, closing the hide flap behind him. They heard him speaking to someone in a language none of them understood, then footsteps moving away.

For a long moment, no one spoke. They sat on the fur-covered floor in a rough circle, processing what had just happened to them. Outside, they could hear the Wapiti moving about the camp, voices calling to each other, the sounds of preparation for something significant.

"This is bad," Dana finally said, her voice small. "This is really, really bad."

"Everyone stay calm," Zuri said, though her own voice shook. "We're going to get through this. They said the ceremony is tonight. After that, they'll have to let their guard down. That's when we make our move."

"Make our move?" Rogerio looked around the dim interior. "There's one door, and it's guarded. We don't know the forest. We don't have weapons. What move exactly are we making?"

"I don't know yet," Zuri admitted. "But I'm not accepting that we're just going to stay here. We're not participating in whatever twisted ceremony they have planned. We're getting out."

"What if we can't?" The question came from Sarah, her voice thick with barely suppressed panic. "What if they really can keep us here? What if no one finds us?"

"Steven knows where we went," Stella said, her practical mind working through the logistics. "He stayed with the canoes. When we don't come back, he'll call for help.

The satellite phone works anywhere. Search and rescue will come looking."

"By which time we could be miles from here," Dave pointed out. "They said the camp moves. They're probably planning to relocate after tonight."

"Then we fight," Stella said flatly. "When they come to take us to this ceremony, we fight. All of us, together. Create chaos, scatter in different directions. Some of us will get away."

"And some of us won't," Ben said quietly. "Some of us will get hurt. Maybe badly. Those men have knives. Did you see them?"

"I saw them," Zuri confirmed. "Which is why we're not doing anything rash. We stay calm. We look for opportunities. And we stick together—no one separates from the group."

Elaine had been sitting silently, her arms wrapped around her knees, her mind racing. "They want me specifically. Ayâs kept looking at me. Did you notice?"

"I noticed," Maureen said from her position near the wall. She'd been so quiet they'd almost forgotten she was there. "You're special. She sensed it the moment you arrived. You have the capacity to bridge worlds. To become what she is."

"What are you talking about?" Elaine's voice rose with fear and frustration. "I'm not special. I'm just—I'm nobody. I run a real estate empire and go to charity galas, and have a miserable marriage. There's nothing special about me."

"You don't see it yet because you've spent your whole life covering it up. Hiding it beneath designer clothes and social obligations and a personality built to please others." Maureen's eyes were bright in the dim light. "But it's there. The potential. The openness. The ability to perceive beyond the purely material world. Ayâs knows. The Napiyaw know. Soon, you'll know too."

"Stop it," Zuri said sharply. "Maureen, I need you to listen to me very carefully. You've been drugged. They gave you something that's altered your judgment. Everything you're saying right now is coming from whatever they put in your system, not from your actual thoughts. Do you understand?"

"I understand you think that," Maureen said gently. "But you're wrong. For the first time in my life, I'm thinking clearly. I'm seeing truly. And I'm trying to help you understand, so tonight won't be so frightening for you."

"Tonight," Elaine repeated. "What happens tonight? What is this ceremony?"

Maureen opened her mouth to answer, but the hide flap opened before she could speak. A young Wapiti woman entered carrying a large wooden bowl and several smaller vessels. Behind her came another woman with a basket of bread and dried meat.

"Food," the first woman said simply, setting the bowl in the center of their circle. "Eat. You'll need your strength."

"We don't want your food," Zuri said.

"Then you'll be hungry." The woman's expression was neutral, unconcerned. "It's not poisoned. It's not drugged. It's just food. But eat it or don't—that's your choice." She set down cups of water and left as quickly as she'd come.

They stared at the food—some kind of stew that smelled surprisingly good, the bread still warm, strips of what looked like venison jerky. Elaine's stomach growled traitorously. They hadn't eaten since lunch, and her body didn't care about the circumstances of captivity.

"We should eat," Dave said pragmatically. "She's right—if we're going to have any chance of escaping, we need energy. And if they wanted to drug us through food, they would have done it already. They have us trapped. They don't need to be subtle."

"He's right," Stella agreed, reaching for the bread. "Starving ourselves won't help anything."

One by one, they ate—some reluctantly, some with obvious hunger they couldn't deny. The stew was rich and savory, the bread dense and filling. Despite everything, despite the fear and anger and uncertainty, the food helped. It gave them something to do, something normal and human in a situation that felt increasingly surreal.

Maureen ate sparingly, her attention divided between the food and the activities outside that only she understood. She kept tilting her head, listening to distant sounds, smiling occasionally at words the others didn't understand.

"What do you hear?" Elaine asked quietly, sitting beside her.

"The drums starting. The singing beginning. The old ones stirring in the forest." Maureen's voice was dreamy. "Can't you feel it? The energy building? Something is waking. Something has been sleeping for a long time, and tonight it's coming here."

"That's the drugs talking," Elaine said, but even as she spoke, she felt something. A change in the air pressure, maybe. A subtle vibration beneath them, as if the earth itself was taking a deep breath. Or maybe it was just fear making her imagine things.

Outside, the sounds of the camp were changing. Voices had dropped to murmurs or stopped altogether. And then, cutting through the evening air, came the sound of drums—slow, rhythmic, hypnotic. Not loud, but pervasive. The kind of sound you felt in your chest as much as heard with your ears.

"It's beginning," Maureen said softly.

The drumming continued, joined gradually by voices chanting in a language none of them recognized. The rhythm was complex, layered, building slowly toward something. And despite themselves, despite their fear and resistance, they found their breathing synchronizing to the beat. Their heartbeats matching the drums.

CHAPTER 22

ESCAPE

The drumming continued for what felt like an eternity, building in intensity, layered with more voices joining the chant. Dave shifted restlessly, his jaw clenched, his eyes moving between the hide flap entrance and the walls of the lodge.

"We can't just sit here," he said quietly, leaning toward Zuri. "Once that ceremony starts, once they have us all outside surrounded by the entire camp, we'll have zero chance. But right now, they think we're cowed. They think we're waiting obediently."

"What are you thinking?" Zuri kept her voice low, aware that guards were posted outside.

"Ben and I go now. Quick and quiet. We get into the forest, make it to the river, follow it back to where Steven took the canoes out. We bring back help—the sheriff, search and rescue, whoever we can find." Dave's eyes were intense. "Two of us have a better chance of moving silently than all of us. And if we get caught, at least you'll still be here with the rest of the group."

"When you get caught!" Stella's voice was sharp with fear for her partner.

"If," Dave corrected, though his tone suggested he had doubts. "Look, they're distracted by this big ceremony. Everyone's focused on the fire, the drums, whatever ritual they're doing out there. The guards outside are probably watching the ceremony more than this tent. This might be our only chance."

Zuri looked around the circle at her group—scared, exhausted, trapped. Every trip director's instinct screamed against splitting them up. But Dave had a point. If they all tried to escape together, it would be chaos. Two experienced runners moving quietly through the forest had a real chance.

"Alright," she said finally. "But you move fast and you move smart. The moment you're clear of the camp, you run. Don't try to be heroes, don't look back. Just get to Steven and bring help."

"Thank you." Dave squeezed Stella's hand, then turned to Ben. "You ready?"

Ben nodded, his face pale but determined. "Let's do this before I overthink it."

They moved to the edge of the lodge, where the hide wall met the ground. Dave tested the hide carefully—it was staked down, but there was six inches of give at the bottom. Enough for a person to wriggle under if they were quiet and careful.

"Now," Dave whispered.

He dropped flat and began working his way under the hide, moving with agonizing slowness to avoid making noise or disturbing the wall enough to be visible from outside. Ben followed immediately behind him.

The rest of the group held their breath, watching the entrance, expecting at any moment to hear shouts, to see guards burst in. But nothing happened. The drumming continued. The chanting rose and fell. And Dave and Ben simply… disappeared into the night.

"They made it," Rogerio breathed. "They actually made it."

"It's a good start," Zuri said. Hope was rising in her chest like a physical force. "They need to get clear of the camp. Into the forest. Then—"

"Where's Dave?" Maureen's voice cut through the whispered conversation like a knife.

Everyone froze.

Maureen stood near the entrance, her head tilted as she considered her own question. "Where's Dave? And Ben? They were here, and now they're not."

"Maureen, don't—" Stella started.

But Maureen was already moving toward the hide flap, pushing it aside, calling out in a clear, carrying voice: "Maskwa! Dave is gone!"

"No!" Zuri lunged for her, but it was too late.

Outside, the drumming faltered. Voices called out in alarm. Heavy footsteps ran past the lodge, moving toward the perimeter.

Maskwa filled the entrance a moment later, his massive frame blocking out the firelight. "Who?" His voice was cold, controlled, but underneath was anger that made them all shrink back. "Who is missing?"

"Dave and Ben," Maureen said calmly, as if she were reporting on class attendance. "They went under the wall maybe two minutes ago. That way, back toward the river."

Maskwa didn't respond to her, just turned and barked orders in his own language. More footsteps—running now, organized, purposeful. Then he stepped fully into the lodge, and his presence was overwhelming.

"You were warned," he said, his eyes sweeping across them all before settling on Zuri. "You were told not to try to leave. Did you think we wouldn't notice? Did you think we wouldn't be ready?"

"They have a right to leave," Zuri said, forcing her voice steady even as her heart hammered. "You can't keep us prisoner."

"Everyone tries," Maskwa said, and there was something almost weary in his voice. "Everyone thinks they're clever, that they can slip away. But we've been doing this for over a century. Do you think you're the first to sit in this tent?"

He moved deeper into the lodge, and instinctively the runners pressed back against the walls. "The forest at night is dangerous even for those who know it. Your friends are crashing through it blind, making noise like wounded elk. My people will have them back here within minutes. And when they return—" he paused, letting the threat hang in the air, "—you will all understand that our patience has limits."

Outside, they could hear shouting in the distance. Then, almost immediately, the sounds of a struggle—branches breaking, voices raised in alarm.

It had taken less than ten minutes.

Maskwa stepped back outside without another word. The hide flap fell closed behind him, leaving the group in dim lamplight and terrified silence.

"How could you?" Stella turned on Maureen, her voice shaking with rage and disbelief. "How could you do that? Dave is out there because of you—"

"Dave is out there because he was foolish," Maureen replied, unmoved by Stella's anger. "The Wapiti are trying to share something sacred, and all any of you can think about is running away from it. Don't you see? You're here because you're meant to be here. Fighting it only causes suffering."

"You've lost your mind," Rogerio said. "They've completely brainwashed you."

"No," Maureen said softly. "They've awakened me."

The sounds outside were getting closer—voices speaking urgently, footsteps approaching the lodge. Then the hide flap opened again, and Dave and Ben were pushed into the tent. Maskwa stepped in behind them.

Both men were disheveled, breathing hard, with scratches on their faces and arms from tearing through brush in the darkness. Maskwa's hand rested on Dave's shoulder—not violently, but with enough pressure to make escape impossible.

"Your friends," Maskwa announced, "thought they could find their way through miles of forest in pitch darkness without being caught. They made it a few hundred yards." His voice carried grim satisfaction. "The men I sent after them didn't even have to hurry."

He pushed Dave forward, and he stumbled to the center of the group. Stella immediately threw her arms around him.

"I'm sorry," Dave muttered. "I thought we had a chance."

"You thought you were smarter than us," Maskwa finished. "You thought because we live in the old ways, we must be simple. Primitive. Easy to outsmart." His eyes swept across all of them. "That thinking is what trapped you here to begin with. Your arrogance. Your certainty that modern education makes you superior to those who choose older paths."

He gestured to one of his men standing outside. "Kai. You stand guard inside the tent. No one goes in or out until Ayâs calls for them. Anyone who tries—" he looked directly at Zuri, "—will be stopped with whatever force is necessary. Am I understood?" Kai stood to the side of the entrance flap, holding a war club they hadn't seen before. It was carved from a single piece of heavy wood—a three-foot shaft, ending with a large wooden ball at the end. There was no mystery in how it was designed to be used.

Zuri said nothing, but her expression was answer enough.

Maskwa studied them for a long moment, his face unreadable in the dim light. When he spoke again, his voice was softer but no less commanding. "You're afraid. I understand. But your fear comes from ignorance, not danger. What happens tonight is sacred—older than your laws, deeper than your understanding. You will witness it. You will be part of it. And afterward, those who wish to leave will simply leave."

They also glanced at Maureen, considering her mental state. Did he mean they would all think like her when they finally left?

"Then let us leave now," Ben said, his voice hoarse. "If you're going to let us go anyway, why force us to stay for this ceremony?"

"Because some things must be witnessed to be believed," Maskwa replied. "Because the modern world has forgotten truths that must not be lost. Because one of you—" his eyes moved to Elaine, "—has a destiny here that's larger than your fears."

He turned to leave, then paused at the entrance. "The ceremony has begun. I suggest you prepare yourselves. Fighting the inevitable only makes the experience more difficult."

He left, and they heard him speaking to the outside guard in low tones. Then his footsteps moved away, back toward the fire and the drums that had never stopped.

For a long moment, no one spoke. They sat in stunned silence, processing what had just happened. The attempted escape had failed spectacularly, and now their situation was even worse—more guards, weapons, Maskwa suspicious and watchful, their captors' patience wearing thin.

"I'm sorry," Dave said again, his voice breaking. "I thought—I really thought we had a chance."

"You did what you thought was right," Zuri said, though the words felt hollow. "We had to try."

"No, we didn't," Maureen said from her position by the wall. "All we had to do was trust. Accept what's being offered. Let go of the need to control everything."

"Shut up," Stella said flatly. "Just shut up, Maureen. I don't want to hear another word from you."

Maureen fell silent, but her expression remained serene, untouched by Stella's fury. She settled back against the wall, her eyes half-closed, listening to the drums that had resumed their full intensity outside.

Elaine watched her with a mixture of horror and fascination. This woman—brilliant, educated, rational just days ago—had been transformed into something else entirely. Was that what waited for all of them? Would they all end up like Maureen, convinced that captivity was enlightenment, that being held against their will was actually freedom?

No, Elaine thought fiercely. *I won't let that happen to me. Whatever they do tonight, whatever they try to make me believe, I'll hold on to who I am. I'll remember my real life. I'll resist.*

But even as she formed the thought, she felt doubt creeping in. Because part of her—a small, treacherous part—was curious. Part of her wanted to know what was so powerful that it could so transform someone like Maureen. Part of her wondered if maybe, just maybe, there was something real and important here.

The drumming grew louder, more insistent. The chanting outside swelled, dozens of voices joined in ancient words that seemed to vibrate in her bones. And despite her determination to resist, despite her fear and anger, Elaine felt herself being drawn toward it.

The hide flap opened again. Ayâs stood in the entrance, backlit by fire, her form seeming larger than her actual size. Behind her, Maskwa and Takoda waited.

"It's time," the old woman announced. "The ceremony calls for you. Come."

"And if we refuse?" Zuri stood, positioning herself between Ayâs and her group.

"Then you'll be carried." Ayâs's voice was patient but implacable. "Willingly or unwillingly makes no difference to the ceremony. But it will make a difference to how much fear you carry. Choose wisdom over stubbornness."

Maskwa stepped into the lodge, his size making the space suddenly feel much smaller. "Please. Don't make this harder than necessary."

For a moment, Zuri looked like she might refuse, might force them to make good on their threat. But then she looked at her group—her responsibility—and made a decision. "We'll come. But I'm telling you right now, if any of you hurt any of them, there will be consequences. Legal, professional, personal. You understand me?"

"I understand you're frightened and trying to assert control in a situation where you have none," Ayâs replied. "That's human. Normal. But pointless. Come now. The drums are calling."

CHAPTER 23

THE CIRCLE

They emerged from the teepee into a transformed camp. The sun had fully set, and darkness pressed in from all sides, held back only by multiple fires scattered throughout the clearing. The Wapiti had gathered in a large circle around the central fire pit, all wearing ceremonial dress—animal skins, elaborate beadwork, faces painted with designs that moved with the firelight.

The drumming came from several sources—deep drums that resonated in the chest, smaller drums with quicker rhythms, and a hollow stick that sounded like rattles or bones clicking together. The chanting rose and fell in rhythmic harmonies.

The Global Runners were led to the center of the circle, positioned near the fire where they could see everything and, more importantly, where everyone could see them. Elaine found herself at the front, closest to Ayâs who had taken a position nearest the flames.

"Witness," the old woman called out, her voice cutting through the drumming. "Witness the old ways. Witness what your world forgot. Witness the truth."

The chanting intensified. The Wapiti moved slowly, circling the fire in a choreographed dance that was ancient—steps that had been performed exactly this way for centuries, possibly millennia. Some dancers wore masks—animal faces carved from wood, with exaggerated features and empty eyes.

"This is insane," Dave muttered beside Elaine. "This is actually insane."

But Elaine couldn't look away. The dance was hypnotic, the firelight casting shadows that seemed to move independently of the bodies that created them. And the smell—smoke, herbs, and roots—everything organic and ancient that triggered parts of her brain she hadn't experienced before.

Ayâs spoke, her voice rhythmic, matching the drums. The language was nothing Elaine recognized—harsh consonants and flowing vowels that sounded like wind through trees, like water over stone, like earth settling.

"She's calling to them," Maureen whispered beside her. "The old ones. The Napiyaw. She's inviting them to witness this. To participate."

"Stop it," Zuri hissed. "Stop feeding into this."

But Maureen wasn't listening. Her attention was fixed on the forest beyond the firelight, and her smile was beatific. "They're coming. Can't you feel them? The Napiyaw. The ancient ones. They're here."

And despite everything—despite knowing this was manipulation, despite understanding on some level that this was theater designed to overwhelm and frighten them—Elaine felt it too. A presence. Multiple presences. Things moving in the darkness between the trees, just beyond the reach of firelight. Watching. Waiting.

The dance intensified. Many of the Wapiti dancers had worked themselves into obvious trances, their movements becoming jerky and uncoordinated, as if something else was moving their bodies. Others maintained perfect control, their steps precise and deliberate.

One dancer—a large figure in an animal mask that looked almost bear-like—broke from the circle and approached the captive runners. Even through the mask, Elaine recognized Maskwa's build. He moved around them slowly, assessing, before stopping directly in front of Elaine.

He pointed at her. A single, deliberate gesture.

"She is chosen," Ayâs announced. "Bring her forward."

"No." Zuri stepped between them. "You're not taking her anywhere."

"Zuri," Takoda said from beside them, his voice apologetic but firm. "Please don't fight this. You'll only get hurt. Let her come forward. She won't be harmed—she's far too precious for that."

"That's supposed to be reassuring?" Stella moved to Zuri's other side, both women forming a human shield in front of Elaine. "You want to do something to her in some drugged-out ceremony? Over our dead bodies!"

Behind the mask, Maskwa growled like a bear. Then in English, he said, "You're going to bridge the two worlds."

"Bridge what worlds? There's only this one place." Elaine asked, her voice surprisingly steady despite the terror coursing through her veins.

"There are infinite places right here where we stand. But seek a connection to just one of them," Ayâs replied. "You will become Nitânis—the daughter who becomes the mother. The priestess who calls the old powers back into full being. The bridge to the world of the Napiyaw."

She gestured, and four Wapiti members moved forward. Two took hold of Zuri, pulling her gently but inexorably away from Elaine. Two did the same with

Stella. The women struggled, but the grip was firm, and more Wapiti moved in to restrain Dave and the others when they tried to intervene.

"Don't hurt them," Elaine heard herself say. "Please. I'll come forward. Just don't hurt them."

"Elaine, no!" Zuri's voice was desperate. "Don't do what they want. Make them force you. Make them show everyone here what they really are."

But Elaine was stepping forward anyway, toward the fire, toward Ayâs. Partly because fighting seemed futile, but partly—and this was the truly frightening part— because something in her wanted to. Some buried, denied, suppressed part of her consciousness was curious. Was drawn to what Ayâs was offering.

What if Bradford could see me now? she thought with something like hysteria. *His perfect wife, about to be transformed into some kind of indigenous priestess in the middle of the Canadian wilderness. This isn't exactly the Junior League.*

Ayâs smiled as Elaine approached, as if she could read these thoughts. "You hide yourself well. But I see you. The real you. The one buried beneath layers of training and expectations. Tonight, those layers will burn away. Tonight, you will become Nitânis—my daughter."

She reached out and touched Elaine's forehead with one gnarled finger. The touch was surprisingly gentle.

"Kneel," Ayâs commanded.

Elaine knelt without deciding to, her body responding to the authority in that voice. The fire was close enough that she could feel its heat on her face, could smell the herbs burning within it. Things that made her head feel light and strange.

Ayâs's fingers dipped into a clay bowl at her side, scooping small amounts of natural pigment from its bottom. Then, her fingers rested lightly on Elaine's forehead, slowly drawing symbols as the firelight flickered. It required just a minute for Elaine's forehead and cheeks to be adorned with the ancient symbols.

From behind her, she heard Zuri still struggling, still arguing, still trying to reach her. But the sounds were distant, muffled, as if traveling through water.

Ayâs began to chant again, and this time Maureen joined her, the professor's voice blending with the old woman's in harmonies that would have been beautiful under other circumstances. The sound surrounded Elaine, entered her, resonated in her chest and skull.

Takoda appeared at Ayâs's side, holding a gourd vessel. He handed it to the old woman with obvious reverence.

"Nature's milk," Ayâs said, holding it before Elaine. "It opens the door to an older reality. Shows you what's always been here but hidden. Transforms the veil between worlds into a window. Drink, and see truly."

"Don't," Zuri's voice cut through the chanting. "Elaine, whatever's in that, don't drink it. It's what they did to Maureen. It's how they control you."

"It's how they free you," Maureen corrected, her voice dreamy and certain. "I was lost before. Now I understand. Let them free you, Elaine. Let them show you what you really are."

Ayâs held the gourd to Elaine's lips. The liquid inside was white and thick, smelling of roots and earth and something sweet. Elaine tried to turn her head away, but Ayâs's other hand came up to cup her jaw, holding her face steady.

"You can drink willingly, or I can have Maskwa hold you while we pour it down your throat," the old woman whispered matter-of-factly. "But you will drink. The ceremony requires it."

Behind them, Elaine heard Dave curse and the sounds of struggle—he or someone else was trying to reach her. But the Wapiti were many, and her group was outnumbered.

This is really happening, Elaine thought with a strange kind of calm. *I'm about to be drugged by an Indigenous cult in the middle of nowhere. Bradford would die of embarrassment if he knew. The Junior League would never recover from the scandal.*

And then, because hysteria had apparently given way to something else entirely, she thought: *Good. Let them be scandalized. Let Bradford be embarrassed. Let my whole carefully constructed life crumble. At least this is real. At least this is something actually happening to me instead of me happening to it.*

She opened her mouth.

Ayâs tipped the gourd, and the liquid flowed onto Elaine's tongue, thick and bitter and strangely warm. She tried not to swallow, but her body's reflex took over. The first gulp went down, then another, then another, until the gourd was empty and Ayâs was smiling down at her with something between satisfaction and anticipation.

"Good," the old woman said softly. "Now we wait. Now we watch. Now you begin to see."

The chanting reached a crescendo. The drums thundered. The dancers whirled faster, their shadows stretching and writhing on the ground like living things. The massive fire in the center of the camp seemed to match the fever of the dancers. Even the trees seemed to join in as their branches swayed rhythmically despite the stillness of the air.

And Elaine felt something opening inside her—doors in her soul swinging wide to let in light and darkness and everything that lived in both.

The world began to change.

CHAPTER 24

TRANSFORMATION

The world around her dissolved.

That was the only way Elaine's fragmenting mind could describe what was happening. Reality—solid, dependable, boring reality—was melting like wax in the fire, reforming into primitive shapes that felt more real than anything she'd experienced in her thirty-five years of careful, curated living.

The fire before her was alive, breathing, a creature of energy that danced and laughed and called to her in its own language. Each flame was a voice telling stories—of forests that grew and burned and grew again, of animals that lived and died and fed the earth, of humans who came and went like mayflies, brief sparks in an eternal cycle.

"It's beginning," she heard Ayâs say, the old woman's voice echoing as if from a great distance. "She's opening up to the real world. Watch as the bridge forms."

Elaine tried to focus on the faces around her—her group, the Wapiti, the ceremony continuing its ancient rhythm—but they kept shifting, becoming transparent, revealing the skeletons beneath skin, the organs pulsing with blood, the electricity firing through neural pathways. She thought could see everything. The complexity of the life around her felt simple, in harmony.

"Elaine!" Zuri's voice cut through the chaos, and Elaine turned toward it like a plant turning toward the sun. Zuri was struggling against the Wapiti members holding her, her face twisted with concern and fury. But around her—behind her—Elaine could see something else. Threads. Thousands of golden threads connecting Zuri to every person she'd ever cared about, every place she'd ever called home, stretching back through time to her childhood in Wales, to her ancestors before her, an unbroken chain of love and responsibility that made her who she was now.

Beautiful, Elaine thought. *She's so beautiful and doesn't even know it.*

"The veil is thinning," Maureen said, appearing beside Ayâs like a ghost materializing from smoke. "She's seeing everything. Seeing the truth. Soon she'll be ready for the marking."

But Elaine wasn't listening. The forest beyond the fire had caught her attention, and what she saw there made her breath stop entirely.

The trees were moving. Not swaying in the wind, but actually moving—walking, their roots pulling free from earth to take slow, ponderous steps. And between them, through them, creatures moved that she didn't recognize at first.

Massive forms covered in dark fur, walking upright like humans but clearly not human. Seven, eight, nine feet tall, with powerful limbs and faces that were disturbingly familiar. Their eyes reflected the firelight like animals', but held intelligence that was unmistakably aware, calculating, ancient.

The Napiyaw, some part of her mind supplied. These are the old ones. The first people.

But these weren't the Napiyaw of now—shadowy, half-glimpsed, existing more in spirit than matter. These were the Napiyaw of centuries before. Before humans and time had worn them down into legend.

The vision deepened, and suddenly Elaine wasn't at the ceremony anymore.

She was in the forest, but it was a different forest. The same mountains, the same valleys, but the trees were older—impossibly old, their trunks wider than houses, their canopy so dense that the forest floor existed in permanent twilight. There were no trails, no signs of human passage, no sounds of modern life. Only wilderness in its original form, untouched and primeval.

And there were the Napiyaw. They moved through this ancient forest with casual ownership. They were everywhere—families, bands, entire communities of them. She watched a mother with two young ones teaching them to hunt, showing them how to read the forest's signs, how to move without sound, how to call to prey in voices that mimicked elk and deer perfectly. The youngsters were clumsy, their movements still awkward, and the mother corrected them with patient touches and soft grunts.

Further into the vision, she saw a gathering—dozens of Napiyaw assembled in a clearing similar to where the Wapiti were now. But this gathering was joyful, celebratory. They were drumming on hollow logs, creating rhythms that made the earth vibrate. Some danced with the same hypnotic grace she'd seen in the Wapiti ceremony, but their movements displayed a power that the human imitations couldn't match. When they danced, the trees leaned in to watch. The animals came to the clearing's edge, unafraid, as if understanding this was a sacred time when the normal rules of predator and prey were suspended.

One of the Napiyaw—larger than the others, his fur darker, his presence radiating authority—stood at the center of the gathering. He raised his arms, and his voice emerged in a sound that was part growl, part song, part radiant authority. The other Napiyaw responded in harmony, their voices blending in a call to all of nature.

This was their world. Their time. They were the apex beings of this wilderness, living in balance with forces that humans would later chase away. They hunted, but only what they needed. They gathered, but never depleted. They existed in equilibrium with the land because they were the land, as much as the trees and stones and rivers.

And they were happy.

Elaine could feel it—the contentment, the belonging, the absolute certainty of knowing your place in the world and being at peace with it. They had no concept of progress or civilization or improvement because they didn't need those things. They had everything that mattered: community, purpose, and connection to something larger than themselves.

But then the vision shifted, darkened.

The humans came.

At first, just a few—nomadic hunters crossing the land bridge from Asia, spreading slowly across the continent. The Napiyaw watched these strange, weak, hairless creatures with curiosity more than concern. They were so small, so vulnerable. Surely, they wouldn't survive the winters, the predators, the harsh reality of wilderness life.

But the humans did survive. They learned. They adapted. They multiplied.

The Napiyaw tried to coexist. There was enough land for both species, enough resources to share. Some of the humans even learned to perceive the Napiyaw, learned to respect them, learned to ask permission before hunting in Napiyaw territory. These humans—the ancestors of the Wapiti and other Indigenous peoples—made agreements, extended courtesies, sought a balance.

But then more came. Different ones. Pale-skinned, carrying metal tools and fire-weapons, claiming ownership of land that had never belonged to anyone. These new humans didn't see the Napiyaw at all, or if they did, they saw only monsters to be destroyed.

The Napiyaw retreated. Into the deeper wilderness, into the places humans couldn't easily reach. Their numbers dwindled—some killed by guns and traps, others simply fading as their territories shrank and their way of life became impossible to maintain.

The vision showed her the decision—made by that same dark-furred leader she'd seen at the joyful gathering. He stood with a handful of his kind, perhaps thirty or forty where once there had been thousands. And he made a choice: they would step back. Not away, but back—into the space between physical and spiritual, into the liminal realm where they could exist without being destroyed by the human tide that seemed unstoppable.

But the cost of that choice was high. Existing partially in spirit meant losing their place in this world. They became shadows of what they'd been—powerful still, but incomplete. Always watching the physical world they'd once dominated, unable to fully inhabit it without risk of discovery and destruction.

The last image of the vision was the dark-furred leader standing at the edge of a forest, watching a human settlement grow where his people had once danced. His expression was unreadable, but Elaine felt his emotions as if they were her own: grief, rage, resignation, and underneath it all, a patient, terrible hope that someday, somehow, the balance might be restored.

Elaine gasped, and the vision released her. She was back at the ceremony, kneeling by the fire, her body shaking from the intensity of what she'd witnessed. But something had changed. The drug—nature's milk—had altered her perception. She could still see the layers of reality, though not as overwhelmingly as before.

And she could see… them.

In the shadows beyond the firelight, they stood. The Napiyaw. Not dozens as in her vision, but seven, maybe eight. Watching the ceremony with ancient eyes that held all the grief and patience she'd felt in the vision.

The largest one—she knew him instantly—was the same leader from her vision. Impossibly, he was the same individual, not a descendant but the actual being who'd made the choice to step back from the physical world all those centuries ago. He stood perhaps thirty feet from the fire's edge, his massive form half-visible in the dancing light, his eyes fixed on her with an intensity that made her skin prickle.

The First Walker, her awakened mind supplied. The old one. The leader who chose exile over extinction.

She could smell him—that musky scent like elk and fish that belonged to no creature she'd ever encountered. She could hear his breathing, slow and deep, the sound of bellows in the dark. She could see details the firelight shouldn't reveal: the individual hairs of his fur, the scarring on his massive hands, the way his chest rose and fell with each breath.

He was real. Absolutely, undeniably real. As real as the fire, as real as her own trembling hands.

Ayâs followed Elaine's gaze. The old woman's face broke into an expression of triumph and reverence. "You see him. You truly see him. Not just shadows, but living form. Substance." She turned to the gathered Wapiti. "She is the one! She has the sight! She can call them fully forth!"

The Wapiti followed their priestess's gesture, looking toward where Elaine was staring. But their reactions were different—confused, uncertain. They could sense something clearly. The way they shifted uneasily, the way their voices dropped to whispers, the way some made warding gestures suggested they felt its presence.

But they couldn't see him. Not clearly. To them, the First Walker was still just a shadow, a suggestion, the half-glimpsed thing they'd been calling to for decades without answer.

Only Elaine and Ayâs could see him fully.

The Global Runners were looking too, following the Wapiti's attention. Zuri's expression shifted from confusion to horror as she stared at the darkness beyond the fire.

"There's something there," she said, her voice shaking. "I can't—I can't see it properly, but there's something there. Something big."

"Multiple somethings," Dave added, his voice tight. "Look at the shadows. They're moving. They're swaying with the drums. Something's definitely there."

Stella had gone very still, her runner's instincts screaming warnings. "We need to leave. Right now. Whatever that is—"

But the First Walker's attention had shifted from Elaine to the gathered Wapiti, and something changed in his posture. His head tilted slightly, assessing. His massive hands flexed, claws glinting in the firelight. Around him, the other Napiyaw moved closer to the fire's edge, their forms becoming more solid, more present, as if Elaine's ability to see them was calling them more fully into the physical world.

Ayâs stepped forward, raising her arms in supplication. "Old ones! We have found her! She can bridge our two worlds! Through her, you can return fully! Through her, you can walk in daylight again, claim your rightful place, drive out the destroyers who stole your land!"

The First Walker made a sound—a low rumble that came from deep in his chest, something between a growl and speech. Elaine understood it, though she didn't know how. It wasn't words exactly, but meaning that bypassed language.

Be careful what you call forth.

Maskwa moved to stand beside Ayâs, his painted face reverent and awed. "They're here. I can feel them.

The Napiyaw are witnessing us. They approve of what we're doing."

We approve of nothing, the First Walker's gesture-thought conveyed. *We watch. We consider. We decide.*

But the Wapiti couldn't understand him. They felt his presence, interpreted his appearance as an endorsement, took his watching as a blessing. They were seeing what they wanted to see, hearing what they'd hoped to hear for decades.

Ayâs turned back to Elaine, her face alight with fanatic certainty. "It's time. The marking. The final step of the transformation. You must become Nitânis—daughter who becomes mother, priestess who calls them forth. Only through you can they return."

She produced something from the folds of her ceremonial garb—a blade. Not metal, but stone, a long, sharp sliver of obsidian that looked older than memory. Its edge caught the firelight, throwing red reflections across Ayâs's weathered face.

"No," Zuri said, fighting against her restraints with renewed desperation. "Absolutely not. You're not cutting her. You're not marking her. This has gone far enough!"

"It's gone exactly as far as it was meant to," Ayâs replied calmly. She knelt beside Elaine, holding the blade up for her to see. "This is ancient. Sacred. It has marked every priestess of the Wapiti for over two centuries. And now it marks you. Not as property, not as a slave, but as something special and revered. Something that matters."

Elaine stared at the blade. The drug made it seem to pulse with its own light, its own life. Part of her wanted to resist, to fight, to refuse. But another part—the part that had seen the Napiyaw in their glory, that had felt their grief and hope, that could still see the First Walker watching with those ancient, patient eyes—that part was curious.

What would it mean to be Nitânis? What would it feel like to be something other than Bradford's wife, other than her mother-in-law's disappointment, other than the hollow shell of a woman who'd spent thirty-five years being what others wanted?

What would it feel like to matter?

"This will hurt," Ayâs said, her voice surprisingly gentle. "Truth always does. But pain fades. What you become will be permanent."

She placed the obsidian blade against Elaine's forehead.

And from the shadows, the First Walker growled.

NAPIYAW APPEARS

The growl froze everyone.

It wasn't loud—not a roar or a challenge—but it carried like the weight of a bear or something larger. It resonated in bone and marrow. It spoke directly to the most primitive parts of the brain that remembered when humans were prey.

Ayâs's hand stopped, the obsidian blade hovering a hair's breadth from Elaine's skin. The old woman's eyes flickered toward the forest shadows, and for the first time since Elaine had met her, uncertainty crossed her weathered face.

"They object?" she whispered, speaking more to herself than to anyone present. "But why? This is what they want. What we've worked toward. Their return to this world."

The First Walker moved, just slightly—a shift in weight that brought him one step closer to the firelight. Still mostly in shadow, still not fully manifested, but more present than before. Around him, the other Napiyaw held their positions, watching with those reflecting eyes that gathered all available light.

You assume our purposes. You assume our plans. You assume too much.

Again, Elaine understood him, though the others clearly didn't. Ayâs cocked her head, listening to something, but her expression suggested she was receiving only fragments, hints, impressions rather than clear communication.

"Speak clearly!" the old woman commanded, her voice cracking with frustration and age. "I've served you my entire life. I've kept the ceremonies alive when everyone else forgot. I've found the one who can bridge our worlds. Tell me what you want!"

But the First Walker's attention had shifted entirely to Elaine. He was studying her with an intensity that made her feel transparent, as if those ancient eyes could see not just her body but every thought, every fear, every secret shame and hidden hope she'd ever carried.

She felt him in her mind—like a weight on the scales of her consciousness. She could feel him assessing her worthiness, her capacity, her truth. It was the most intimate violation she'd ever experienced, and yet it felt necessary. As if she'd been waiting her whole life to be truly seen.

You wear many masks, his thought-voice said directly into her awareness. *Daughter. Wife. Woman of privilege. Each one false. Each one hiding what you are beneath.*

"I don't know what I am," Elaine heard herself respond aloud, her voice strange and distant.

Then let them show you. Let the blade mark what you choose to become. But understand—once marked, you cannot return to what you were. Your path forward is with us.

"Everything has already changed," Elaine said, and realized she meant it. Even if she escaped tonight, even if she returned to New Jersey, to Bradford, to her carefully constructed life—she could never pretend again. She'd seen too much. Felt too much. Her masks were already broken beyond repair.

Ayâs had been watching this exchange, understanding perhaps half of it from Elaine's responses and the First Walker's postures. Now she spoke with renewed confidence: "They permit it. They witness it. The marking will proceed."

"No!" Zuri's voice cut through, desperate and furious. "Elaine, you don't have to do this! They're drugging you, manipulating you! This isn't real!"

But was it? Elaine couldn't tell anymore where the drug's influence ended and her own desires began. The nature's milk had opened doors in her mind, yes, but it hadn't created the feelings behind those doors. The dissatisfaction, the hunger for meaning, the desperate wish to be something more than decorative—those had always been there, buried beneath breeding and expectations.

"I'm sorry," she said to Zuri, and meant it. "But I need to move on. I need to become someone different from what I was taught to be."

"This is insane," Dave said, his voice thick with horror and helplessness. "This is actually insane, and we're just watching it happen."

"We're not just watching," Stella said quietly. She'd stopped fighting against her captors, but her body had gone tense in a different way. Her eyes were moving constantly, assessing angles, counting Wapiti members, calculating the odds. "We're waiting for the right moment."

Ayâs placed the obsidian blade against Elaine's forehead once more. "This marks you as Nitânis—daughter who becomes mother, priestess who bridges worlds, keeper of ancient knowledge. Do you accept?"

The question hung in the smoke-thick air. Elaine could feel everyone waiting—the Wapiti with hope, her group with horror, the Napiyaw with certainty.

Do you accept? The First Walker's thought-voice echoed Ayâs's words, but with a deeper meaning. *Do you choose to be our priestess? To know our people? To carry the weight of truth and responsibility?*

"Yes," Elaine whispered.

The blade bit into her forehead, and pain bloomed white-hot behind her eyes.

Ayâs's hand was practiced and sure despite her age. The obsidian sliced through skin with precision, carving a design Elaine couldn't see but could feel—curves and lines that followed patterns older than language. Blood ran down her face, hot and wet, dripping from her chin onto her expensive running gear that would never be clean again.

The chanting intensified. The drums thundered. Maureen's voice rose above the others, clear and strange, singing in a language she shouldn't know but somehow did. The Wapiti dancers whirled faster, their movements becoming frantic, ecstatic.

And through the pain, through the blood and smoke and sound, Elaine felt the world inside her grow. It was not the drug this time. It was real and permanent. Something that had been locked away her entire life broke free and filled her.

She could feel the forest. Every tree, every animal, every living thing connected in a vast web that pulsed with life and purpose. She felt the Napiyaw in their half-existence, trapped between worlds by necessity and time. She felt the land itself, ancient and patient, waiting for humans to remember they were its guests, not its owners.

"I see," she breathed, the words barely audible. "I see everything."

Ayâs stepped back, the bloody blade still in her hand. "It is done. You are marked. You are Nitânis."

The old woman turned to the Wapiti, raising her arms in triumph. "Witness! The new priestess is born! Through her, the old powers return! Through her, the Napiyaw can walk in flesh again! Through her—"

The First Walker's growl cut her off. This time it was louder, carrying a clear warning.

She is ours, not yours. We will direct her actions. We will decide when to return.

But the Wapiti couldn't fully understand him. They saw his presence as an endorsement, his appearance as a blessing. They were lost in their own fervor, their own hope, too desperate to hear the warnings he offered.

Elaine touched her forehead, her fingers coming away slick with blood. The cut was still bleeding freely, and she could feel the design carved into her skin—a stylized face with features that were both human and animal. The face of the Napiyaw. She'd been marked with their image, claimed as their bridge to the physical world, exactly as she'd desired.

"I am Nitânis," she whispered.

Yes. Now you see. Now you are connected to us.

The ceremony was reaching its crescendo. Some of the Wapiti had worked themselves into full trance states, speaking in tongues, convulsing with what looked like seizures. The air felt thick, charged, knowing something important had occurred.

And in that chaos, Zuri moved.

She'd been watching, waiting, calculating. She'd noticed that the Wapiti members holding the Global Runners were as caught up in the ceremony's fervor as everyone else. Their attention waned. Their focus had shifted to the spectacle of Elaine's marking and Ayâs's triumphant declarations.

Zuri yanked her arm free from the distracted man holding her, and her elbow came up fast and hard, catching him in the throat. He went down gasping, and before anyone could react, Zuri was moving—a blur of athletic efficiency and desperate courage.

"Now!" she shouted. "Everyone, now!"

It was the signal they'd been unconsciously waiting for. The Global Runners erupted into motion all at once.

Dave twisted free from his captors, his basketball player's reflexes serving him well as he dodged a grasping hand and delivered a punch that sent another Wapiti member stumbling backward. Stella bit the hand restraining her—literally bit it—and when the man yelped and released her, she was running, grabbing Dana's arm and pulling her along.

Rogerio, true to form, immediately tripped over his own feet and went sprawling. But Ben and the Austin couple helped him up, and together they pushed through the circle of dancers whose trance made them obstacles but not active threats.

"Elaine!" Zuri screamed, turning back. "Come on!"

But Elaine was still kneeling by the fire, blood streaming down her face, her mind reeling from the marking and the visions and the presence of the First Walker who still watched from the shadows. She wasn't leaving, caught between two worlds, watching the events and letting them happen.

Maskwa lunged for Zuri, his massive hands reaching to grab her. He would have caught her—he was too large, too fast—but something happened.

The First Walker appeared.

It wasn't fully manifest, wasn't completely stepping into the physical world. But his massive presence became solid enough that when he positioned himself between

Maskwa and the fleeing runners, the giant Wapiti man couldn't ignore him.

Maskwa stopped short, his eyes going wide. He could see the First Walker now—more clearly than before. It was more massive and terrifying than he had ever imagined. He could see the dark fur, smell the musky animal scent. Suddenly he was no longer the largest predator in the camp. For the first time, Maskwa was dwarfed by a predator far larger than himself.

"Don't let them go," Maskwa pleaded, his voice shaking. "This is our ceremony. They know us. They must stay."

No. They go. We have what we need, a new priestess.

Takoda moved to help Maskwa, but he too stopped when he saw the massive being blocking their path. Around the fire, other Wapiti members could see it too, pointing, their voices rising in confusion and awe and fear.

"They're protecting the runners!" someone shouted. "The Napiyaw are protecting them!"

"No," Ayâs said, her voice sharp with denial. "No, this is wrong. You're supposed to help us keep them! You're supposed to—"

We are supposed to do nothing, the First Walker's thought-voice boomed, and even those who couldn't fully hear him felt its weight. *You do not command us. We need Nitânis. We do not need the others.*

"Elaine!" Stella called back to the camp, hoping to convince the women to join their escape.

But Elaine just watched as her last connection to her old life and the modern world disappeared into the forest. *That is not my life now, not my path. You can return, but I stay here.*

The runners couldn't hear these thoughts, but the Napiyaw could. They honored their new priestess' wishes.

The Wapiti were in chaos. Some were giving chase, but others were paralyzed by the Napiyaw's presence. Ayâs was screaming orders that no one seemed to hear. The drums had stopped. The chanting had dissolved into shouted arguments and confusion.

And in the shadows, the First Walker watched the humans scatter in all directions—some fleeing, some pursuing, all of them tiny and temporary and utterly predictable in their panic.

He made a gesture to his band, and the other Napiyaw moved. Not to pursue, but to create obstacles. They positioned themselves in the paths of the Wapiti pursuers, not attacking but simply being there—massive, undeniable presences that stopped the pursuing Wapiti in their tracks. It slowed the chase, bought the fleeing runners the advantage they needed.

Why? one of the younger Napiyaw asked in their gesture-language. *Why help them escape?*

Because we don't need them. The Wapiti were afraid to let them go. But we don't want them as slaves. We are already free.

CHAPTER 26

FLIGHT

The forest was absolutely black beyond the fire's reach. No moon, no stars visible through the dense canopy, nothing but darkness that seemed to have a physical weight. The Global Runners crashed through it anyway, branches whipping their faces, roots catching their feet, terror propelling them forward faster than wisdom would suggest.

"Stay together!" Zuri shouted, though staying together was nearly impossible when they couldn't see each other. "Call out! Keep talking so we know where everyone is!"

"Here!" Dave's voice came from the left.

"Here!" Dana echoed from slightly behind.

"Still here!" Rogerio added, though his voice suggested he was falling behind. "Although I've already fallen twice, and I'm pretty sure I'm bleeding!"

"Which direction?" someone asked—Ben, maybe. "Which way back to the river?"

"I don't know!" Zuri admitted. "Just away from the camp. Away from them. We'll figure out the direction when we're far enough away that they can't catch us."

But some of the Wapiti were still following. Not the whole camp—most had been paralyzed by the Napiyaw's manifestation—but a handful of the younger, bolder men who either hadn't seen the forest creatures or hadn't believed what they'd seen. Zuri could hear them crashing through the forest behind, could hear voices calling in their own language, coordinating the pursuit.

"They're still coming!" Stella called from somewhere ahead. "Keep moving! Don't slow down!"

The group pushed forward through the darkness, their lungs burning, legs screaming, fear giving them energy their exhausted bodies shouldn't have possessed. Two days of trail running had prepared them somewhat for this—their legs knew how to navigate uncertain terrain, their breathing stayed controlled even in panic— but nothing had prepared them for fleeing through pitch-black wilderness from pursuers who knew these forests intimately.

Rogerio, true to his disaster-magnet nature, went down hard. His foot caught on a root, and he crashed face-first into the forest floor with a grunt of pain and surprise.

"Rogerio's down!" someone shouted.

Zuri heard it and immediately doubled back, her responsibilities overriding her own survival impulse. She couldn't leave anyone behind. Not again. They'd already lost Elaine and Maureen to the Wapiti's madness. She wouldn't lose anyone else.

"I'm coming!" she called, crashing back through the undergrowth toward where she could hear Rogerio groaning.

She found him by feel more than sight, her hands locating his shoulder in the darkness. "Can you stand? Are you hurt?"

"Just my pride," Rogerio gasped. "And possibly my face. Definitely my face. I think I'm bleeding again."

"Up. Come on." Zuri hauled him to his feet.

Behind them, the sounds of pursuit were getting closer. Voices in the darkness, moving fast, knowing the terrain in a way the fleeing runners didn't.

"Move!" Zuri commanded, pushing Rogerio ahead of her. "I'm right behind you. Just keep—"

The smell hit her first.

It was wrong—too strong, too animal, too wild to belong to any creature in these mountains. Elk and fish and something else, something musty that made the hair on her neck stand up and her lizard brain scream warnings.

Then she saw it.

Between them and the pursuing Wapiti, the darkness became solid. A massive shape materialized from the shadows—not walking into the space but rather becoming visible when it had been there all along, watching.

The Napiyaw stood seven feet tall, its dark fur absorbed what little light penetrated the forest. Its eyes reflected the starlight or the distant glow of the Wapiti camp—twin points of amber fire in a face that was almost human. The features were too heavy, the jaw too powerful, the brow too pronounced. And the body—lean but impossibly muscled, with arms that hung too long and hands that were too big.

It wasn't attacking. It was just there. Standing between the fleeing runners and their pursuers. A living barrier that couldn't be dismissed as a shadow.

Zuri stopped breathing. Her entire body locked up, every instinct screaming contradictory commands: *Run! Hide! Fight! Freeze!* Her mind couldn't process what she was seeing because what she was seeing couldn't exist. This was the legend, the myth, the kind of thing that lived in blurry photographs and disputed eyewitness accounts, not a solid, smelling, breathing reality standing just a few feet away.

"Oh my God," Rogerio whispered beside her, his voice tiny and broken. "Oh my God, oh my God, it's real. It's actually real. I was joking about Sasquatch, but it's REAL—"

The Napiyaw turned its head slightly, acknowledging their presence with eyes that held too much intelligence, too much awareness. It wasn't an animal. Whatever it was, it was thinking, planning, making choices.

Behind the creature, the pursuing Wapiti stopped. Zuri could hear them talking urgently in their language, their voices carrying awe and fear. They could see it too— clearly enough to know they weren't getting past it.

The Napiyaw made a sound—low and rumbling, something between a growl and speech. It wasn't directed at Zuri and Rogerio but at the Wapiti. A warning. A command. Whatever it meant, the Wapiti got the message.

As one, they stopped in their tracks, momentarily frozen. Then they backed away, afraid to turn their backs on the beast before them. Once out of reach, they turned and ran back the way they'd come, chattering in their native language.

The only word clearly discernible to Zuri was "Napiyaw."

For another endless moment, the creature stood there, still as stone, watching the two remaining humans with those ancient, reflective eyes. Then, as abruptly as it had appeared, it stepped backward into shadow and was simply gone. Not running away, not hiding exactly, just blending completely with the darkness.

But Zuri could still smell it. Could still feel its presence in the darkness, watching.

"Run," she whispered to Rogerio. "Run now."

They ran.

The group crashed through the forest for what felt like hours. Eventually—whether because they'd truly lost the Wapiti or because the Napiyaw's intervention had ended the pursuit—the sounds behind them faded entirely. No voices calling. No footsteps. Just the normal sounds of the wilderness at night: wind in trees, distant water, small animals going about their nocturnal business.

They slowed to a walk, then stopped in a clearing to catch their breath and count heads.

"Everyone here?" Zuri's voice was hoarse from running and shouting. "Dave?"

"Here."

"Stella?"

"Here."

"Dana?"

"Here, and I got some of it on video. Not much—too dark—but some."

"Rogerio?"

"Here and definitely bleeding from multiple locations, but alive."

"Ben?"

"Here."

One by one, the group accounted for themselves. Everyone who'd fled the camp was present. But not everyone who'd entered the forest was accounted for.

"Maureen?" Zuri called, though she already knew. "Maureen, if you can hear us, call out!"

Silence.

"Elaine?"

More silence.

"They didn't come," Stella said quietly. "Maureen never ran. She stayed with them. And Elaine—I called for her, but she just stayed by the fire. She chose to stay."

"No." Zuri's voice cracked. "No, they wouldn't choose that. They're drugged. Whatever that nature's milk is, it's controlling them. They're not making real choices."

"Maybe," Dave said carefully. "But they stayed. And we left them. We left two people behind."

The weight of that settled over the group like a physical thing. They'd escaped. But the cost had been two members of their group—two people Zuri was responsible for, two people who'd trusted her to keep them safe.

"We'll get them back," Zuri said, her voice hard with determination and guilt. "As soon as we reach civilization, we'll call the authorities. Search and rescue, the police, whoever we need to get them out of there."

"If the Wapiti are still there," Ben pointed out. "They said the camp moves. They might already be gone."

"Then we find them." Zuri's British accent was getting stronger with stress, her words sharp and clipped. "I don't care if they move. I don't care if they hide. We find them, and we bring Maureen and Elaine home."

"What about what we saw?" Rogerio asked, his voice still shaky. "What Zuri and I saw? That… thing. That creature that stopped the Wapiti from following us?"

"What did you see?" Stella asked.

"I don't know what to call it." Zuri struggled to find words for something that defied description. "It was massive. At least seven feet tall, maybe more. Covered in dark fur. It walked on two legs like a human, but it wasn't human. The face was thick. The proportions were wrong. And the eyes—" She stopped, shuddering. "The eyes were intelligent. Whatever it was, it was thinking. It positioned itself between us and the Wapiti deliberately. It stopped them from following us."

"Why would it do that?" Dana asked. "If it's part of whatever they're doing, if they worship it or whatever, why would it help us escape?"

"I don't know," Zuri admitted. "But I saw it. Rogerio saw it. It was real. It was there."

"The Napiyaw," Dave said quietly. "That's what Maureen kept talking about. The old ones. The forest creatures from Indigenous legends. She said the Wapiti were trying to call them, trying to bring them fully into the physical world."

"Legends aren't real," Ben said, but his voice lacked conviction.

"We saw something," Zuri insisted. "I don't care if you call it Napiyaw or Sasquatch or anything else. We saw it. And it helped us. That's all that matters right now."

"We need to keep moving," Stella said practically, pulling them back to their immediate concerns. "Even if they've stopped chasing us, we're still lost. We don't know where we are, we don't know which direction leads back to civilization, and we're all exhausted and some of us are injured. We need a plan."

"We walk through the night," Zuri decided. "Pick a direction and maintain it. Eventually we'll hit a road, a trail, a river—something. We can't just sit here."

"Which direction?" Dave asked the obvious question.

Zuri looked up at the canopy, trying to see stars. The forest was too dense. She tried to think about the sun's position when they'd been captured, about the direction they'd fled, about any landmarks she could remember. But terror and darkness had erased all sense of geography.

"We keep the rising terrain to our left," she finally said. "That means we're heading generally east, back toward where we came from. The hotel is east. Banff is east. Eventually, if we keep on that bearing, we'll hit something recognizable."

It was barely a plan, but it was better than standing still. They formed a loose line, staying within arm's reach of each other, and began walking.

The night was endless.

They walked through terrain that shifted from dense forest to rocky slopes to areas where the trees thinned enough to see stars. They helped each other over fallen logs, around suspected cliffs in the darkness, through streams cold enough to make their feet go numb. Dana twisted her ankle but kept walking. Ben cut his hand on a sharp branch and had to wrap it with a torn piece of his shirt.

Zuri kept them moving, kept them talking, kept them from giving up. Every time someone suggested stopping to rest, she pushed them forward. Rest meant time for the Wapiti to catch up, time for exhaustion to turn into sleep they might not wake from, time to think about what they'd lost and seen and survived.

"Tell me about your families," she said as they climbed yet another slope. "Dave, what's waiting for you and Stella back in Phoenix?"

"Her parents," Dave said, and despite everything, he managed a weak laugh. "The ones who worry about us every time we depart on one of these vacations." He adopted a falsetto voice, "'You'll get lost' they say. Or 'What if you can't leave the country?' or 'What if you're captured by a cult and brainwashed?' You know, just the normal stuff."

Everyone laughed at the voice and the last joke.

All Stella said was, "Not wrong."

"What about you, Dana? Your social followers are going to want the real story."

"They're not getting it," Dana said firmly. "I'll post the scenic running stuff. Maybe mention that we had 'an intense cultural experience' or something vague. But the kidnapping? The ceremonies? The… whatever those things are in the forest? No one would believe it, anyway. They'd think it was staged clickbait."

"Rogerio?"

"I'm just glad I'm still alive to disappoint everyone with my next disaster," Rogerio said. "Although this one's going to be hard to top. Attacked by an Indigenous cult, chased through the forest by something that may or may not be Bigfoot, lost in the wilderness overnight—pretty solid entries for my disaster resume."

Despite everything, people laughed. Exhausted, slightly hysterical laughter, but laughter nonetheless. It kept them human. It kept them moving.

The sky was just beginning to lighten—not dawn yet, but the deep black fading to charcoal gray—when they emerged from the tree line onto a rocky outcropping. And below them, impossibly, spread out in the valley like a miracle, were lights.

"Oh my God," Stella breathed. "Is that—"

"Banff," Zuri said, her voice breaking. "That's Banff."

The town sprawled below them, its lights still glowing in the predawn darkness. From their vantage point high on the mountainside, they could see the main street, the hotels, the train station—civilization, safety, help.

"We made it," Dave said, disbelief evident in his voice. "We actually made it."

"How far?" Ben asked. "How long to get down there?"

Zuri studied the terrain. They were on the eastern face of the mountains ringing Banff, probably Cascade or Rundle based on their position. The town was perhaps two miles away as the crow flies, but getting down the mountain would take time—a couple of hours at least.

"We're close," she said. "By full sunrise, we'll be there. Just a bit more. Can everyone make it?"

Exhausted nods. Determined faces. They'd come this far. They could finish.

As the sky continued to lighten, they began the descent, picking their way down the rocky slope toward the town below. Behind them, the forest they'd fled through stood silent and dark, keeping its secrets.

And somewhere in that forest, in a camp that might already be packing to move, two women who'd started this journey as tourists were living a new reality—one they'd been drugged into accepting, one they'd chosen under influence, one they might never escape from.

Zuri tried not to think about that. Tried to focus on getting her remaining group to safety. But the guilt was already settling in, heavy and permanent.

I lost them, she thought. *I brought them here, and I lost them.*

Below them, Banff was waking up. Lights in windows. Cars beginning to move on the streets. Normal life resuming for people who had no idea what had happened in the mountains above their town.

"Come on," Zuri said, forcing strength into her voice. "Let's get home. And then we bring them back."

DAY 4

THE PAST IS ALIVE

CHAPTER 27

RETURN TO CIVILIZATION

The descent took three hours.

What looked like a relatively straightforward slope from above revealed itself to be a treacherous maze of loose scree, sudden drop-offs, and areas where the rock face was too steep to navigate directly. They had to backtrack twice, finding alternate routes that added time and exhausted legs that were already past their limit.

But the sight of Banff below them—real, solid, normal—kept them moving. Every time someone stumbled or suggested they stop to rest, someone else would point at the town growing larger below and say, "Almost there. Just a bit more."

The sun had fully risen by the time they reached the outskirts of town, emerging from a hiking trail that led down from Cascade Mountain. A couple of early-morning dog walkers stopped and stared at the bedraggled group—torn clothing, visible cuts and bruises, expressions of exhausted trauma—but Zuri waved them off before they could ask questions.

"We're fine," she said, her voice hoarse. "We just need to get to the police station. Where is it?"

One of the dog walkers pointed down the street, giving directions to the small building that served as Banff's law enforcement headquarters. "Are you sure you're alright? You look like you've been through something terrible. Should I call an ambulance?"

"We're fine," Zuri repeated, though they clearly weren't. "Thank you. We just need the police."

They walked through the awakening town like ghosts, drawing stares from the few people already on the streets. A barista opening her coffee shop paused mid-unlock to watch them pass. A delivery driver unloading boxes did a double-take. They must have looked like disaster survivors, which, Zuri supposed, they were.

The sheriff's office was a modest single-story building on a side street, its parking lot empty except for two patrol vehicles. Through the windows, Zuri could see lights on inside, suggesting someone was already at work despite the early hour.

She pushed through the door, and a bell chimed cheerfully—an absurdly normal sound given what they'd been through. Behind the front desk, a young officer in uniform looked up from his computer, and his eyes widened.

"Jesus Christ," he breathed, standing immediately. "What happened to you people? Do you need medical attention?"

"We need Sheriff Adaire," Zuri said, her trip director voice still functioning despite exhaustion. "It's urgent. We need him now."

"He's not—" the officer started, then stopped as a door behind him opened and Sam Adaire himself emerged, coffee mug in hand, reading something on a tablet.

The sheriff looked up at the interruption and stopped mid-step. His green eyes swept across the group, taking in their condition with a professional's assessment. "Officer Morrison, call for two ambulances. These people need medical—"

"We don't need ambulances," Zuri interrupted, stepping forward. "We need you to listen. We need you to organize a search and rescue. Two of our group are still out there. They're being held by the Wapiti band, the one you told me was harmless. They're not harmless. They're dangerous, and they've got two of my people."

Adaire's expression flickered—something Zuri couldn't quite read passing across his face before professional concern replaced it. "Slow down. Start from the beginning. Who are you?"

"Zuri Davies, Global Runners Travel. We spoke on the phone three days ago. You told me the Wapiti band was safe, that they'd been coming here for years without incident. You were wrong. They kidnapped us. They held us at their camp. They drugged at least two of my people, possibly all of us. And when we escaped, two stayed behind—Maureen O'Sullivan and Elaine Whitmore-Calhoun. We need to go back for them. Now."

Adaire set down his coffee mug carefully, his movements deliberate. "You're saying you were kidnapped by an Indigenous group?"

"Not just any group—the specific one I asked you about. The Wapiti. The ones who camp a few miles from here every summer." Zuri's exhaustion was giving way to anger. "You said they were safe. You said there'd never been any trouble. But they grabbed us, they forced us to participate in ceremonies, they drugged us with something they call 'nature's milk,' and they tried to—" She stopped, realizing how insane the next part would sound.

"Tried to what?" Adaire prompted, his voice carefully neutral.

"Tried to make Elaine their new priestess. They marked her. Carved something into her forehead during a ceremony. And now she's still there, along with Maureen, who went voluntarily yesterday and came back confused or drugged. They're both still at that camp, and we need to get them out."

The sheriff pulled out a notepad, and Zuri felt a flicker of relief—he was taking this seriously, documenting it, preparing to act. "How many of you were taken initially?"

"Twelve, not counting our guides, who weren't with us. We all escaped except Maureen and Elaine."

"And where exactly is this camp?"

"I—" Zuri stopped, realizing the problem. "I don't know exactly. We were on the river, one canoe leaked, we followed a trail inland and found the camp. It's maybe a couple of hours' hike from the Bow River, but I couldn't tell you precise coordinates. But you said you knew where they were. You said you'd visited them yourself."

Something in Adaire's expression shifted—just slightly, just for a moment, but Zuri caught it. "I know the general area they frequent. But their camp moves. They don't stay in one place. Finding them might take time."

"We don't have time!" Zuri's voice rose despite her efforts to stay calm. "Two of my people are there. Being held against their will. Or at least—" She faltered, remembering Elaine's stillness by the fire, Maureen's serene acceptance. "At least being influenced by drugs that affect their judgment. We need to get them out before the Wapiti move the camp. You said yourself they move. If we wait, we might lose them entirely."

"I understand your concern," Adaire said, his voice maddeningly calm. "But I can't just rush into the wilderness without proper planning. I need to organize a search team, coordinate with Parks Canada, possibly bring in RCMP if this is a criminal matter—"

"If?" Stella stepped forward, her voice sharp. "They kidnapped us. They drugged us. They cut one of our people with a knife and marked her face. What part of that isn't criminal?"

Adaire's attention shifted to her, and Zuri noticed his hand move to his wrist, fingers absently touching something beneath his uniform sleeve. "I'm not saying it's not serious. I'm saying we need to do this properly. A hasty search helps no one. Now, I need statements from all of you. Detailed accounts of what happened—"

"We don't have time for statements!" Zuri's control was slipping. "While we sit here talking, they could be moving camp. They could be taking Maureen and Elaine deeper into the wilderness. We need to act now!"

"Ms. Davies." Adaire's voice hardened slightly. "I understand you're upset. You've clearly been through something traumatic. But I'm the law enforcement officer here, and I decide how to proceed. Now, you and your group are going to sit down, you're going to give detailed statements, and then I'm going to organize an appropriate response. That's how this works."

Zuri opened her mouth to argue, but Dave put a hand on her shoulder. "He's right," he said quietly. "We're exhausted. We're not thinking clearly. Let's give our statements, let him do his job, and then get somewhere we can rest and clean up. We're not helping Maureen and Elaine by collapsing from exhaustion."

It went against every instinct Zuri had—the need to act immediately, to not waste a single second while her people were still captive—but she recognized the wisdom in it. They were all running on adrenaline and terror, and adrenaline eventually ran out.

"Fine," she said through gritted teeth. "We'll give statements. But I want search and rescue teams mobilized today. Not tomorrow. Today."

"We'll do everything we can," Adaire assured her, though something in his tone felt off. "Officer Morrison, set up the interview room. We'll take statements one at a time. Ms. Davies, you first. The rest of you, there's a waiting area with coffee and water. Help yourselves."

The interview room was exactly what Zuri expected—bland walls, fluorescent lighting, a simple table with chairs on either side, and a recording device sitting obviously in the center. Adaire gestured for her to sit, then took the opposite chair and activated the recorder.

"This is Sheriff Sam Adaire, conducting an interview with Ms. Zuri Davies regarding an alleged incident involving the Wapiti Indigenous band. Ms. Davies, please state your full name and occupation for the record."

Zuri went through the formalities, then launched into her account of the past three days. She tried to keep it factual, chronological, focused on verifiable events rather than subjective interpretations. The canoe trip. The leak. Following the trail to the camp. Being held there. The ceremony. The escape.

Adaire took notes, asked clarifying questions, and maintained a professional demeanor throughout. But Zuri kept noticing small things that bothered her. The way he seemed unsurprised by certain details. The way he didn't react when she mentioned the "nature's milk" drugging. The way his questions seemed designed to establish whether they'd been physically restrained rather than exploring the coercive nature of their captivity.

And most troubling—the way his hand kept returning to his wrist, fingers rubbing at something beneath his sleeve.

"You mentioned a ceremony where Ms. Whitmore-Calhoun was marked," Adaire said. "Can you describe this marking?"

"I didn't see it completed. We escaped during the ceremony. But the old woman—their priestess, Ayâs—was using some kind of stone blade. Obsidian, maybe. She was carving something into Elaine's forehead. Something ceremonial. Symbolic."

"And Ms. Whitmore-Calhoun didn't resist this?"

The question felt loaded somehow. "She was drugged. Whatever they gave her affected her judgment. She wasn't capable of meaningful consent."

"But she didn't physically resist? Didn't try to stop them or escape?"

"She was surrounded by dozens of people, including several very large men. Where would she have escaped to?"

"I'm just trying to establish the facts, Ms. Davies. Did she verbally object? Say no? Ask for help?"

Zuri tried to remember. The ceremony was a blur of firelight and drums and terror. "I—I'm not sure. Everything was happening so fast. But she was under the influence of their drugs. That's the important point. They drugged her to make her compliant."

"Did you see them forcibly administer this 'nature's milk' to Ms. Whitmore-Calhoun?"

"During the ceremony, yes. The old woman held her jaw and poured it into her mouth."

"And before that? When did Ms. Whitmore-Calhoun first consume this substance?"

Zuri opened her mouth, then closed it. She didn't know. Elaine had been at the camp for several hours before the ceremony. Had they drugged her during that time? Or had the ceremony been the first dose?

"I don't know," she admitted. "But Maureen—Dr. O'Sullivan—she was definitely drugged the day before, when she visited voluntarily. She came back disoriented. Vacant stares. And she stayed that way. That's how we know it's not just suggestion or fear. They have some chemical or substance that acts like LSD or peyote."

Adaire made a note. "And you believe both women are currently being held against their will?"

"Yes, absolutely."

"Even though neither one physically tried to escape during your group's flight from the camp?"

Zuri's frustration flared. "They were drugged! Do you not understand what that means? They weren't capable of making rational choices. That's why we need to get them out—before whatever they were given causes permanent damage."

"I understand," Adaire said calmly. "I'm just trying to establish the exact nature of the situation. Because if these women are there of their own free will, even if influenced by substances, that changes the legal framework considerably."

"They're not there of their own free will. They're prisoners."

"With respect, Ms. Davies, you don't actually know that. You escaped. They didn't. There could be multiple interpretations of that fact."

Zuri stared at him, a cold suspicion forming. "Whose side are you on?"

"I'm not on anyone's side. I'm trying to understand what happened so I can respond appropriately." Adaire's expression remained professional, but Zuri noticed his hand had moved to his wrist again, fingers touching something beneath the fabric.

"What's that?" she asked suddenly, pointing at his wrist. "What are you touching?"

Adaire's hand stilled. "Nothing. Just a nervous habit."

"Show me."

"I don't see how that's relevant—"

"Show me your wrist." Zuri's voice carried command despite her exhaustion.

For a moment, she thought he'd refuse. Then, slowly, deliberately, Adaire pulled back his uniform sleeve.

A leather bracelet circled his wrist. Woven into it was a wooden amulet, carved with a crude face—heavy features, prominent brow, an image that was almost human but not quite. The Napiyaw.

The same symbol Zuri had seen carved into Elaine's forehead.

"You're one of them," she breathed, standing so quickly her chair fell backward. "You're with the Wapiti. That's why you told me they were safe. That's why you're asking all these questions about consent and free will. You're protecting them."

"That's an absurd accusation," Adaire said, but he didn't sound offended. He sounded careful. "This bracelet is just—it's local Indigenous art. It doesn't mean—"

"Bullshit." Zuri backed toward the door. "You're working with them. That's why all those hikers went missing and were never found. You covered it up. You're covering this up right now."

"Ms. Davies, please sit down. You're clearly exhausted and not thinking rationally—"

"I'm thinking perfectly rationally." Zuri's hand found the door handle. "And I'm not giving you any more information until I talk to someone else. Someone who isn't wearing the symbol of the cult that kidnapped us."

She yanked the door open and practically ran into the waiting area where her group sat with styrofoam cups of terrible coffee, looking exhausted and shell-shocked.

"We're leaving," Zuri announced. "Everyone up. We're going back to the hotel."

"What?" Dave looked confused. "But we haven't all given statements—"

"We're not giving statements to him." Zuri pointed back at the interview room where Adaire had appeared in the doorway, his expression unreadable. "He's one of them. He's working with the Wapiti. We need to find someone else—RCMP, Parks Canada, anyone but him."

"Ms. Davies, you're making serious allegations—" Adaire began.

"Show them your wrist," Zuri challenged. "Show them what you're wearing."

Adaire's jaw tightened, but he didn't move to reveal the bracelet. That hesitation told the group everything they needed to know.

"Oh my God," Dana breathed. "She's right. Look at his face. He's guilty."

"This is ridiculous," Adaire said, his voice hardening. "I'm trying to help you, and you're accusing me of—what exactly? Being part of some cult conspiracy?"

"I'm accusing you of covering up kidnappings and letting people disappear into the wilderness without proper investigation," Zuri said flatly. "How many others were there? How many 'missing hikers' were actually taken by the Wapiti and never came back?"

Adaire's green eyes went cold. "You need to leave. You're clearly not in a state to give coherent statements. Come back when you've rested and can think clearly."

"We're not coming back to you." Zuri held his gaze, refusing to be intimidated despite the uniform and authority he represented. "We're going to the Royal Canadian Mounted Police. We're going to Parks Canada. We're going to keep going until we find someone who'll actually help us instead of protecting a cult."

"Good luck with that," Adaire said quietly. "The Wapiti have been here longer than any police force. They know these mountains better than any search team. If they don't want to be found, they won't be. And if those two women don't want to be rescued…" He let the sentence hang.

"They need to be rescued whether they want it or not," Zuri insisted. "Because they're not capable of wanting anything right now. They've been drugged and brainwashed."

"Or they've found something meaningful," Adaire countered. "Something the modern world can't offer. Did you ever consider that?"

The statement hung in the air between them—admission and accusation combined.

"Let's go," Zuri said to her group. They filed out quickly, eager to leave the small building and its compromised sheriff behind.

Outside, the morning sun was bright and warm, Banff was fully awake now, tourists and locals moving about their normal routines, completely unaware that twelve people who looked like disaster survivors were standing outside the police station, trying to figure out what to do next.

"The hotel," Stella said decisively. "We need to get back to the hotel. Shower, change, eat something substantial. Then we figure out our next move from there."

"But Maureen and Elaine—" Zuri started.

"Are probably safer right now than we were last night," Dave interrupted gently. "The Wapiti aren't going to hurt them—they're too valuable. We're not helping anyone by collapsing from exhaustion. We need food, rest, and clear heads. Then we figure out how to rescue them properly."

Zuri wanted to argue, wanted to insist they act immediately, wanted to do something—anything—that felt productive. But she recognized the wisdom in Dave's words. They were all running on empty, physically and emotionally. Making decisions in this state would only lead to more disasters.

"Fine," she agreed reluctantly. "We go to the hotel. We clean up and eat. But then we're calling the RCMP, Parks Canada, and anyone else we can think of. We're not letting this go."

They found a taxi company willing to send vehicles to pick up ten exhausted, disheveled people who looked like they'd been through a war. The drivers took one look at them and didn't ask questions, just loaded them into multiple vans and started the drive to the Louise Mountain Lodge.

Zuri sat in the back of one van, staring out the window at the mountains that looked so beautiful and peaceful in the morning light. Somewhere up there, in those pristine forests that tourists came from around the world to photograph, two of her people were prisoners. Or converts. Or something in between that she didn't have words for.

And the one person whose job was to help them was instead protecting their captors.

"We'll get them back," Stella said beside her, reading her thoughts. "I don't know how yet, but we will. I promise you that."

Zuri nodded but didn't speak. She didn't trust her voice. The guilt was overwhelming—she'd brought these people here, she'd vouched for the safety of the trip, she'd let Maureen go to that camp alone.

This was her fault. And somehow, she had to make it right.

The Louise Mountain Lodge looked exactly as they'd left it—pristine, comfortable, normal. The front desk staff's expressions shifted from professional welcome to shock when they saw the state of the returning group.

"My God, what happened?" the concierge—James, the same man who'd guided them on the Chester Lake run—rushed around the desk. "We were worried when you didn't come back last night. I thought you might be camping. Are you alright?"

"We just need to get into our rooms. We don't have our keys," Zuri said, too tired to explain. "And we need food sent up. A lot of food. Please."

"Of course, of course." James was already typing rapidly on his computer to make new key cards. "Here you are." He looked up at the group as he laid out the key cards, concern evident on his face. "Should I call for medical assistance? You all look—"

"We're fine," Zuri lied. "Just exhausted. Food and rest will help. But please—have breakfast sent up to my room. Enough for everyone."

"Right away."

They collected their room keys and dispersed toward the elevators. Most headed straight for their rooms, desperate for showers and privacy. But a core group of six— Zuri, Stella, Dave, Rogerio, Dana, and Ben—agreed to meet in Zuri's room in thirty minutes.

Zuri's shower was the best thing she'd experienced in her entire life. The hot water washed away blood, dirt, sweat, and some small portion of the trauma. She stood under the spray until it cooled, watching the water run brown and red down the drain.

When she finally emerged, wrapped in the hotel's plush robe, she checked the time: 9:47 AM. They'd been gone over eighteen hours since the canoe trip yesterday afternoon. It felt like weeks.

A knock at her door announced the arrival of breakfast. A hotel staff member wheeled in two carts laden with food—scrambled eggs, bacon, sausage, pancakes, fruit, pastries, coffee, juice. Enough to feed a small army.

"Will this be sufficient?" the young woman asked.

"Perfect. Thank you."

Within minutes, the others began arriving—freshly showered, in clean clothes, looking more human but still carrying the weight of what they'd experienced. They descended on the food like starving wolves, loading plates and eating with the focused intensity of people whose bodies desperately needed calories.

For several minutes, no one spoke. The only sounds were eating, drinking, and the occasional sigh of satisfaction as real food hit empty stomachs.

Finally, Rogerio broke the silence. "So. That happened."

Despite everything, several people smiled.

"That happened," Dave agreed. "We were kidnapped by an Indigenous cult, drugged, witnessed some kind of priestess transformation ceremony, saw cryptid shadows in the forest, and escaped through the wilderness overnight. That's our vacation story."

Rogerio glanced meaningfully at Zuri at the mention of cryptid shadows. They'd agreed to keep what they'd seen private until they could talk it through so they didn't come across as crazy.

"And no one's going to believe us," Dana added. "I got some of it on video, but it's too dark, too chaotic. It just looks like shaky footage of people running through a forest. Without context, it's meaningless."

"The sheriff doesn't believe us," Stella said. "Or rather, he believes us, but he's protecting them. That bracelet. He's part of it somehow."

"We need to go over his head," Zuri said, pulling out her phone. "RCMP. Parks Canada. Maybe even federal authorities if needed. Someone has to take this seriously."

"Do they, though?" Ben asked quietly. "Think about what we're claiming. An Indigenous group practicing ancient ceremonies, drugging people with homemade substances, worshipping forest creatures that may or may not be real. How does that sound to a rational law enforcement officer?"

"Like complete madness," Dave admitted.

"Exactly. We sound like we're having a collective breakdown. Or like we're racists trying to demonize the original natives here. Or like we took some hallucinogens and had a really bad trip." Ben set down his coffee cup. "I'm not saying we shouldn't report it. But we need to be realistic about how it's going to be received."

"Maureen and Elaine are still out there," Zuri insisted. "That's not hallucination or racism or anything else. Two people from our group are missing. That's a fact."

"Are they missing, though?" Stella's question was uncomfortable. "Or did they choose to stay? Because that's what Sheriff Adaire is going to claim. That they made choices, even if influenced by substances. And proving otherwise is going to be nearly impossible."

Zuri opened her mouth to argue, then closed it. She remembered Maureen's serene face, her calm insistence that everything was fine. She remembered Elaine kneeling by the fire, not resisting, not calling for help. She remembered how neither woman had tried to escape when the rest of them fled.

"They were drugged," she said, but her voice lacked conviction.

"We were all there," Rogerio pointed out. "We all breathed the smoke from their fires. We all drank the water they gave us. But only Maureen and Elaine stayed. What if—" He hesitated, then pushed forward. "What if they both just wanted a way out of their normal lives? Maybe the drugs just gave them the excuse they were looking for?"

"Maureen was desperate for academic recognition," Dana said slowly. "She talked about it constantly. About needing a breakthrough for tenure. What if she saw this as her opportunity and convinced herself it was worth any cost?"

"And Elaine…" Stella trailed off, uncertain how to continue.

"Was running from something," Zuri finished. "She talked about how controlled and artificial her life was, how her husband controlled her. She came here to escape her life. Maybe the Wapiti offered the escape she actually wanted."

The implications of that hung heavy in the air.

"So, what do we do?" Dana asked. "Do we report it? Try to rescue them? Or do we accept that maybe—just maybe—they chose this?"

"We report it," Zuri said firmly. "We tell the Mounties everything. We give them all the information we have. And then we let them decide how to proceed. Because I'm not going to be the one who abandons two people on the assumption that being drugged and marked with knives is something they wanted."

Nods around the room. They might doubt, they might question, but they couldn't live with doing nothing.

Zuri searched for the RCMP emergency number and dialed it. The call was answered immediately. "Royal Canadian Mounted Police. What is your emergency?"

Zuri gave a brief explanation of her tour group, the kidnapping, and her location.

The officer responded, "We'll send someone immediately. Please wait there."

Then she disconnected.

"We need to sleep," Dave added. "We've been up all night. We're not making good decisions right now. Just until they arrive." He nodded at Zuri's phone to indicate the authorities.

Reluctant agreement rippled through the group. The adrenaline that had kept them moving was finally wearing off, and the exhaustion beneath was profound.

One by one, they finished eating and drifted back to their own rooms, promising to reconvene. Zuri found herself alone in her room, the breakfast carts still laden with half-eaten food, the morning sun streaming through windows that looked out on mountains that hid terrible secrets.

She pulled out her phone again and opened her contacts. Then, almost against her will, she opened her messages and typed out a text to Maureen's number, knowing it probably wouldn't go through in the wilderness, knowing it was futile, but needing to try anyway:

We're safe. We made it back. If you can see this, if you get any signal at all, please call me. Please let me know you're okay. We can come get you. Just let me know. Please.

She hit send and watched the message sit in pending state, waiting for a signal that would probably never come.

Then she crawled into bed, still wearing the hotel robe, and fell into dreamless, exhausted sleep.

AUTHORITY

The knock on Zuri's door came exactly one hour after she'd called the RCMP. She jolted awake from a sleep so deep it felt like drowning, her body protesting every movement as she dragged herself out of bed and stumbled to the door.

Two officers stood in the hallway, both in the distinctive uniform of the Royal Canadian Mounted Police—not the famous red serge of ceremonial dress, but the practical dark blue operational uniform with its recognizable yellow stripe down the leg and the RCMP shoulder flash. Still, even in working dress, the uniform carried an authority that the local sheriff's office had lacked. The woman was perhaps forty, with sharp eyes and dark hair pulled back in a tight bun. The man was younger, maybe thirty, with the kind of alert watchfulness that suggested he was still proving himself.

"Ms. Zuri Davies?" the woman asked.

"Yes. Come in." Zuri stepped back, suddenly aware she was still wearing the hotel robe, her hair a disaster, her face probably showing every hour of the sleepless night. "Give me one minute to get dressed and wake the others."

"Take your time," the woman said, though her tone suggested time was actually quite important. "I'm Corporal Elena Ruiz, this is Constable James Park. We're with the RCMP detachment for this area. We received your call about a kidnapping incident involving an Indigenous group?"

"Yes. Multiple kidnappings. My entire tour group—twelve people—were held against our will. Two are still missing." Zuri was pulling clothes from her bag as she spoke, moving toward the bathroom. "I'll be two minutes. Please, sit. There's still coffee from breakfast—it might be cold but it's drinkable."

She dressed in record time, splashed water on her face, and sent a rapid text to the group chat: *RCMP here. Come to my room NOW.*

When she emerged, both officers were standing rather than sitting, and Corporal Ruiz was examining the breakfast remnants with the eye of someone trained to read crime scenes. The amount of food consumed, the scattered plates, the evidence of multiple people eating desperately—it all told a story.

"Your group was hungry," Ruiz observed.

"We hadn't eaten properly in over twenty-four hours. We were held at the Wapiti camp from yesterday afternoon through the night. We escaped around midnight and walked through the wilderness until dawn, then came down the mountain into Banff this morning."

Ruiz's expression sharpened. "You walked through wilderness overnight? In the dark?"

"We didn't have a choice. They were chasing us. We had to keep moving."

A knock at the door announced the arrival of Stella and Dave, both looking barely more awake than Zuri felt. Within minutes, the others trickled in—Rogerio with his hair standing in multiple directions, Dana with her phone already recording, Ben looking grim and exhausted.

"Thank you all for coming so quickly," Ruiz said, her voice carrying authority despite not being particularly loud. "I understand you've been through a traumatic experience. We're going to need detailed statements from each of you, and we need to move quickly if two of your group are still in danger. Ms. Davies, can you give me the basic overview first? Then we'll take individual statements."

Zuri launched into the account—the second time she'd told this story in less than two hours, and it was already taking on a rehearsed quality that bothered her. The canoe trip. The leak. The trail to the camp. Being held there. The drugging. The ceremony. The escape.

Ruiz took notes in a small notebook, asking clarifying questions, her expression remaining neutral throughout. Constable Park was doing the same, and Zuri noticed he was drawing a rough map based on her descriptions.

"And you say you reported this to Sheriff Adaire in Banff?" Ruiz asked when Zuri finished.

"Yes. This morning, around seven. We went straight to his office."

"And his response?"

Zuri hesitated, then decided there was no point in softening it. "He was unhelpful. He asked questions that seemed designed to establish that the women might have stayed voluntarily rather than being held against their will. And when I pressed him, I noticed he was wearing something on his wrist—a leather bracelet with a carved wooden amulet. The symbol on it was the same design they carved into Elaine's forehead during the ceremony."

Both officers' attention sharpened considerably.

"You're saying Sheriff Adaire is connected to this group?" Ruiz's voice remained neutral, but Zuri could hear the underlying intensity.

"I'm saying he's wearing their symbol, and he showed more interest in protecting them than helping us. You can draw your own conclusions."

Ruiz and Park exchanged a glance—a professional communication that Zuri couldn't interpret.

"That's a serious allegation," Ruiz said carefully.

"It's a serious situation," Zuri countered. "Two of my people are still out there. One of them—Dr. Maureen O'Sullivan—is a university professor from Virginia. She was drugged with something they call 'nature's milk' that altered her judgment and personality. The other—Elaine Whitmore-Calhoun—was marked during a ceremony. They carved something into her forehead with a stone blade. These aren't willing participants in some cultural experience. They're victims who need to be extracted."

"Can anyone else verify what you saw regarding Sheriff Adaire's bracelet?" Ruiz asked.

"I can," Stella said. "We were all there. We saw him touching his wrist throughout the interview, and when Zuri confronted him, he pulled back his sleeve. The bracelet was there, and the carved symbol matched what we saw at the camp."

"I saw it too," Dave confirmed. "Same symbol."

Zuri wondered at the accuracy of their statements. But their support was making a difference.

Ruiz made notes, her expression giving nothing away. "Alright. We're going to need individual statements from each of you—detailed accounts of everything that happened. Constable Park will set up in one of the hotel's conference rooms for interviews. This will take an hour. But first, I need exact location information. You said you followed a trail from the Bow River to the camp. Can you show me on a map approximately where?"

Park had pulled out a tablet with topographical maps already loaded. Zuri studied it, trying to remember landmarks from their panicked flight.

"We were somewhere in this area," she said, indicating a section of the Bow River between Banff and Canmore. "The canoe leaked, they beached it on a peninsula—I can't tell you which one specifically, but our guide Steven Waters would know. He was at the take-out point when we went back to search for them. He stayed with the damaged canoe."

"We'll need to speak with Mr. Waters as well," Ruiz said. "What about the trail from the river to the camp? Direction? Distance?"

"Generally northwest, I think. Could be five or ten kilometers? It felt longer because we were panicking, but objectively it probably wasn't far. The trail was well-maintained, clearly used regularly. And the camp itself was large — multiple structures, fire pits, maybe thirty or forty people."

"Thirty or forty?" Ruiz's eyebrows rose. "That's a substantial group."

"They've been coming here every summer for decades," Zuri said. "Or at least that's what Sheriff Adaire told me when I asked about them three days ago. He said they were harmless, that they'd never caused any trouble. He lied."

"Or he was misinformed," Ruiz suggested neutrally, though her tone suggested she didn't believe that any more than Zuri did.

"There's one more thing," Rogerio said, his voice hesitant. "Something Zuri and I saw during the escape. Something that's going to sound completely insane, but I swear it's true."

Ruiz turned her attention to him. "What did you see?"

"There was something in the forest. Something that stopped the Wapiti from chasing us. It was—" He glanced at Zuri for support. "It was like a Bigfoot. Or what people describe as Bigfoot. Tall, covered in dark fur, walking on two legs but clearly not human. And it deliberately positioned itself between us and the people chasing us. That's why they stopped pursuing us. They were scared by it—the Wapiti were."

Park's pen had stopped moving. Both officers were very still.

"You saw a cryptid," Ruiz said flatly.

"I know how it sounds," Zuri interjected. "But we both saw it clearly. It was real. Solid. It smelled like—like animal and earth. And it wasn't just us. The Wapiti called them Napiyaw. They worship them, or work with them, or something. That's what the ceremony was about—calling these creatures, bringing them into the physical world or something like that."

"The symbol on the bracelet," Stella added. "And the mark they carved into Elaine's forehead—it was a face. A crude, almost-human face. The Napiyaw, I think."

Ruiz closed her notebook with deliberate slowness. "Let me be very clear. You're telling me that you were kidnapped by an Indigenous group that worships Sasquatch, and that actual Sasquatch creatures intervened to help you escape?"

When she said it like that, it sounded completely absurd. Zuri felt her credibility crumbling in real time.

"I'm telling you what I saw," she said firmly. "Whether or not you believe the part about the creatures, the kidnapping is real. The drugging is real. Two women are still missing. That's what matters."

Ruiz studied her for a long moment, and Zuri couldn't read the expression in her eyes. Professional skepticism?

Concern about their mental state? Calculation about whether any of this was actionable?

Finally, the corporal spoke: "Here's what's going to happen. We're going to take detailed statements from all of you. We're going to locate this camp and verify your account. If we find evidence of kidnapping, drugging, or assault, we'll take appropriate action. But I need you to understand something—if these two women say they are there voluntarily, if they refuse to leave, our options become very limited."

"They were drugged," Zuri repeated, feeling like a broken record. "They can't make voluntary choices under the influence of mind-altering substances."

"That will be for medical professionals to determine," Ruiz said. "Now, let's get those statements. I'll put together a search team right now based on the location you gave us. Then we can give them more specific details once they're in the field."

The hotel provided a small conference room for the interviews. One by one, the Global Runners were called in to give their accounts to Constable Park while Corporal Ruiz coordinated with other RCMP units and Parks Canada rangers to organize a search team.

Zuri went first, walking through the entire timeline again—when they'd arrived in Canada, the tours they'd taken, Maureen's first visit to the camp, the canoe trip, everything. Park asked detailed questions, drilling down on specifics about times, locations, names, physical descriptions of the Wapiti members.

"This old woman—Ayâs—can you describe her?"

"Small, maybe five feet tall. Very old, though I couldn't say exactly how old. Weathered skin, deeply tanned. Gray-blonde hair in elaborate braids. Stooped posture. And the tattoo on her forehead—the same symbol I described, the Napiyaw face."

"And she was clearly the leader?"

"Absolutely. Everyone deferred to her. When she gave orders, people obeyed without question."

"What about the man you called Maskwa?"

"Large—six-four, maybe six-five. Very muscular. Quiet, intimidating. He was clearly the enforcer. The physical presence that kept people in line."

Park took meticulous notes, building profiles of each person Zuri mentioned. By the time her statement was complete, nearly sixty minutes had passed.

Stella went next, then Dave, then the others. Through the conference room's windows, Zuri could see Corporal Ruiz on her phone, making call after call, her expression growing increasingly focused.

Around two hours into the process, Ruiz stuck her head into the waiting area where Zuri and the others who'd already given statements were trying to stay awake with increasingly desperate amounts of coffee.

"We've located Steven Waters," she announced. "He confirmed your story about the damaged canoe and the location. He guided our officers to the exact peninsula where you beached. We have a team there now to follow the trail to the camp."

Relief flooded through Zuri. "Thank you. How long until they reach it?"

"They should reach the site within an hour, assuming they can follow the trail. They'll have satellite communications, so we'll get updates as they progress." Ruiz paused. "I also need to inform you—we're sending an officer to speak with Sheriff Adaire. Not accusing him of anything, just getting his statement about your visit this morning and asking about his knowledge of the Wapiti group."

"He'll deny everything," Zuri predicted.

"Perhaps. But we'll have his statement on record either way." Ruiz's expression was unreadable. "In the meantime, I'd suggest you all try to rest. This is going to take most of the day to resolve, and you're not helping anyone by sitting here exhausted and anxious."

"I can't rest while Maureen and Elaine are out there," Zuri protested.

"You can and you will, because if this becomes a longer operation, you'll need your strength." Ruiz's voice carried the authority of someone used to being obeyed. "We have this handled. We're taking your report seriously. We're acting on it. Now let us do our jobs."

It was a dismissal, gentle but firm. Zuri wanted to argue, wanted to insist on being part of the search, wanted to do something. But she recognized the wisdom in the corporal's words. They were all running on empty, and empty people made bad decisions.

"Alright," she conceded. "But you'll call me the moment you have any information? The instant you find them?"

"You'll be my first call," Ruiz promised. "Now go. Rest. We'll contact you as soon as we know something."

CHAPTER 29

EVIDENCE

The group wandered into the hotel lobby, unsure what to do next.

"Well, I can't go back to sleep now," Zuri said. She kept seeing Maureen's serene face at the camp, kept hearing Elaine's silence when they'd called for her to run, kept wondering if she'd made the right choices or catastrophically wrong ones.

Everyone shook their heads, agreeing that they couldn't either.

"So, what do we do? I'm much more comfortable in this group than in my hotel room," Stella replied.

After thinking for a minute, Zuri answered, "We have tickets for the Cave and Basin Historic Center this afternoon. Does anyone feel like getting back to our vacation itinerary while we wait?"

Rogerio answered immediately, "Yes! I'm in. I'd rather do that than hang out here."

It seemed absurd—going tourist sightseeing while two of their group were missing. But the alternative was sitting in paralyzed anxiety, and that wasn't helping anyone.

"Okay then," Zuri said slowly. "We stay together. We stay reachable. But we give ourselves something to focus on besides worst-case scenarios."

One by one, the others agreed. They gathered their things, double-checked that all phones were charged and ringers on maximum, and headed out into the Canadian afternoon.

The weather was beautiful—clear skies, warm sun, the mountains spectacular in every direction. It felt wrong that the world could be this beautiful while such darkness existed in the forests above.

They walked the short distance to the Cave and Basin in relative silence, each person lost in their own thoughts. The historic site was moderately busy with other tourists, all of whom looked refreshed and happy, clearly having normal, uncomplicated vacations.

"We look like disaster survivors," Dave muttered as they entered. "Everyone's staring."

"We are disaster survivors," Stella replied. "We just survived something no one's going to believe."

They presented their tickets and began moving through the exhibits, trying to focus on the history of Banff's founding, the discovery of the hot springs, the role these thermal waters played in creating Canada's first national park.

But Zuri's attention drifted to displays about the Indigenous peoples who'd used these springs for thousands of years before Europeans arrived. The Stoney Nakota, the same nation the Wapiti had broken away from. Their traditional territories, their sacred sites, their forced relocation to reservations.

"It's complicated, isn't it?" Ben said quietly beside her. "Everything we've been through — it exists in this context. Their anger, their desire to preserve what's being lost. I'm not saying what they did to us was right. But I'm starting to understand where it comes from."

"That doesn't excuse kidnapping," Zuri replied, but her voice lacked heat. She was thinking about the same things, wrestling with the same uncomfortable questions.

They moved through the exhibits, and then Stella called out from across the room. "Zuri. Rogerio. You need to see this."

The urgency in her voice drew them immediately. Stella was standing in front of an ancient photograph—black and white, dated 1895, showing a group of early Banff residents. Miners, hunters, farmers, a few Indigenous people. All dressed in the clothing of their time, all looking stiffly at the camera the way people did in that era of long-exposure photography.

And there, in the second row, barely five feet tall even next to the other women, was a figure Zuri recognized instantly.

"That's impossible," she breathed.

But it wasn't impossible because it was right there in the photograph. Weathered face, elaborate braids, stooped posture, and the distinctive way she held herself—as if the camera was beneath her notice, as if she was humoring these modern people with their strange technology.

Ayâs.

Not someone who looked like Ayâs. Not a relative or ancestor. The same woman. The same face. The same presence that Zuri had seen in the firelight just hours ago.

The placard beneath the photograph read: Early Residents of Banff, 1895. A mix of European settlers and local Indigenous peoples gathered for the dedication of the Cave and Basin hot springs as a public facility.

"That's her," Stella said unnecessarily. "That's the same woman who led the ceremony last night. Which would make her—"

"Over one hundred and thirty years old," Zuri finished. "At least. Probably older."

"That's impossible," Rogerio said, but he was staring at the photograph with the same certainty they all felt. That was Ayâs. No question.

"So is a seven-foot-tall creature covered in fur that walks on two legs and communicates telepathically," Zuri countered. "But we saw that too. Maybe we need to recalibrate our sense of what's impossible."

"Look at this," Rogerio called from a display case in the corner. He was staring at something mounted on a stand, his face pale.

They joined him and faced a triangular case set into the corner of the room. On a stand in the center sat what appeared to be a large, misshapen coconut—brown, weathered, with tufts of dark hair still clinging to it.

The placard read:

This is the only known artifact of the legendary Napiyaw that was worshipped and feared by the Stoney Nakota tribes of this area. It is believed to be the skullcap of one of the beasts, still adorned with tufts of the animal's hair. Legend says that it was taken by a hunter who killed one of the beasts in the woods in the mid-1800s. The DNA of the hair has been tested. Results are inconclusive. It's not human, but neither does it match the other animals in the area.

Behind the skull fragment, mounted on the wall, was a painted hide—a deerskin with faded but still visible artwork. A massive figure standing upright, towering over an elk, covered in fur, with a face that was disturbingly almost-human but not quite.

The same face Zuri had seen in the darkness. The same creature that had stood between them and their pursuers.

"They're real," Rogerio whispered. "They've always been real. Not legend. Not myth. Real."

"And that's what the Wapiti are trying to bring back?" Dave added. "Not just preserve knowledge of, but actually bring back into physical existence. That's what the ceremonies are for? That's what they needed Elaine for—someone who could reach across to wherever those things are and pull them into our reality? I don't think that works for me."

Zuri's phone rang, loud and jarring in the quiet museum space. She grabbed it so fast she nearly dropped it.

"Ms. Davies?" Corporal Ruiz's voice was tight, professional. "We've reached the site. We need to talk."

RECOVERY

"What did you find?" Zuri asked, her voice tight with barely controlled fear. Around her in the museum, the others had stopped pretending to look at exhibits and were watching her intently, trying to read the conversation from her side of it.

"The camp is there," Corporal Ruiz said. "Exactly where you described. We found the structures, the fire pits, clear evidence of recent occupation. But—"

"But what? Are Maureen and Elaine there? Are they safe?"

"Dr. O'Sullivan is here. We're bringing her back to town now. She's physically unharmed but disoriented. Possibly still under the influence of whatever substance she ingested. We've called for medical personnel to meet us at the hotel."

Relief flooded through Zuri so powerfully her legs went weak. "Thank God. What about Elaine?"

A pause on the other end—the kind of pause that preceded bad news. "Ms. Whitmore-Calhoun is at the camp. We spoke with her at length. She's lucid, coherent, and insists she's staying voluntarily. She refused to leave with us."

"She's drugged," Zuri said automatically. "She can't make that decision rationally."

"That was our initial assessment as well," Ruiz said carefully. "But Ms. Calhoun demonstrated a clear awareness of her situation, her choices, and the consequences. She answered our questions without confusion or obvious impairment. She explicitly stated she's there by choice and does not want to be removed."

"She has a carved symbol on her forehead! They cut her with a knife during a ceremony! How is that voluntary?"

"She acknowledged the marking. Said it was part of a spiritual transformation she accepted. She showed no signs of being held against her will, no physical restraints, no one preventing her from leaving if she chose to."

Ruiz's voice carried professional distance, but Zuri could hear the discomfort beneath it. "Ms. Davies, I understand this isn't what you want to hear. But legally, we cannot remove an adult who's not demonstrably incapacitated and who explicitly refuses our help."

"What about the kidnapping? The forced drugging? The ceremony where they held her down and carved her face?"

"We asked about all of that. She said the initial situation was confusing and frightening, but that she ultimately chose to participate in the ceremony. She said no one held her down—that she knelt voluntarily. As for the substance they gave her, she described it as a sacrament in a religious practice she's chosen to join."

Zuri wanted to scream. "You can't possibly believe that. She's been brainwashed. That's what cults do—they make victims believe they're there by choice."

"I don't disagree with you," Ruiz said, and for the first time there was real sympathy in her voice. "But I'm bound by law. I can't forcibly extract someone who says they don't want to be extracted, who shows no signs of immediate danger, and who appears to be making informed choices. If we did that, we'd be the ones committing a kidnapping."

"Then what about the rest of it? The fact that they held twelve of us against our will? That they drugged people? That they forced us to participate in ceremonies?"

"We're investigating all of that. We've documented the site, taken photographs, collected samples of substances we found. We've interviewed members of the group who were present, including Ms. Calhoun. But, Ms. Davies, I need you to understand—everyone we spoke to, including Ms. Calhoun, claims your group came to the camp voluntarily, that you were offered food and shelter, and that you were free to leave at any time. They deny any coercion or drugging beyond offering traditional ceremonial substances that were refused by most but accepted by some."

"That's a lie," Zuri said flatly. "They physically blocked us from leaving. They surrounded us. They—"

"Created a frightening situation, yes. But physical restraint and creating an intimidating environment are different things legally. And without physical evidence of restraint, without injuries consistent with being held against your will…" Ruiz trailed off, the implication clear.

"So, they get away with it," Zuri said, hearing the bitterness in her own voice. "They kidnap tourists, drug them, and get away with it because they're clever enough not to leave marks."

"I didn't say that. We're still investigating. But I want you to have realistic expectations about what we can prove and what charges we can bring." Ruiz paused. "There's one more thing you should know. The old woman you described — Ayâs — she's not at the camp."

Zuri's attention sharpened. "Where is she?"

"No one knows. Or at least, no one's saying. The members we spoke to claim she left sometime during the night, after your group left. They say she does this periodically — goes into the wilderness alone for extended periods. They don't expect her back."

"That's convenient," Zuri said. "The leader disappears right before you arrive? They're protecting her. She's probably twenty feet away, hiding in the trees."

"We searched the surrounding area. If she's nearby, she's very well hidden. And legally, she hasn't committed a crime we can charge her with based on current evidence." Ruiz's frustration was evident now. "I know this isn't the outcome you wanted. But we did find Dr. O'Sullivan, and we're bringing her back. That's something."

It was something. But it felt like a pyrrhic victory when Elaine was still there, marked and converted and claiming it was all her choice.

"When will you be back with Maureen?" Zuri asked.

"Thirty minutes, maybe forty. We're taking her directly to the hotel. I'd suggest you gather your group there to meet us. Dr. O'Sullivan specifically asked to see you."

"We'll be there," Zuri promised. "And Corporal Ruiz? Thank you. For finding her. For trying with Elaine. I know you did what you could."

"I wish I could have done more," Ruiz said quietly, and disconnected.

Zuri lowered the phone and looked at her group, all of them watching with desperate hope. "They found Maureen. They're bringing her back. But Elaine—"

"Won't leave," Stella finished when Zuri couldn't. "She told them she wants to stay."

Zuri nodded, not trusting her voice.

"At least we got one of them back," Dave said, trying to find the positive. "That's more than we had an hour ago."

But the victory felt hollow. They'd lost Elaine—whether to drugs, brainwashing, spiritual transformation, or actual choice, the result was the same. She wasn't coming back.

"We should go," Rogerio said quietly. "If Maureen asked to see us, we should be there when she arrives."

The hotel had prepared a suite on the ground floor for Maureen's arrival—somewhere with more space than a regular room, somewhere the RCMP and medical personnel could work without being cramped. Zuri and her group waited in the adjacent sitting area, tension building with each passing minute.

When Corporal Ruiz and Constable Park finally arrived, supporting a figure between them, Zuri's breath caught.

Maureen looked like a ghost of her former self. Her red hair was tangled and dirty, her clothes—still the same running gear from days ago—were stained and torn. But it was her face that was most disturbing. Her eyes were unfocused, tracking movement slowly as if she were underwater. Her expression was slack, empty, like someone had reached inside and turned off essential parts of her personality.

"Maureen," Zuri said, stepping forward carefully. "It's me. It's Zuri. You're safe now. We've got you."

Maureen's eyes found her, and there was a flicker of recognition. "Zuri," she said, her voice hoarse and uncertain. "I was… I was with them. The Wapiti. The ceremony. I saw…"

"I know," Zuri said gently, taking Maureen's hand. It was cold despite the warm day. "You don't have to talk about it now. You're safe. We're going to take care of you."

"Elaine," Maureen said with sudden urgency, her grip tightening. "Elaine is still there. She's staying. She's Nitânis now. The new priestess. The old woman is gone."

"Gone where?" Ruiz asked, her professional attention focusing.

"Just… gone." Maureen's eyes drifted, losing focus again. "Ayâs said her time was complete. That she could finally rest. That Elaine would continue the work. She walked into the forest and…" Maureen's voice trailed off. "She became the trees. Or she was always the trees. I'm not sure anymore. Nothing is sure."

A medical technician had arrived and was gently guiding Maureen toward a chair, checking her vitals, shining a light in her eyes. "Pupils are dilated but responsive," she reported. "Heart rate elevated. Blood pressure is slightly high but not dangerous. She's definitely under the influence of something, but I can't say what without blood tests."

"We'll do those tests," Ruiz said. "Full toxicology screen. I want to know exactly what substances are in her system."

"Of course. We'll get you all that."

Maureen suddenly focused on Zuri again, her hand reaching out with desperate urgency. "You have to understand. It's real. All of it. The Napiyaw are real. I saw them. Not just shadows—I saw them in the flesh. During the ceremony, when Elaine was marked, they came. They watched us. I think they approved." Her voice dropped to a whisper. "They're not animals. They're not monsters. They're the first people. And Elaine can call them now. She has the sight. She can bridge the two worlds."

"Maureen, you were drugged," Zuri said gently. "What you saw—"

"Was real," Maureen insisted, her voice cracking. "I know how it sounds. I know what you think. But I'm a trained academic. I study religions and spiritual practices. I know the difference between a hallucination and an authentic spiritual experience. What happened there was real."

"Dr. O'Sullivan," Ruiz said carefully, "did anyone force you to stay at the camp? After the ceremony, after the others escaped, did anyone prevent you from leaving?"

Maureen's brow furrowed, as if the question required immense effort to process. "Force? No. No one forced me. I wanted to stay. I wanted to learn more. The ceremony was the most significant thing I've ever witnessed. My entire academic career was building toward that moment. How could I leave?"

"But you're here now," Zuri pointed out. "You left. Or they sent you."

"Elaine asked them to send me back." Maureen's eyes filled with tears. "She said I wasn't ready to join them yet. That I was still too connected to the old world, the academic world. That I needed time to integrate what I'd experienced before I could return." She looked at Zuri with a desperate need to be understood. "She knows best. She's Nitânis. This is what's best for me right now."

"She's still heavily influenced by whatever they gave her," the medical technician said quietly to Ruiz. "Her judgement is clearly altered. She needs proper medical care and probably psychiatric evaluation."

"No," Maureen said, hearing this despite the whispered tone. "I don't need psychiatry. I just need some time. I need to process all of this. I need…" She swayed suddenly, and multiple hands reached to steady her. "I'm very tired."

"Let's get you lying down," the technician said, guiding her toward the suite's bedroom. "You need rest, hydration, and probably some good food. Then we'll talk about next steps."

As Maureen was led away, still maintaining that she was fine and murmuring about ceremonies and the old gods, Zuri felt her heart break a little more. They'd gotten Maureen back physically, but mentally, spiritually—she was still at that camp. Still converted or confused.

"What happens now?" she asked Ruiz.

"Medical evaluation, as we discussed. Psychiatric consultation. We'll document everything she says, every detail about what happened at the camp. And we'll build a case—if we can." Ruiz's expression was grim. "But I need to be honest with you, Ms. Davies. This is going to be difficult to prosecute. Ms. Calhoun, Elaine, is claiming voluntary participation. Dr. O'Sullivan says she wasn't forced to stay. Without clear evidence of coercion or restraint, without the cooperation of the alleged victims…"

"What about the rest of us?" Dave asked. "We were held there. We were surrounded, prevented from leaving. Doesn't that count?"

"It helps establish a pattern of behavior," Ruiz acknowledged. "But again—they'll claim you were free to leave at any time, that you chose not to because you were frightened by the cultural situation. They'll say any intimidation you felt was a cultural misunderstanding, not criminal intent."

"That's bullshit," Stella said bluntly. "How is all of this not criminal?"

"It is criminal," Ruiz agreed. "If we can prove it. But proving it requires evidence that holds up in court, and so far, what we have is contested by the primary victims themselves." She looked at each of them. "I'm not giving up. We're still investigating. But it's going to be tricky. And how many of you want to stay here in Alberta to support the legal process?"

Ruiz looked at each of the runners. It was a point they hadn't considered. Everyone was due to leave the country the next day. Pressing charges, making statements, and going through the court process would require staying longer and returning multiple times in the future.

Receiving no positive responses, Ruiz said, "You see what I mean? I suspect each of you is eager to return to your normal lives, and hopefully happy to be unharmed. Elaine Calhoun is choosing to stay, but her story is very different."

"What about Sheriff Adaire?" Zuri asked. "He's wearing their symbol. He lied to me about them being harmless. He's clearly connected to them somehow. Doesn't that matter?"

"We sent Constable Park to interview Sheriff Adaire this afternoon," Ruiz said. "He confirmed that he's familiar with the Wapiti band, that he's visited their camps over the years as part of community policing, and that he's accepted gifts from them including the bracelet you mentioned. He claims the relationship is purely professional and cultural—building bridges between law enforcement and Indigenous communities."

"And you believe that?" Zuri asked incredulously.

"I believe it's possible," Ruiz said carefully. "I also believe it's possible he's more involved than he admits. But belief isn't evidence. The good news is that the RCMP is now aware of the situation here. Any disappearances will no longer be handled solely by the local sheriff's office. We'll certainly step in—and he knows that. If he has been protecting them, that won't be happening anymore."

"So, they just get away with it," Zuri said, her voice hollow.

"Definitely not," Ruiz replied. "What you and your group have done in reporting to us is open this up to a much larger law enforcement lens. Because of you, we can prevent this from happening again. There won't be any lost hikers or tourists who aren't investigated by RCMP and Parks Canada, at a minimum. You are to be congratulated for making that possible for everyone who hasn't disappeared yet."

"So you do suspect Sheriff Adaire of colluding with them," Dave said, reading between the lines.

Ruiz raised an eyebrow, unable to confirm his suspicion, but not denying it either. She said nothing.

It wasn't enough. It would never be enough. But it was all they were going to get.

From the bedroom, they could hear Maureen's voice, still talking—a stream of consciousness about ceremonies and ancient powers and the old woman who walked into trees. The medical technician was trying to get her to drink water, to rest, to stop talking and sleep.

"She's going to need a lot of support," Ruiz said quietly. "Professional help, certainly. But also friends. People who believe her even when what she's saying sounds impossible. People who'll help her reintegrate into normal life—if she can."

"We'll be here for her," Zuri promised, though she had no idea how to do that. The tour was ending the next day. People would scatter back to their homes, their normal lives. How many would stay in touch? How many would want to be reminded of what they'd experienced here?

"There's one more thing," Ruiz said, pulling out her phone and scrolling to a photo. "Dr. O'Sullivan mentioned that the old woman—Ayâs—disappeared into the forest. That no one knew where she went. But one of the Wapiti members told us something interesting. He said that when a new priestess is anointed, the old one's time is complete. That she's released from her service and can finally rest."

"Rest," Stella repeated. "You mean die?"

"That's what I assumed he meant. But he said it differently—that she 'returns to the forest' or 'becomes one with the land again.' That her physical form is no longer needed once the succession is complete." Ruiz showed them the photo on her phone—the 1895 image from the Cave and Basin museum, showing Ayâs standing among the early Banff residents. "You saw this earlier today. This woman, who looks exactly like the person you describe as Ayâs, photographed over a century ago."

"You think it's the same person?" Zuri said, not quite making it a question.

"I think it's impossible for it to be the same person," Ruiz corrected. "But I also think impossible things keep happening in this case. And I think if Ayâs—whoever or whatever she was—truly has disappeared into the wilderness, we're never going to find her. Because I don't think she exists to be found anymore."

The implication hung in the air—that Ayâs had been something other than human, something that defied normal biology, and that her disappearance wasn't death but dissolution. Return to whatever force had animated her for over a century.

And Elaine had taken her place.

"I need to go back," Zuri said suddenly. "To the camp. I need to talk to Elaine myself. If she looks at me and tells me she wants to stay, if she's really making that choice freely, then… then maybe I can accept it. But I need to hear it from her. Face to face."

"I can't authorize that," Ruiz said. "You're a civilian, and that camp is now part of an active investigation."

"Then take me with you. As a witness. As someone who knows Elaine and can assess whether she's acting normally. However you want to justify it, just take me there. Please."

Ruiz studied her for a long moment, then shook her head. "I understand why you want that. But it's not going to help. Ms. Calhoun made her position clear. Seeing her again will only cause you more pain."

"That's my choice to make," Zuri insisted.

"No," Ruiz said firmly. "It's my choice to make, and I'm making it. You've been through enough. Your group needs you here, helping Dr. O'Sullivan, processing your own trauma. Going back to that camp will only upset all of that. Trust me on this."

Zuri wanted to argue, wanted to insist, wanted to demand her right to try one more time to reach Elaine. But she saw the finality in Ruiz's expression and knew it was futile.

"What happens to the camp now?" Dave asked. "Do they stay there? Do you shut it down?"

"We can't shut down a temporary Indigenous camp on Crown land without specific criminal charges," Ruiz said. "They have as much right to be there as any other group camping in the wilderness. We've documented the site, we've interviewed the people there, and we've made it clear we're watching. I think that will be more than enough."

"What do the rest of us do now?" Rogerio asked the question they were all thinking.

"You take care of Dr. O'Sullivan," Ruiz said. "You give your final statements if we need any clarification. And tomorrow, most of you go home. You try to put this behind you and move forward with your lives."

"Can we?" Dana asked quietly. "Can we really just go back to normal after this?"

"I don't know," Ruiz admitted. "But you'll have to try."

LEAVING IT BEHIND

CHAPTER 31

DEPARTURE

The morning arrived with a perfect weather that mocked the runners' harrowing experience. Clear skies, warm sunshine, mountains glowing gold in the early light—it was the kind of day that Zuri wished for to start every one of her trips—not filled with goodbyes weighted with trauma and unanswered questions.

The event director stood in the hotel lobby watching her group gather for the last time, their luggage clustered around them like small fortresses. Most were heading to the Calgary airport for afternoon flights that would scatter them back across the United States—Phoenix, Austin, Seattle, Savannah. Back to their normal lives, their jobs, their families who had no idea what had really happened in the Canadian Rockies.

The energy was subdued, awkward. No one quite knew how to say goodbye after what they'd been through together. The friendly camaraderie that had developed during the first two days of the trip—the jokes, the competitive banter, the shared excitement for adventure—felt like it belonged to different people in a different lifetime.

"Well," Stella said, breaking the uncomfortable silence, "this was definitely the most memorable Global Runners trip I've ever been on. And I've been on twelve of them now, so that's saying something."

A few people managed weak smiles at his attempt at humor.

"I think we can all agree this one was… unique," Dave offered, his arm around Stella's waist as if physical contact could anchor them both to reality.

Dana had her phone out, but for once she wasn't filming. "I don't even know what to post about this trip. 'Great running, beautiful scenery, got kidnapped by a cult, saw a cryptid, lost two friends to spiritual transformation—five stars, would recommend?'"

"Maybe just stick with the scenery photos," Ben suggested quietly. He looked exhausted, dark circles under his eyes suggesting he'd slept as poorly as the rest of them.

The Austin couple—Sarah and Luke—had barely spoken since giving their statements to the RCMP yesterday. They stood slightly apart from the group, their body language broadcasting their desperate need to leave, to get on a plane, to put as much distance between themselves and this place as possible.

"I want you all to know," Zuri said, her voice carrying the authority that had guided them through five days of adventure and one night of terror, "that what happened here wasn't your fault. It wasn't anyone's fault except the people who chose to drug and kidnap and convert vulnerable tourists. You did everything right—you stayed together, you escaped when you could, you reported it to the authorities, you gave detailed statements. You should all be proud of how you handled an impossible situation."

"We left Maureen and Elaine behind," Sarah said, her voice thick with guilt. "That's not handling it right."

"Maureen is back with us," Zuri corrected gently. "She's upstairs, recovering. And Elaine…" She paused, struggling with how to frame it. "Elaine made her own choices. Whether those were truly free or influenced by drugs and manipulation, we may never know. But we tried. The RCMP tried. Sometimes trying isn't enough, but it's all we can do."

"Is there any update on her?" Marcus asked. "Any chance she'll change her mind and come back?"

Zuri shook her head. "Corporal Ruiz called me this morning. The Wapiti camp is still at the same location, and Elaine is still there. The Mounties have established that she's not being physically restrained, that she has access to food and water, and that she's explicitly stated she doesn't want to leave. Legally, there's nothing more they can do."

"What about charges?" Ben asked. "Is anyone being prosecuted for what they did to us?"

"The investigation is ongoing," Zuri said, repeating what Ruiz had told her. "But I want you all to understand—and I say this so you can make informed decisions about your own lives—any criminal prosecution would require many of you to stay in Canada or return multiple times for court proceedings. It would mean depositions, testimony, possibly months or years of legal process. Corporal Ruiz wanted me to make sure you understood that before expecting quick resolution."

The implications settled over the group. Most of them had jobs, families, obligations. The idea of being pulled back here repeatedly for a legal case that might not even succeed was discouraging.

"I can't do that," Sarah said, her voice breaking. "I can't come back. I can't relive this in court testimony. I just need to go home and try to forget it happened."

"No one's judging you for that," Stella assured her. "We all need to do what's right for our own healing."

"There is one positive thing," Zuri continued. "Corporal Ruiz assured me that going forward, the RCMP and other agencies will be actively involved in any lost hiker or tourist cases in this area. They won't leave it to the local sheriff to handle alone. They're aware now of the Wapiti's practices, and they'll be monitoring the situation. So even if we can't get justice for what happened to us, we may have prevented it from happening to others in the future."

It was small comfort, but it was something. A reason to believe their suffering hadn't been entirely pointless.

"When do the buses leave?" Mario asked, clearly eager to begin the journey away from this place.

"Thirty minutes," Zuri checked her watch. "Two buses—one heading directly to Calgary airport, the other stopping in downtown Calgary for a few hours of sightseeing—for those who have later flights or are staying longer."

"I'm on the direct bus," Sarah said immediately. "First one out."

Several others nodded their agreement. The desire to leave was palpable, as if lingering in Banff even a few extra hours might somehow pull them back into the nightmare.

"Before everyone scatters," Dana said, "can we do one thing? Can we at least exchange contact information? Stay in touch? We went through something together that no one else is going to understand. We might need each other in the future—to talk, to process, to remember we're not crazy."

It was a good idea, and Zuri was grateful Dana had suggested it. They spent the next several minutes sharing phone numbers and email addresses, creating a group chat that already felt like a lifeline to people who couldn't imagine explaining what they'd experienced to anyone who hadn't been there.

"I want to see Maureen before I go," Ben said. "Say goodbye properly. Is she up for visitors?"

"She's awake," Zuri confirmed. "The nurse said she had a much better night—the drugs are clearing her system. She's still processing everything, still insistent that what she experienced was real, but she's coherent. I think she'd appreciate seeing you all."

The group moved as one toward the elevator, riding up to the third floor where Maureen had a larger suite with space for the nurse who'd been assigned to monitor her recovery. They found her in the sitting area, dressed in regular clothes for the first time in days. Her red hair was washed and braided, and she looked almost as perky as the day she'd arrived.

But her eyes were still a bit unfocused. They held something they hadn't before—a depth that couldn't be erased even as the drugs left her system.

"You're all leaving today," Maureen said as they filed in. It wasn't a question.

"Most of us," Rogerio confirmed. "Some are staying a little longer. But yeah, the official tour is over."

"I'm sorry," Maureen said, and tears welled in her eyes. "I'm so sorry. I brought you all to that camp. It was so safe and special for me. I thought it would be the same for you."

"You didn't bring us there," Zuri said firmly, sitting beside her. "That canoe leaked because they sabotaged it. The trail was there because they wanted it to be found. They engineered the whole thing. You were a victim too, Maureen. Don't blame yourself for their manipulations."

"But I stayed," Maureen whispered. "Even after you all escaped, I stayed. I chose to stay. What does that mean?"

"Human," Stella said gently. "It means you're human. They gave you something that altered your thinking, that made you see what they wanted you to see. You can't blame yourself for that."

"I did see things though," Maureen insisted, her voice gaining strength. "Things that were real. The Napiyaw—I saw them. Not hallucinations, not drug-induced visions. I saw them physically in the forest. And Elaine—what they did to her, what she became — that was real too. I'm a trained academic. I know the difference between genuine spiritual transformation and drug-induced delusion. What happened there was real."

The group exchanged uncomfortable glances. No one wanted to return to that discussion.

"Whether it was or not," Dave said carefully, "you're safe now. And when you're ready, you'll go home to Virginia, and you'll have all the time you need to process what happened and decide what it means."

"I'm going back to my research," Maureen said with surprising firmness. "This is the most significant fieldwork I've ever done. The discovery of a functioning Indigenous spiritual practice that has a genuine connection to something we can't explain — do you understand what that means academically? This could change my career. But I have to be careful about the mystical claims — regardless of what I believe personally."

"Just promise me," Zuri said, "that you won't go back there. That you won't try to return to the Wapiti. Promise me you'll focus on healing first, research second."

Maureen met her eyes, and Zuri saw the conflict there — the academic hunger warring with the recognition of danger. "I promise I won't go back alone. And not until I'm fully recovered. But I can't promise I won't go back — eventually. If Elaine is there, if she's truly their priestess, then I have an obligation to document it. To understand it. To share it with the world—if she permits it."

Not the promise Zuri wanted, but it was probably the best she'd get.

One by one, the group said their goodbyes to Maureen—hugs, well-wishes, exchanges of contact information. There was an understanding that she was still part of their shared trauma, even if her perspective on it differed from everyone else's.

"Take care of yourself," Dana said, hugging Maureen tightly. "And if you ever need to talk to someone who was there, you call me. Day or night. Promise?"

"I promise," Maureen said, returning the embrace.

When everyone had said their goodbyes, they headed downstairs to where the buses were waiting. Luggage was loaded, last-minute bathroom trips were made, and then it was time.

Zuri stood on the hotel steps watching her group board the buses. She'd guided dozens of groups over the years, had said goodbye to hundreds of travelers. But this one was different. These people carried wounds that would take years to heal, memories that would haunt them, questions that would never have satisfactory answers.

"You're staying?" Rogerio asked before boarding, his duffel bag slung over his shoulder.

"Until Maureen is ready to travel," Zuri confirmed. "I can't leave her here alone. Not after everything."

"That's good," Rogerio said. "She needs someone. We all do, but especially her." He hesitated, then added, "For what it's worth, I believe her. About what she saw. About it being real. We saw it too, remember? I know what we saw, and it wasn't a hallucination or a bear or anything normal. It was exactly what she described—something ancient and powerful that shouldn't exist but does."

"Yes. I can't forget it either," Zuri said carefully. "But I still can't explain it to someone who wasn't there."

"Maybe that's the point," Rogerio suggested. "Maybe some mysteries aren't meant to be explained. Maybe we just have to live with not knowing." He gave her a quick hug. "Take care, Zuri. And thank you for getting us home safely. I know it doesn't feel like success, but it is. You saved us."

He boarded before she could respond, and Zuri was grateful because she didn't trust her voice.

The buses pulled away, and she watched them disappear down the road toward home. Her group was gone, scattered back to their normal lives where they'd have to figure out how to explain the unexplainable to people who hadn't been there.

"Well," a familiar voice said behind her, "that was harder than expected."

Zuri turned to find Stella and Dave standing there, their own luggage still in the lobby behind them.

"You didn't get on the bus?" Zuri observed.

"Nope," Stella confirmed. "We decided we're staying in Banff for a few more days. Not for the tour—that's officially over. Just as tourists. Regular, normal tourists who want to enjoy the area."

"And maybe avoid the woods," Dave added with a weak smile. "Stick to the town. The shops. The restaurants. Places where cults don't hang out."

"You don't have to stay for me," Zuri said, though she was grateful they were. The thought of being alone with Maureen and her nurse and the weight of everything that had happened was overwhelming.

"We're not staying for you," Stella joked, deflecting the sentiment. "Well, not entirely. We're staying because we started a vacation together and we want to finish it properly. We want to make some good memories in this place to balance out the terrible ones. And yes, we'd like your company if you're available. But if you need to focus on Maureen, we understand."

"I'd like that," Zuri admitted. "I'd like that very much. Maureen has a nurse with her, and honestly, she seems more stable today. I don't think she'd want me sitting in the hotel hovering over her."

"Then it's settled," Dave said. "The three of us will be tourists. We'll eat good food, buy overpriced souvenirs, take photos of mountains, and pretend we're normal people having a normal vacation."

"Sounds perfect," Zuri said, and meant it.

They headed back into the lobby together, and Zuri felt some of the weight lift from her shoulders. She had people who understood, who'd been there, who could help her process the experience without thinking she was crazy.

Upstairs, Maureen sat by the window of her suite, staring out at the mountains. Her notebook was open on her lap, and she was writing—recording everything she could remember about the ceremonies, the practices, the transformation she'd witnessed. The academic in her couldn't let it go, couldn't walk away from the most significant discovery of her career.

But part of her mind was still at that camp, still connected to Elaine, who was living a new life now, still hearing Ayâs's ancient voice promising truth and transformation. The drugs had cleared her system, but the experience hadn't cleared from her soul.

I'll go back, she thought, pen moving across paper. *Not today. Not this week. But eventually. I have to. I have to understand it better. I have to document it. I have to share at least some of it with the world.*

The nurse knocked softly and entered with lunch on a tray. "How are you feeling, Dr. O'Sullivan?"

"Better," Maureen said, and it was true. "Much better. Thank you."

But as she ate and made polite conversation with the nurse, her eyes kept drifting back to the mountains, to the forests. Somewhere out there, Elaine—Nitânis—was learning what it meant to lead an entirely different life.

I hope you're alright, Maureen thought toward her friend. *I hope you chose wisely. I hope it brings you the meaning you were searching for.*

CHAPTER 32

THE VIEW FROM BELOW

Zuri woke in her hotel room, momentarily disoriented by the silence. No alarm for an early morning run. No itinerary to review. No group to shepherd through another adventure. The official tour was over.

She checked her phone and found a text from Stella: *Breakfast? Meet in the lobby in an hour? Let's be normal tourists today.*

Perfect, Zuri replied. *See you there.*

She took her time getting ready, enjoying the luxury of a leisurely morning. A long shower. Careful attention to makeup she hadn't bothered with in days. Clothes chosen for comfort and style rather than athletic function—jeans, a soft sweater, walking shoes that weren't running shoes.

When she arrived in the lobby, Stella and Dave were already there, looking similarly refreshed. The trauma was still visible in small ways—the way Stella's eyes scanned the room constantly, the way Dave positioned himself with his back to a wall—but they were trying. Choosing to be present rather than paralyzed.

"How's Maureen this morning?" Stella asked as Zuri joined them.

"I checked on her before coming down. Much better. She was eating breakfast, talking to the nurse about academic journals and publication timelines. I think her brain has switched fully into researcher mode—planning for a paper on the Wapiti."

"Whatever helps her cope," Dave said. "I'm not ready to go back to real estate yet. Just one more day of vacation."

They headed to a café Stella had found online—a local place off the main tourist strip, known for excellent coffee and homemade pastries. The walk there was pleasant, the morning air crisp and clean, the mountains spectacular in every direction.

Zuri relaxed incrementally with each step away from the hotel. She was still in the shadow of the mountains that hid the Wapiti camp, but she wasn't responsible for anyone's safety right now. She was just a person walking through a beautiful town on a beautiful morning.

The café was exactly as advertised—cozy, welcoming, smelling of fresh bread and excellent coffee. They ordered generously—lattes and cappuccinos, croissants and scones, breakfast sandwiches that were far more elaborate than necessary. They found a table by the window and settled in.

"So," Dave said, spreading jam on his scone, "what do normal tourists do in Banff?"

"According to this," Stella said, consulting her phone, "they shop on Main Street, visit art galleries, take photos of the Three Sisters, eat at overpriced restaurants, and generally pretend they're in a postcard."

"Sounds perfect," Zuri said. "Let's do all of that."

They did. They spent the morning wandering through shops that sold local art, Indigenous crafts—Zuri felt a complicated twist in her stomach at those—outdoor gear, and the kind of upscale home décor that somehow seemed essential when on vacation but absurd when you imagined shipping it home. They didn't buy much, but the browsing was soothing. Normal. Safe.

They stopped for photos at every scenic overlook, taking turns with each other's phones, capturing images of themselves with the mountains as a backdrop. Evidence that they'd been here, that they'd survived, that they were choosing to make good memories in this place that had given them such terrible ones.

Around noon, they felt the surge of tourists joining them on the streets. They looked happy and oblivious to the darkness that existed just beyond their manicured trails and scenic overlooks. They blended into the crowds on the main street, moving through shops and restaurants that catered to people who'd never experienced anything more threatening than a missed dinner reservation.

"This is surreal," Stella said, watching a family pose for photos in front of a candy shop. "They have no idea. This whole town—all these people—they have no idea what's happening in the forests around them."

"Maybe that's for the best," Dave suggested. "Ignorance isn't always bad. They get to enjoy the beauty without the fear."

"Or maybe they deserve to know," Zuri countered. "Maybe they deserve to understand that their hiking trails lead to places where people disappear, where ancient things still exist, where the wilderness isn't just a scenic backdrop but actually wild."

They walked in silence for a moment, each processing their own relationship with that idea.

As they passed the sheriff's office, Zuri noticed something. "Look."

Two RCMP vehicles were parked outside—the same ones that had been at their hotel for the past two days. Through the window, she could see Corporal Ruiz and Constable Park inside, apparently in conversation with someone—Sheriff Adaire, based on the uniform visible through the glass.

"They're still investigating," Stella observed. "Still here, still working the case."

"Good," Zuri said. "I hope they make his life miserable. I hope every day they're here reminds him that his protection of the Wapiti has consequences."

They didn't stop, didn't go inside. There was nothing more they could contribute, and seeing Adaire again would only dredge up anger they were trying to erase. They kept walking, past the police station, past the tourist shops, toward the edge of town where the buildings gave way to parkland.

"I want to see something," Zuri said, angling toward a trailhead that led upward, toward the lower slopes of the mountains that ringed Banff.

"Are we going back into the woods?" Dave asked, concern evident in his voice.

"Just a little way. I want to see where we came down. Where we emerged that morning." Zuri couldn't quite explain the compulsion, but she needed to see it from this side—the path they'd descended in exhaustion and terror, now just a hiking trail like any other.

The trail was well-maintained, popular with tourists based on the number of people they passed heading up or down. They climbed for perhaps twenty minutes, gaining elevation until Banff spread out below them—a small town nestled in an enormous valley, dwarfed by mountains on all sides.

"There," Zuri said, pointing. "That's roughly where we came down. That slope."

They stood at a scenic overlook, catching their breath, admiring the view with dozens of tourists passing by them. It looked so ordinary in daylight. So manageable. Nothing like the terrifying descent through the darkness that had brought them here three days ago.

"It's strange," Stella said quietly. "Seeing it like this. It's just a mountain. Just trees and rocks and trails. In my head, it's the place of nightmares. But standing here, looking at it—it's just geography."

"Yes, you're right," Dave added. "Just a normal place."

Zuri's attention shifted upward, scanning the slopes above them. The wilderness they'd fled through. The forests that held the Wapiti camp. The territory of the Napiyaw.

And then she saw her.

"Oh my God," she breathed, her hand reaching out to grip Stella's arm. "Look. Up there. On that rocky outcrop."

Perhaps half a mile away and several hundred feet higher, a figure stood on a prominent stone formation.

Even at this distance, even without binoculars, Zuri recognized her.

Elaine.

She was dressed entirely differently from the last time they'd seen her. Gone were the expensive running clothes, the carefully coordinated athletic gear. She wore animal skins now—a dress or tunic that fell to her knees, decorated with elaborate beadwork that caught the sunlight. Her blonde hair, previously always perfect, now hung in elaborate braids similar to how Ayâs had worn hers. And even from this distance, Zuri could see the mark on her forehead—the carved symbol that proclaimed her as Nitânis, priestess of the old ways.

But it was Elaine's posture that struck Zuri most. She stood different. Not the careful, controlled stance of someone always aware of being watched and judged, but something looser, stronger, more grounded. She looked comfortable in her own skin in a way she never had during the tour.

As if sensing their attention, Elaine turned toward them. For a long moment, she simply looked down at the three figures on the trail below. Then, slowly and deliberately, she raised her hand and waved.

It wasn't a call for help. It wasn't a desperate signal from a prisoner begging for rescue. It was a simple greeting. An acknowledgment of their presence. A gesture of connection across the distance.

Zuri raised her own hand and waved back, her throat suddenly tight with emotions she couldn't name.

Elaine smiled—even at this distance, Zuri could see it—smile, genuine and unforced, so unlike the polite, carefully measured expressions she'd worn throughout the tour. Then she placed her hand over her heart, held it there for a moment, and then extended the hand toward them. Then she turned away. She walked back from the overlook and disappeared into the forest, moving with the confidence of someone who belonged there, who knew exactly where she was going.

"She's really staying," Stella said softly. "She's really chosen this."

"Maybe she has," Zuri admitted. "I certainly hope so. I wish the best for her. I can't even imagine the life ahead of her."

"She looked happy though," Dave observed. "Didn't she? That smile—that wasn't the smile of someone being held prisoner. That was someone at peace."

"At peace wearing animal skins and living in the wilderness at primitive camps," Stella countered. "At peace might not be comfortable."

"Or," Zuri said slowly, working through new thoughts, "at peace can be someone who found what they were looking for. Even if it looks like madness from the outside."

They stood in silence, staring at the place where Elaine had been. The forest had swallowed her completely, showing no sign that anyone had been there at all.

"Did you see the strength in her?" Zuri asked. "The way she held herself? She's definitely different now. Not the woman who started this trip. That Elaine is gone."

"Do you think she's safe?" Stella asked. "Really safe? Not just 'appears to be safe' to law enforcement?"

"Yes, I think she is," Zuri admitted. "Maybe she's safer than she ever was in New Jersey."

"Or maybe we're rationalizing," Dave said gently. "Maybe we're telling ourselves she's okay because we can't stand the guilt of leaving her there."

They started back down the trail, moving slowly, each lost in their own thoughts. Other hikers passed them, cheerfully discussing trail conditions and photo opportunities, completely unaware that they'd just witnessed a moment of profound significance on the slopes above.

"What do we do now?" Dave asked when they reached the bottom. "Go back to the hotel? Keep wandering?"

"I think I need food," Stella said. "Real food. And maybe alcohol. Definitely alcohol."

They found a restaurant on Banff's main street— nothing fancy, just a pub with good burgers and local beer. They sat in a corner booth and ordered with a

hunger that comes from a mixture of emotional and physical exhaustion.

Returning to the hotel hours later, they found Maureen in the lobby, dressed in street clothes, using her phone.

"You're leaving?" Zuri asked, surprised.

"Tomorrow," Maureen confirmed. "The nurse cleared me this morning. The drug is completely out of my system. I'm physically fine. And mentally—well, I'm as fine as I'm going to get. I need to go home, see my own doctors, return to my own life. But I wanted to say goodbye properly this time."

They sat together in the lobby's comfortable chairs, the four of them forming a small circle separate from the other guests coming and going around them.

"Are you really okay?" Stella asked gently.

"No," Maureen said honestly. "I'm not okay. But I'm functional. I can get on a plane tomorrow and go home and resume my life. That's more than I had two days ago."

"What will you tell people?" Dave asked. "About what happened?"

"The truth, mostly. That I took part in Indigenous ceremonies, that I was given substances that opened my mind, that I had extraordinary experiences I'm still processing. The academic world will either embrace that as groundbreaking fieldwork or dismiss me as having had a breakdown. Either way, I have to document it. I have to try to understand it. That's who I am."

"And Elaine?" Zuri asked. "What will you say about her?"

Maureen's expression grew complicated. "That she found what she was looking for. That she underwent a transformation I witnessed but can't fully explain. That she chose a new life. Whether anyone believes that, whether they understand it—that's not my problem. I know what I saw. I know she's there by choice now, whatever circumstances led to that choice initially."

"We saw her today," Stella said. "Up on the mountain. She was watching the town. She waved to us. She looked… different. Stronger. At peace."

"Good," Maureen said softly. "I'm glad. I was worried the Mounties might try to force her back, or that she'd be scared or hurt. If she looked at peace, then maybe the transformation was successful. Maybe she really is Nitânis and whatever that means."

"Do you believe that?" Zuri asked. "Really believe it? That she's some kind of priestess to ancient forest creatures? That any of that is real and not just hallucination?"

Maureen met her eyes steadily. "I believe I saw things that shouldn't exist but do. I believe Elaine has a capacity for spiritual awakening that most people lack. I believe the Wapiti have maintained practices and knowledge that connect to something ancient and powerful. Beyond that—I don't know. I may never know. But I'm going to spend the rest of my career trying to find out."

They talked for another hour, making promises to stay in touch, acknowledging that they were bound together now by an experience that would shape the rest of their lives. Finally, Maureen excused herself, claiming exhaustion and the need to finish packing.

"Take care of yourself," Zuri said, hugging her tightly. "And if you ever need anything—if you're struggling, if you're scared, if you just need to talk to someone who was there—you call me. Promise?"

"I promise," Maureen said. "And Zuri? Thank you. For getting me back. For believing me even when what I'm saying sounds insane."

"You're welcome," Zuri said. "And you're not insane. None of us are."

After Maureen left, the three of them remained in the lobby, too drained to move just yet.

And somewhere in those forests, a woman from New Jersey who'd been running from her life had found a different one. Whether that was tragedy or transformation, Zuri would probably never know.

But she'd seen Elaine wave. Seen her smile. Seen the strength in how she held herself.

And maybe—just maybe—that was the assurance she needed.

EPILOGUE: NITÂNIS

SIX MONTHS LATER · WINTER IN THE ROCKIES

The snow had come early this year, blanketing the forest in a silence that was peaceful and profound. Elaine—though she rarely thought of herself by that name anymore—stood at the edge of the winter camp, watching the smoke from cooking fires rise straight up into the still morning air.

Nitânis. Daughter. Mother. Bridge.

The names meant different things depending on who spoke them, but they all pointed to the same truth: she was no longer the woman who'd arrived in Canada six months ago, desperate to escape a life that had never fit her.

She touched the mark on her forehead—habit now, a gesture of reassurance. The carved lines had healed months ago, leaving raised scars that she traced with her fingertips during moments of contemplation. The Napiyaw face. Her face now, in a way. The symbol of her role, her purpose, her connection to ancient creatures and legends.

"Nitânis." Takoda approached from the nearest lodge, his breath misting in the cold air. "The council is ready."

She nodded, pulling the heavy bearskin cloak tighter around her shoulders. The animal skins had felt strange at first—rough, primitive, nothing like the designer fabrics she'd worn in her old life. But now they made her feel strong. Natural. Her body had always known it was meant to be wrapped in fur and leather rather than silk and cashmere.

The winter camp was smaller than the summer ceremonial site—just eight lodges arranged in a circle around a central fire pit, housing the core members of the Wapiti band. Thirty-seven people in total, including herself. Some had dispersed to other locations for the cold months, but this group stayed together, maintaining the practices, keeping the connection to the earth and the past alive.

Inside the largest lodge, the council waited. Maskwa sat to the right of where she would sit, his massive presence as reassuring as ever. He'd been skeptical of her at first—this soft city woman who'd stumbled into their ceremony—but over the months, he'd become her staunchest protector. To the left sat three elders, their weathered faces expressionless as she entered. Across from her position, Takoda took his seat, completing the circle.

The empty space at the head of the circle was hers now. Ayâs's place. The priestess's seat.

She still felt the weight of Ayâs' absence. She had simply walked into the forest that night—the night of Elaine's marking—and never returned. The Wapiti spoke of it as a natural transition, as if the old woman had completed her purpose and dissolved back into the land she'd served. But Elaine sometimes wondered if Ayâs was still out there somewhere, watching, judging whether her successor was worthy of the role.

"We need to discuss the spring," one elder said once everyone was settled. His name was Chaska, and he'd been with the band longer than the others. "The ceremony site near Banff. Do we return?"

This was the question they'd been avoiding for weeks. The summer ceremonial site was compromised—the RCMP knew of it, had documented it, had interviewed the Wapiti who'd been there during the incident with the runners. Returning would mean increased scrutiny, possible interference.

"The site is sacred," Maskwa said, his voice rumbling with conviction. "We've gathered there for generations.

The threshold between worlds is thinnest there. We cannot simply abandon it."

"But we cannot afford to draw more attention from the authorities," another elder countered. "They're watching it now. They suspect us now. Every missing hiker, every tourist who strays too far into the wilderness — they'll blame us. Come looking for us. Eventually they'll find cause to move us away as they did our ancestors."

All eyes turned to Elaine — Nitânis. The one who was supposed to have the answers.

She closed her eyes, reaching for the connection that had become second nature over these months. It was like diving beneath the surface of visible reality, feeling for currents that flowed deeper than sight or sound. The Napiyaw were always there, just beyond the veil, watching and waiting. And among them, one presence was stronger than the others.

First Walker, she called silently. *Do we return to the summer site? Or do we seek new ground?*

The response came not in words but as impressions, images, feelings that her mind translated into something approaching language. She saw the summer site as the Napiyaw perceived it — a thin place, a wound in the fabric between worlds that had been carefully maintained for centuries. Abandoning it would be a loss. But loss was sometimes necessary for survival.

The images shifted. She saw new places—sites further north, deeper in the wilderness, where humans rarely ventured. Places where the threshold could be rebuilt, where ceremonies could continue without the watchful eyes of authorities who would never understand what the Wapiti were preserving.

"We don't return," Elaine said, opening her eyes. The council waited, attentive. She'd learned that they listened to her not because she was wise or experienced, but because she could hear what they couldn't. Her gift—or curse—was a clear reception of the Napiyaw's will. "The First Walker shows me new sites. Further north. Remote. We will create new thin places. The old site has served its purpose."

Maskwa's jaw tightened—he hated change, hated abandoning tradition—but he nodded. "If that is their will."

"It is," Elaine confirmed, though part of her wondered if she was truly receiving their will or projecting her own desires. The connection was real—she was certain of that—but where her perceptions ended and the Napiyaw's guidance began was sometimes impossible to determine.

"Then we begin scouting in the spring," Chaska said. "Before the snow fully melts. We'll establish the new site before the summer ceremonies."

The council continued, discussing logistics, supplies, and the challenge of moving the band to unfamiliar territory. Elaine participated, her input valued now in ways it never had been in her old life. In New Jersey, in her marriage to Bradford, her opinions had been decorative at best—pretty thoughts to be smiled at, but seldom taken seriously. Here, when she spoke, people listened. When she saw things, they believed her.

Even if what she saw was impossible.

After the council ended, Elaine walked alone into the forest. She needed this—the solitude, the silence, the chance to shed the role of Nitânis and remember who she'd been before. Or try to remember. That woman felt increasingly distant, as if Elaine Whitmore-Calhoun was a character she'd played in a long-running performance that had finally closed.

The snow was deep here, untouched except by animal tracks. She moved through it easily now, her body adapted to the terrain in ways her old self would never have imagined possible. Six months of constant physical activity, of hiking and carrying and working with her hands, had transformed her from the decorative creature of New England social circles into something functional. Strong. Capable.

She didn't miss it. That was the most surprising thing. Six months ago, she'd thought leaving her marriage was a temporary escape, a rebellion that would eventually end with her return to the familiar comforts of her old life. But now, thinking about Bradford felt like thinking about a stranger. That marriage, that life, those careful social performances—they belonged to someone else entirely.

Do you regret it?

The thought-voice wasn't her own. Elaine stopped walking, her breath misting in the cold air, and looked around. The forest appeared empty, but she knew better now. They were always there when she called, and sometimes when she didn't.

"No," she said aloud, her voice steady. "I don't regret it."

The First Walker materialized gradually, as if the shadows between the trees were coalescing into something solid. Even after six months of regular contact, his appearance still made her breath catch. Eight feet of muscle and dark fur, moving with impossible silence, eyes that held intelligence beyond human understanding.

He tilted his head, studying her with that unblinking attention that made her feel seen and assessed. *You are certain? You could still return. They would take you back. The authorities. The woman named Zuri. Even the man you were bound to—he could be convinced to accept you again.*

"I don't want to be accepted back," Elaine said firmly. "I want to be here. This is where I belong."

Belonging and choosing are not the same thing. You chose here before. You continue to choose every day, even as Ayâs did.

It was a test. The Napiyaw tested her constantly, pushing at her certainty, making sure her commitment was genuine rather than manufactured by the nature's milk or the ceremony that had awakened her identity.

"I chose then," Elaine acknowledged. "I'm still here. I'm still choosing this. Every day I choose this. It's who I am—not a single decision made in one moment, but a continuous choice, renewed each morning when I wake up and decide to continue."

The First Walker made a sound that might have been approval—a low rumble that resonated in her chest. *You are stronger than the old woman guessed. She accepted her end. But she also feared that you might not be what the Wapiti needed.*

"Ayâs is gone," Elaine said, and felt the familiar pang of relief. The old priestess had been powerful, wise, and also terrifying in her absolute certainty. "I am Nitânis. I am what the Wapiti need. I will be worthy of that."

Worthiness is demonstrated through action, through time, through the choices you continue to make when no one is watching to judge them.

"You watch me," Elaine challenged. "Judge me. I'm not afraid of your judgment anymore."

The First Walker stepped closer, and Elaine held her ground. Six months ago, this proximity would have terrified her. Now it felt almost comfortable. He reached out with one massive hand and touched her forehead, his claw tracing the carved lines on her forehead.

You carry us on your skin. You hear us in your mind. You speak for us to the humans who would destroy what little remains of our kind. This is a burden, not a blessing.

"Yes," Elaine said quietly. "It is. This role isn't an escape. It's a sacred responsibility. It's harder than anything I've ever done. And it matters. For the first time in my life, what I'm doing actually matters."

The First Walker withdrew his hand and stepped back. *The old woman walked into the forest and became the trees. She served for over a century, and when her service was complete, she dissolved back into the land. That is the fate of all who take this role. You will never return to your human life. You will never grow old in comfort, surrounded by the softness your previous world offers. You will age here, in the wilderness, serving purposes that most humans will never understand or appreciate. And when your service is complete, you too will walk into the forest and not return.*

It was the most direct statement of her fate that anyone had offered. Not veiled in ceremony or mysticism, but blunt and clear. This path had an endpoint, and that endpoint was dissolution.

"I accept it," Elaine said, and meant it. "Better to dissolve into something meaningful than to spend decades as a decoration in a life I never chose."

Then you are truly Nitânis. And we will walk with you until your service ends.

He faded back into the shadows as gradually as he'd appeared, leaving Elaine alone in the winter forest. But not lonely. Never lonely. The Napiyaw were always there, just beyond sight.

She turned back toward camp, her footprints the only marks in the fresh snow. Smoke from the cooking fires guided her home—because that's what the camp had become. Home. Not the mansion in New Jersey with its empty rooms and emptier marriage. Not the hotel suites and vacation rentals of her previous life. This collection of crude lodges in a frozen forest, surrounded by people who now looked to her for guidance.

That night, after the evening meal, after the quiet conversations around the fire, after most of the band had retired to their lodges, Elaine sat alone by the dying flames. She'd pulled out a piece of paper—precious and rare in the camp—and a pencil stub she'd been saving.

She'd tried this several times over the past months. Writing to someone from her old life. Explaining.

Justifying. Making them understand. But the words never came out right. How do you explain an entirely different world to someone who didn't believe in it? How do you describe choosing a life of primitive hardship over modern comfort to people who were afraid she was brainwashed?

She tried again:

Zuri—

I saw you on the mountain, so many months ago. I waved. I hope you understood that it wasn't a call for help but a greeting. An acknowledgment that we shared something extraordinary, even if we each took different paths afterward.

I know you tried to rescue me. I know you reported everything to the authorities. I know you feel responsible for leaving me behind. Please don't. You didn't leave me—I chose this. That's very different.

I'm writing this to tell you that I'm well. More than well. I'm fulfilled in ways I never was before. The work is hard. The conditions are harsh. The responsibilities are enormous. But for the first time in my life, I feel like I'm exactly where I'm supposed to be, doing exactly what I'm meant to do.

You'll probably never understand that. Most people won't. They'll think I'm brainwashed, delusional, a victim of Stockholm syndrome or drug-induced psychosis. But I'm happy. Genuinely, deeply happy in a way I never was in New Jersey.

Thank you for caring enough to try to save me. Thank you for seeing me when most people looked through me. Thank you for being kind to the woman I was, even though she was difficult and spoiled and lost.

I hope you're well. I hope you've processed what happened and found peace with it. I hope you keep leading tours, keep bringing people to beautiful places, keep sharing your joy in the wilderness with others. The world needs people like you — people who love nature and want to share it, even knowing the darkness it might hold.

Be well, Elaine/Nitânis

She read it over, then slowly fed it to the dying fire. The paper caught, flared bright for a moment, then crumbled to ash. The smoke rose and dispersed, carrying her words beyond the physical paper. The message and its meaning would find Zuri not through the postal mail, but through the connections that bound them — their shared experience, caring about each other, and the hope for a resolution. As long as Zuri retained these, the message would reach her and she would feel the comfort of knowing that all was well with Elaine, with Nitânis.

She looked up at those stars—the same stars she'd seen from her mansion in New Jersey, from hotel rooms around the world, from every place she'd ever been in her previous life. But they looked different now. Brighter. More significant.

Nitânis. Daughter. Mother. Bridge.

The names settled around her like the bearskin cloak, heavy and warm and chosen.

She was home.

THE END

AI DISCLOSURE

The text of this novel was written by the human author. I used GPT-4 and Claude as research tools to collect cultural, historical, geographical, and geological information on the region and people of Alberta, Canada, past and present.

ABOUT R.D.D. SMITH

R.D.D. Smith writes science-fiction, medical thriller novels featuring advanced surgical devices, AI, telesurgery, simulation, and speculative diseases; and global travel adventures that follow running tourists through exotic countries. The medical series is inspired by his career in healthcare and experience with robotic surgery devices. The travel novels are inspired by his actual vacations in the countries featured in the books.

He holds a doctorate and MBA from the University of Maryland, a master's from Texas Tech University, and a bachelor's from Colorado State University.

He lives with his wife, dogs, and cats in sunny Florida, frequently escaping to cooler climes during the beastly Florida summers.

STAY IN TOUCH

Review:
Please leave a review of this book on Amazon or
your favorite book site.

Join Us:
Join our community of readers to receive fascinating
news related to the story.

www.rddsmith.com/free

ACKNOWLEDGMENTS

As an author, I am infinitely grateful to my readers who invest their time, money, and imaginations in following my stories and characters through their challenges, failures, and transformations.

First, to my wife and children, who have endured decades of fanatic immersion into whatever my latest passion is, most recently, these novels. Your patience, dedication, and love are appreciated every day.

For this adventure story, I am indebted to Vacation Races Global Adventures (USA) for organizing the fantastic trip that inspired the events in this novel. Special thanks to Cheri Santiego, Zoe Calcott, and Salem Stanley for creating a business, an adventure, a community, and a family all in one. Thank you to my fellow vacationers and runners for your enthusiastic encouragement as we created and discovered each chapter of this book together.

For my editor Kaitlin Travis, book layout artist Adina Cucicov, and the many advisors who made this book far better than I could have accomplished alone.

REAL GLOBAL TRAVEL ADVENTURES

If you're looking for running adventure travel:

Runseek Adventures
https://www.runseekadventures.com/

Photo Credit: Barbara Cole, Used with Permission from Vacation Races
www.barbaracolephoto.com